NEWPORT
JANE

NEWPORT JANE

A Novel

Katie Bieksa

Publication Data
Katie Bieksa
Newport Jane
ISBN-13: 9781546606796
ISBN-10: 1546606793

Editor: Lori Bamber
Cover Design and Illustration: Cathryn John © 2017
Author Photograph: Duke Loren Photography
Publishing: The Self Publishing Agency

For information, visit www.KatieBieksa.com

To my husband, Kevin, for keeping our life an adventure.

*To my children, Cole and Reese, who
inspire me to use my imagination.*

To my family and friends for their encouragement.

*To the women of the Port Streets, like the women
in Vancouver and everywhere, who welcome
the new moms and who comfort the new kids
with playdates and cookie deliveries.*

1

The airport is buzzing with vacationers cheerfully checking into their flights, handling the crowds and frustrations with the optimism of sunny days ahead.

I'm guarding our luggage like a porter as my husband Trevor returns a call to his new practice.

All around us, travelers are buried in their phones, probably updating their status (#imalsoobsessed #butthisisdifferent). But Trevor isn't throwing likes around on Instagram. He's trying to figure out how to save the lives of his next three patients, which doesn't make it easy for me to complain. Instead, I stand here refusing to look at my phone.

It's been almost twenty minutes, and I can see security turning into the lineup for the latest attraction at Canada's Wonderland. Two young men toting hockey bags walk past me and fail to even glance in my direction. Have I really gotten that old? Combined with my growing impatience and anxiety, this triggers a rampage of insecure thoughts. If I'm average here in Toronto, I can't imagine what my status will be in California. How much longer do I have before men stop finding me attractive altogether? Five years? Ten, if I drink a lot of water?

Trevor walks toward me, still on the phone. He plants a kiss on my forehead and mouths, "Sorry, babe." Restless, I make myself take a seat as he paces back and forth.

With nothing to do and everything to think about, I lean back and focus on all the passersby. Most women who pass us check Trevor out. As a rule, I try not to be jealous. More realistically, I try to keep it contained in my head with all the other doubts.

Trevor is never jealous, not ever. This bothers me. I don't know if it's his absolute trust in my fidelity and morals, or if he just doesn't think I'm that pretty. He certainly doesn't have any reason to worry. When we're together, men usually look at him before me. Still, I don't think it's wise to admit to your wife that you're never jealous. It's true, possessive guys can be scary as hell, particularly the ones in the Lifetime movies I've watched all summer, but it's also kind of a turn-on to feel wanted.

When Trevor and I first started dating, my best friend Annie shared a fabulous tip, knowing he attracted most of the attention. It's both simple and effective, and no, it's not the "bend and snap" from

Legally Blonde. The idea is to walk slightly in front of him when we're out together and sneakily smile at all the men who pass, just enough that they look in my direction. As far as he knows, they are checking me out. I thought about doing that now, just to remind him I'm still here, but instead I get up and point at the watch I'm not wearing.

He holds his finger up to me, signaling he's about to say goodbye. He nods a few times, smiling at the person on the other end, and hangs up.

"Soooooo sorry, babe," he says, picking me up in a bear hug. "You all set?"

"I don't want to miss our flight—look at security!" I snap as I point toward the insanity that awaits us.

"Relax," he says, "business class, remember?" Shit. Right. I smile on the outside.

We breeze through security, and I grab coffees while he works on his laptop just outside our gate. I wander through the airport wondering if I look as hollow as I feel. I find it a bit alarming that I feel this bored about moving to another country with the hottest guy in the airport. I think about ordering him a decaf just to be mean.

We're flying into LAX, which explains the array of characters waiting to board our plane. I scan the crowds for someone I recognize, but all I see are disguises today: a few unnecessary hats and oversized sunglasses, along with people who remain faceless by refusing to look up from their phones.

I don't even blame all the women staring at Trevor. He's always smiling with those blue eyes, and it's likely they think he's a television doctor prepping for his role. By default, that would make me his assistant, or PR.

We're called to board: elite travelers first (they don't say that, but it's implied). I almost don't want to get in line with all these people who know exactly what they're doing, passports and tickets ready, faces blank, eyes straight ahead, pretending not to notice how they're boarding before struggling parents and the disabled. They're rich, after all. A complete contrast with the regular passengers who are now fumbling with their documents, looking panicked and utterly unprepared.

Today it's mostly businessmen, pretending to be rich while their companies foot the bill. There is also one family with two small children who are impatiently waiting for their freshly baked cookies. How annoying for the oversized man to walk by before squeezing himself into 25B. And then there are the young ones with Gucci carry-ons who you know are either professional athletes or have trust funds. I suppose the only thing worse might be a miserable, privileged, straight white woman, judging everyone and everything.

I never thought of myself as the judgmental type. But the more I think these thoughts, the more I've come to terms with the possibility that, despite my mom's best efforts, I'm less happily confident and more bitterly insecure, less carefree dog person and more crazy cat lady.

When we're comfortably seated, in our pods no less, and I've managed to avoid making eye contact with any of the other passengers, I read all my good-bye messages. I refuse to reply: not to my older sister Audrey whose tears are evident in her text even without an emoji, nor to Annie who is obviously jealous and keeps it short. I turn off my phone.

Here we go…

I must have fallen asleep, because when I wake up there is a note folded into an origami heart on my lap. I glance over at Trevor but he is occupied with a file, his full lips pressed around the Montblanc pen I got him years ago, which I would have lost six times by now. I hold the tiny note in my hand, looking at how delicately it's folded, the edges perfectly round and smooth. Work only a seven-year-old who has mastered her cartwheels and has a lot of time on her hands or a skilled surgeon could produce. What he can do with those giant hands is crazy, especially considering my little ones are a blundering mess.

I'm absolutely famished, and I've likely missed lunch. What's the use of sitting up here if I don't take advantage of the free food? I wipe my eyes and press the call button. It's not until I have a ginger ale and cheese tray that I open the note.

*Elly—You promised to keep an open mind
about the house.
Also, last night was unbelievable.
Wow.
-T*

Really? Unbelievable seems a stretch considering I went to bed alone after. Love notes after five years of marriage and nine years of dating are sweet. But this one also annoys me. It's a two-faced note, a little reminder to keep me in line about this move. Now I have to be appreciative. Not to mention that he knows it makes me uncomfortable when he brings up stuff we've done in the bedroom (or kitchen, in this case).

"That might be the most darling thing I have ever seen!" a flight attendant in a droll 1950s-style uniform whispers as she leans alarmingly close to my face, as if trying to sneak a peek at the note.

"Excuse me?" I ask, smiling as I flip it over.

"The little bitty heart note?" she says, pretending to fold with crazy, exaggerated fingers.

"Oh, yeah, he can be pretty romantic," I say, keeping the scowl on the inside.

"You have to be the luckiest woman in the world!" I smile, because my parents taught me to be polite and because it makes me look prettier, and I know she's already decided I'm out of my league. Inside I scream: "How do you know he isn't the lucky one?!"

Focus. An open mind about the house—that part worries me. I recognize I relinquished all house-hunting control to Trevor and his brother Danny last month, but last month this move didn't seem real. Now, I question that decision. Typically, Trevor tends to care little about material things. He wants to drive a nice car, not a douchebag sports car but a subtle SUV like his Audi, and to wear a good suit. But as for our home, he's always left it up to me. He doesn't notice things like floors, marble counters or square footage. A realtor showed him around Newport, some gated communities along the coast that are relatively close to his new office. Ideally, I would have preferred they look at little cottages on the beach, although the idea of gated security didn't sound terrible.

Confession: I have an irrational fear of being alone at night, so it may not have been the smartest decision to marry a surgeon. But when I was younger, I thought it was something I would grow out of. I haven't yet.

I can tell it is an irrational fear because once I rule out criminals in the house, I start sensing the supernatural. I'm scared to leave the hallway light on, fearful I'll see two soundless, shadowy feet outside our bedroom door.

Another bonus of having my parents just down the street until now was that my father could bike over at every little noise. "It's probably the house settling," he'd say. But what I heard is, "It's definitely a home invasion." For a while, I forbid myself from watching any crime show, especially *Criminal Minds*, which I'm sure gives psychopaths an extra push toward sadistic brilliance. But even when I don't watch, I find that the seed of future home invasions has been deeply planted.

In the first year we were married, I once awoke alone to the dreaded *Beep! Beep! Beep!* of our security alarm, enough to send even the brave into sheer panic. I sprang straight up in bed, telling myself it was just my dream. I sat perfectly still, holding my breath, frozen.

Beep! Beep! Beep!

Someone's in the house! I bolted out of bed, popped the screen out of our ground floor window, climbed through like a ninja and sprinted down the street to my parents. I had a home invasion route planned out like many do for fires—and thank goodness I did. I was at my parents, damp from the cold winter air, in less than two minutes.

It turned out the alarm battery had expired, choosing two in the morning as the perfect time to let me know. But I still spent that night at my parents, curled up safely in the bed I grew up in.

As we land, the pilot comes over the speaker, cheerfully welcoming visitors to the Los Angeles area and everyone else a happy homecoming. Trevor gives me his goofiest grin and leans over to whisper, "Welcome home, babe!"

Way too soon for that!

We fight our way through the busy airport. Mickey Mouse ears and Disney bags are everywhere. It's hard to take yourself too seriously amidst children on cloud nine, headed to or from the Happiest Place on Earth. This is a whole new world for me.

In the car, Trevor seems particularly tense. Our luggage came out first and he had arranged a driver to meet us, a big man with a red face who was waiting for us with a HUNTER sign as we came down the escalator. Despite its reputation, LAX was easy to navigate. We had our luggage and were in the car within twenty minutes.

I can't think of a reason Trevor would be so nervous, other than the fact that his wife is an ungrateful bitch, and perhaps this traffic. Traffic from hell—motorcyclists legally speeding by on solid lines, weaving in and out without warning, their engines backfiring as they sneak up on us, each time causing our tourist bodies to jump.

"Okay, what's wrong with you?" I ask finally. "You haven't seemed this anxious since your MCAT." I playfully nudge his arm. "You worried you won't be the smartest?"

He takes a deep, thoughtful breath and turns his body toward me. "I guess I'm nervous about the house."

"The house? Trevor, seriously, we didn't exactly live in a palace."

"Well, I know you can't stand Mediterranean style, and it's everywhere here, Elly. And rentals are tough."

"You're scaring me now. You and Danny were quite impressed with yourselves when you got back. You said you found a great house. I think you even said I would love it."

"To be honest, Ellen, you seemed a little happier then. I knew you weren't thrilled with the idea of moving here, but I figured you would get over it."

I let him talk, but I don't like where this is going.

"You've been moping around for months now. You've barely said two words all day."

I can tell he's passive-aggressively angry, but he keeps his voice even until it cracks a little before he delivers the final blow. "I don't know if any house would be good enough for you when you're like this."

At least he lowered his voice enough to save us from awkwardness with the driver. Still, I can't believe he is choosing now to pick a fight. I've been so positive this whole trip. "Okay, so let me get this right, you're not actually nervous about the house, you're nervous about my shitty attitude?"

I'm mad, but mostly I'm embarrassed because I know he's right. (Surely, I've said more than two words, though.)

"Why do you do that? That's not what I said."

"Let's just drop it, okay? We'll be there soon, and I promise I'll make all kinds of dramatic oohs and ahhs in front of what's-her-name."

"Her name is Sarah. And she's really going out of her way to meet us today."

"Oh, I'm sure it just kills her. Sorry, Sarah, you have to show some handsome rich guy properties and collect a huge commission. Excuse me if I don't explode with gratitude."

I know I sound awful, but maybe I am awful. Even worse, I don't care.

"She's like sixty, Ellen. She is a very nice person. And none of this is the point. Do me a favor when we get there and just keep your thoughts to yourself."

"Sure, Trev. Anything you want."

It's silence for the next twenty minutes, which is torture because we only move a few miles. I make sure to sigh heavily just so he knows how irritated I am with this traffic. R.E.M's *Losing My Religion* comes on and the driver turns the barely audible radio up as if throwing me a bone. I allow the song to transport me the way music does, and suddenly I'm Brenda Walsh from 90210 and the whole world is against me. In my head, I curse Kelly and Dylan—and then Trevor—and sing the relevant parts louder, *trying to keep up with you and I don't know if I can do it….*

Eventually, he caves and puts his hand on my knee. "Elly, we have to stick together here. If you don't like the house, we'll move. Besides, it's more the neighborhood I'm worried about." I jerk my head toward him, re-kinking muscles that have only just started to relax. What does that mean? I'm ready to pounce, but he has this bug-eyed, don't-be-mad smile. I resist my urge to give him my Elvis lip and instead grab his face and kiss his cheek. "Don't worry, it'll be great." *Oh, no I've said too much, I haven't said enough….*

2

As we pull off the freeway, the driver lets us know we are nearly there. We breeze down palm-lined streets alongside a wide array of luxury vehicles. It's a relief being off the 405—I've made a mental note to avoid it at any cost. The relief almost becomes excitement as I take in what appears to be a movie backdrop. I try not to blink, fearing it may get rolled away and replaced with a set more suited to my current state of mind. Rainy Seattle probably.

My sister Audrey's piercing voice is in my head now, urging me to change my mind.

"You must be insane," she'd said, never one for subtle advice. "No woman in her right mind would send Trevor and Danny, of all people, to pick out a house. You'll end up in some swanky bachelor pad with one bathroom."

I'd told Trevor and everyone else I couldn't go look for houses because I had to be available in case my boss, now my former boss, needed me to edit some last-minute submissions. In reality, the little publishing house I worked for accepted my notice with so little protest it made me question my worth to them to begin with. Not only did I not get assigned any summer projects, I didn't even get a goodbye card, and Lord knows I'd signed dozens of them in my three years there. I told no one this, not even Trevor. My station in this family was at an all-time low already, so I made up some story about how the rest of the staff felt lost without me; panicked, really. For the first time in my life, I felt completely insignificant. *Fifth Business*-level insignificant.

But here I am driving down what must be one of the most beautiful streets in the world, on our way to our overpriced home, a home that we can afford no less, sitting next to my real-life McDreamy. Life is good. But am I good enough for this life? This isn't my success. I try to erase the doubt as quickly as it comes. I practice my belly breathing, in and out, and try to employ some of the methods I learned in my *Mind over Mood* workbook, but it's to no avail.

No surprise, my negative thoughts triumph. The view outside becomes a blur as my gaze settles on my reflection in the car window. I stare at the outline of my face, acknowledging how the daylight magnifies what appears to be the beginning of jowls, pulling down the corners of my once happy mouth. The tiny lines around my eyes seem to claw at any sparkle that's left there, trying to smother it.

When my focus returns to the road, we are driving through a gateway without an actual gate. I bite my tongue and hope it's a detour, but then it hits me: this is what Trevor was hinting at.

This neighborhood could be Wisteria Lane, complete with a redhead overwatering roses that peek through her white picket fence. The Nantucket-style homes are so beautiful and different from the cookie-cutter neighborhoods I'm used to that my worry almost eases. But as uniquely detailed as each home is, even the roses seem to be in competition with each other. (I'm guessing the ones with the most thorns are winning.)

Trevor is talking, his mouth moving quickly, spitting out words like Port Streets, opportunity, established and then: *family*. The word blasts through my ear canal like a derailed train before it smashes into my brain. I am all steam but somehow manage to ignore it, not wanting to sound ungrateful to the driver. By the time the car slows in front of our place I've already counted nine basketball nets.

"This one on the right," Trevor says to the driver, leaning into the front. I can tell he is avoiding my eyes, waiting for me to make the first move.

"Wow, we're really living the American dream," I say as I open the door, ignoring the driver's attempt to get there first. I have to admit the house is lovely. It's not the nicest on the street, but it's almost exactly the house I imagined raising our family in.

Green vines climb over the garage and onto a beautiful porch, stopping just above a large black Dutch door. Tea out here with a book, listening to the birds sing and children play—it could be perfect. Today, however, my mood is more cold tile and concrete; the sound of angry waves crashing onto the shore.

"Beautiful home," the driver mutters as he struggles to carry two more suitcases up the driveway. I can't tell if he is being sweet or cheeky, having already decided he's Team Trevor.

"Yes, it's a beautiful home," I agree, "for a family."

"You can just leave them there. We're waiting for our realtor," Trevor says, handing him a rolled-up twenty.

"You sure you wouldn't rather wait in the car, sir? It's awfully hot out here."

And just then I realize I am practically panting. The air is so heavy I feel like I'm about to melt into the red brick driveway. Why is it so hot? I can't breathe. I drop my bags and tear off my sweater. How did I not notice it's forty degrees?

"How hot is it?" I ask him, as if I'd never considered that California might be hotter than Ontario.

"I think it's close to 100 degrees today," he says, reminding me that I have to start thinking in Fahrenheit. "Been like this for a while now. Why don't you come sit in the car?" he reasons as sweat runs down the back of his neck and makes the collar of his suit jacket shine.

I follow him back to the car, ignoring Trevor's claim that we're used to the heat. I plunk into the backseat and pull my phone out of my pocket. At this point I could not care less about roaming charges, and type "Newport Beach Rentals" into my Google search. I love the house. I do, I love it. But why the F would we live in this neighborhood, surrounded by families? There is not a chance I am staying here all day while he is at work. I should be in some beach house pretending to be happy and at least making my frost-ridden friends jealous.

My search could not be any slower. I'd hoped that by the time Trevor joined me in the car I would have something way better to show him, in time to intercept our moving truck and redirect our already late realtor, Sarah.

"Dave wouldn't get in if I didn't," Trevor says, referring to the driver as he slides in beside me.

"Texting Audrey already?"

I'm about to lie, but he glances at my phone just as the Zillow listings pop up.

"So much for giving it a try. You can't even get inside before you start complaining?"

"I wasn't complaining, Trevor. I was sitting in here alone and I was curious what else there was that's not… here."

With that, Dave gets back out of the car.

"Jesus, Ellen! You're acting like a spoiled brat. You could at least say thank you."

"Thank you, Trevor!" I yell. "Thanks for rubbing it in my face that I have absolutely nothing going on in my life. 'Oh, how many children do you have?'" I say, mimicking our new neighbors. "Ummmm, none! No, no job, either. Can't work in the US. Wrong visa. I'm here for my husband, who is at work eighteen hours a day, seven days a week."

"I don't get you. You don't want to live in a flashy neighborhood, you're scared at the beach. Whatever, I can't win with you anymore."

"Well, maybe if you thought about what I..."

"All I do is think about what you want, Ellen, and what's good for our future. You think I want to live here?? There are two condos right by the office we could have rented, but you wanted space for visitors, you wanted to get a dog, you want a ba..."

"A baby. Yes, I want a baby and you don't, so why would we live here?" I say, violently pointing around the street like a lunatic, forbidding my tears to come.

"Shit, here's Sarah," he says. "Try to get it together until she leaves. Then I promise we'll find some other place for you to complain about."

He coldly climbs out of the car, offering no sympathy. I flip the camera view around on my iPhone and check my eyes. I look horrible on this thing even when I'm not on the verge of tears, but this is particularly offensive. Dave stands outside my door, eagerly awaiting the moment he can close it behind me and speed away.

3

I wasn't always like this.

Like a lot of kids, I guess, I grew up thinking that finally being a grown-up would be the best thing that ever happened to me. No one tells you that it is little girls who live the magic: cloud pictures in the sky, butterflies carrying invisible fairies, and dreams of someday having someone look at us the way Daddy looks at Mom.

Then we grow up. We search for happy; then we settle for happy enough. We learn about what it's like to be disappointed—what it's like *to disappoint*.

I don't know if my current situation is the product of my bad judgement or if it was inevitable from the beginning, predetermined by my belief that I am so completely ordinary. The record speaks for itself: I'm the second daughter of parents who wanted a boy and a girl but only two children. For no reason at all, they called me Ellen. Not as common as Jennifer or Sarah, perhaps, but as plain as Jane. Yes, I'm basically Jane.

My older sister, Audrey, on the other hand— named after our beloved paternal grandmother, she has always been vivacious, mischievous and endlessly forgivable. Her first words were, "Watch me!" (Mine were, "Watch Audrey!") She had bouncing golden curls while my hair was poker-straight and brown. I was, and still am, reserved. According to our roles in the family, Audrey is the beautiful one. I am the smart one; "sharp," as Mom puts it.

The air is heavy today. It's the kind of weather that makes it hard to have a clear thought, but there is one that won't let me go: I'm not happy.

It's thirty degrees, and the humidity makes my thighs stick to each other despite my slight, celebrated thigh gap. For the first time in almost two months, I have to pull myself together to go out, which isn't easy in this state of mind.

Yes, we're moving to California, Trevor and I. Not forever, maybe, but for at least three long years.

I grew up in the kind of small town that could be anywhere. Ordinary people, juggling it all. Working all week, spending their weekends driving hundreds of miles to other small towns scattered along highways to their kids' hockey games, happy with their Tim Horton's coffee, scheduling sex when they can. The life I grew up thinking I would be lucky enough to have.

Being successful was as important to my parents as being well-behaved. In fact, the two were considered very much the same at our house. But I guess I didn't think about what success would mean for me. It was just always part of the plan, and I've been pushing and working for it since I can remember.

I certainly never imagined that success would force me to leave the people I love. Especially success that wasn't even mine. I didn't see it coming until it crushed me. And now that it's here, I have no choice but to go along, like a child whose father gets transferred.

I've been wandering around our house all summer, lamenting misused moments. I understand now that I never fully appreciated its quaint lines and exposed brick. We didn't have enough afternoon teas or late night glasses of wine on the screened-in porch, and now I already miss every bit of its low-key homeliness. That's the thing: it's so easy to miss how precious "ordinary" is until it's too late.

Even now, as I sit in front of the mirror trying to cover my latest stress breakout, all I can see in the reflection is the beautiful bedroom I foolishly saw as flawed before I knew we had to leave it behind. Unapologetically seventies inspired, exactly in time for a seventies comeback—how did I miss how great that was?

A house doesn't truly become a home until you fall in love with it, and right now I'm besotted.

Yesterday, during a melodramatic but quiet tantrum, I added my height to a make-shift growth chart in the spare room. I awkwardly drew a line above my head and labelled it with my name, hoping the new owners would be as sentimental as I am and refuse to paint over history.

I need more time here, more time to become me before I succumb to something...else. It's more than just that *you don't appreciate something until it's gone* bullshit. This empty room that was my life is desolate now. *Ellen was here...*

Now I have exactly fifteen minutes to get ready. "If you're not five minutes early, you're late," Trevor will come in to remind me soon, as he always does, even if it's just my family we're going to see.

When I focus on my face again, I realize I hardly recognize myself. My brown eyes look sullen and wary. I'm still what people call "fresh faced," but the years are starting to show around the edges. I look tired. I cut my long hair a few weeks ago, fully aware it was one of my few selling features—a ridiculous rebellion against all the blond with which I would soon be surrounded. It now brushes my collarbones. Hardly sexy, but cute. I suppose I'm happy enough with the way I look. (Happy enough seems to be theme these days.) At five-foot-three, I'm petite and pretty, not beautiful, but innocent-looking. "Someone men want to take care of," as Annie says.

For now, the idea of being a dark-haired "plain Jane" in California satisfies my negativity, my silently screaming resistance to this move.

You know that designer handbag you find in the outlet store? It doesn't exactly suit your style, but it's Prada. And it's almost within your budget, so there is no question that you're taking it home with you. That's sort of how it is with Trevor and me.

We met in the campus bookstore in my first year at Queens. He was a senior. He was alone, looking serious even then. He seemed to notice no one. In a sweater vest worn unzipped over a white t-shirt, he had a quiet arrogance that no one in a sweater vest should have.

It was impossible to look away. Trevor has the type of beauty that is hauntingly clichéd: tall, dark and handsome, with mesmerizing, unexpected blue eyes.

I watched him for maybe a minute, but the seconds seemed to slow, making it feel like forever. He was older than the boys I usually gravitated toward. He could almost be one of my professors, although the backpack hugging his shoulders suggested otherwise.

I'd bought my books as soon as the lists were posted, so I didn't need anything that day. But my roommate Annie, also my best friend since fifth grade, dragged me in the way she dragged me everywhere. We were already a full month into first semester and she was still debating the necessity of certain books. She's the type who could get through just by listening and taking notes. She always said, "Do one or the other, Ellen, go to class or do the reading; doing both is wasted time we could be living." Good advice if you can get away with it.

In my eyes, Annie is remarkable, intellectually and physically. She's tall, but not freakishly tall; chiseled cheekbones, blond hair from birth, and the type of large breasts women over five-ten tend to have. Trevor says Annie is girl-pretty, like the outfit your husband hates but your girlfriends rave about. Her boyfriends were generally first-string jocks or ambitious fraternity types, guys who valued a hot girl above an interesting one. This is not a slight at Annie; she is fascinating. If you looked for her in the pages of a great novel, she'd be Daisy "Annie" Miller (wildly beautiful and beautifully wild), the type of girl who seems shallow but that you can't stop trying to figure out. Annie, like Audrey, is not ordinary.

That day, she wasted no time. And not that I would have, but before I could even consider approaching him she was headed in his direction. "Hi," she said. That's her big move. She then offers just a small, closed-lip smile that somehow says, "Your turn."

He returned a book to the shelf before acknowledging her, which suggested he was used to being approached by gorgeous women. It was like watching the big cats at the zoo playing off each other's confidence, strutting and claiming territory.

When he finally turned toward her, I felt a slight tinge of uncalled-for jealousy and unconsciously held my breath. He just stared for a minute, his crystal-blue eyes locking onto hers as if they'd recognized a perfect genetic match. And yet after the briefest of moments, he seemed to blink away her magnificence as if it was a speck of dust on his long lashes. With a slight frown that made it clear he wasn't happy about being distracted from what he was doing, he finally said, "Do you work here?"

I watched as Annie tensed. "Oh, no, no," she interrupted, raising her hand as if to block his words and save herself from a possible slight. "I thought you were someone else." Her cheeks were rosy, but her perfect head was high. Only someone who knows her as well I do would guess she was embarrassed.

From the look on my face, she knew I'd seen it all. She mouthed, "What the fuck?" to me. That is the kind of confidence Annie has: Obviously, something must be wrong with him.

I didn't feel too sorry for her. I've seen the damage Annie's done. Leading people on is not something she considers to be an actual thing.

When she doesn't get the usual high volume of attention, it reenergizes her. She just ups her game. She finds a way: she laughs louder, smiles like she has a secret, thinks of something way more fun to do if she is too far behind in the game. Annie's unspoken motto is something like, "You can't fail if you don't give a fuck," and so she never does.

That day in the bookstore was a first, but she recovered quickly. Everyone else in the store was drawn to her, their eyes following her wherever she went. Except for Trevor's.

I snuck the quickest peek back toward him. As I watched her, he was watching me. With the same kind of confidence that Annie has—and that he claims not to have—he walked right over to me. "I thought she worked here," he said coolly, nodding in her direction.

"Sure, you did," I replied, just a bit sarcastically.

"I'm Trevor, Trevor Hunter," he said, offering his hand.

"Hi, Trevor. Ellen," I said, returning his almost comically mature handshake. "I see you met my roommate Annie.

"So…you need an employee?" I asked, laughing.

"Nah, I found it." He held up some medical journal with a name I couldn't read, said, "Pre-med," and then winked. Looking back, I'm not sure if the wink was meant to be funny or was a slightly pompous come-on. Because if Trevor has a flaw, it would have to be his relatively limp sense of humor. At the time, I was charmed, but smart enough not to let it show.

"I don't think you can say you're pre-med until you've been accepted to med school," I baited, stage-whispering to him from behind my hand as if to save him from embarrassment.

He went blank for a second as if processing the validity of my statement. "You don't worry about that—I'm sort of a sure thing," he responded, not even cracking a smile. He put his book down and wiped a hair off my cheek. "Coffee?"

Like my outlet store Prada, which never really felt like mine, when Trevor chose me over all the beautiful women looking his way there was no saying no. Comparing my husband to a designer handbag I couldn't afford but bought anyway is dehumanizing and insulting, I know. And at the time, I didn't think about fashion metaphors. I didn't analyze my immediate, intense attraction to him at all. He was irresistible, and I was all the way in before he even approached me. The fact he chose me after passing on Annie made me feel incredibly special. For a while, it even made up for all those years of loving her just as much as I hated feeling like I lived in her shadow.

It's only now I wonder if I may have focused too much on how special Trevor made me feel and not enough on what a future together might look like.

Having perfection thrust upon you is exhausting. Knowing that you don't measure up, continuously failing to rise to the occasion. Trevor wasn't tricked into loving me. I didn't put a spell on him, make promises of daily blowjobs. I didn't even pad my bra, which Annie says is false advertising. Yet whenever I skip an early morning hike or pass on an alumni event, his time to shine, he gives me this look that says, "You can do better."

At the same time, he's great. Even when he comes home after a twenty-hour day and the sink is still full of last night's dishes, he doesn't roll his eyes or sigh. He just rolls up the sleeves of his perfectly pressed dress shirt (pre-scrub clothing, one of his two very sexy uniforms), turns on the tap and asks how my day was.

He's perfect.

But perfect can be unsettling, annoying really, when you're personally just barely hanging onto the last thread of *fucking disaster.*

Dating in your own league is substantially under-rated. I'm still self-conscious when we're in public. I always assume people are thinking, "What the...?!" Sort of like Bella and Edward, before she was a vampire. Honestly, I would like it if he were less attractive. And like all good-looking men, his attractiveness seems to grow with age, along with his bank account. He's also a genuine genius. In a weird way, my plainness only adds to his perfection, like he knew that if he had paired up with another perfect ten, it might make him seem superficial and therefore slightly less flawless. Looking at our wedding picture now, it's all him, his windblown hair captured at exactly the right moment. Even with the sun directly above the two of us, he somehow caught the best light.

4

According to the e-vite my mom sent out, tonight is our "farewell soirée;" more accurately, one of the backyard barbecue shindigs she is notorious for throwing for every little occasion, complete with balloons and deviled eggs. She grew up poor and the thought of wasting a cent sends her into absolute panic, so she insists on hosting in the backyard as a way of keeping the Southern Ontario flies out and the air conditioning in. Anytime someone goes into the house, she yells, "Close the door!" before it's even opened.

Despite the soirée reference, I know I'll be way overdressed in my prized Philip Lim dress. When I picked it out I was feeling sentimental and had forecast a sunnier attitude. Audrey bought the army-green shift dress for my thirty-first birthday last summer. It was a splurge for her, but she's a lawyer, and she had made me cry the week before by announcing her second pregnancy. Last year, for a brief second, Trevor, contrary to his careful ten-year plan, agreed to try for a baby. After a few months with no luck, we (he) decided it was a sign that "timing is everything and everything should be timed precisely." Heartbroken, I half-joked that he'd picked up some undetectable pregnancy prevention trick in med school. "Yeah, it's called sleep deprivation," he'd said.

I'm wearing the dress, my consolation prize, hoping it will do its trick and supply some happiness.

Since finding out about our move, I haven't been my usual self. I'm resentful. I know I have been a bitch to Trevor. Like a woman who has been cheated on, I just can't stop punishing him.

I worked incredibly hard to get to where I am, was, as an editor. Just like that, I'm expected to give it up for his next career move.

The night Trevor told me he had been offered the position didn't go the way he had hoped. I knew it was coming. He'd been dancing around the subject for weeks: "I'm going to interview for this position, but I won't get it." Liar.

I straight-faced said, "Tell them to forget it."

"What the hell is wrong with you, Ellen? This is an opportunity for us to make some serious money and for me to finally get some recognition." His reasoning was solid, and if he'd stopped there, I might have eventually come to terms with it on my own. There would have been some pouting and slammed doors, natural-ly, but I'd like to believe I would have accepted my fate with more grace had it not been chosen for me.

He didn't stop there, though. He kept going. "I'll turn them down, Ellen... I'll turn them down when you can bring home this kind of money."

The way he said my name made me feel sick. "ELLL-LEN." And just like that, I knew where I stood in this marriage: second. He didn't care about me as much as he loved his work. He didn't care about my happiness as much as he cared about Newport Beach-style money.

"So, it's settled then?" I said quietly, coldly furi-ous. "Whatever happened to me and you and five bucks?" It was a line I stole from *Reality Bites* one day years ago when Trevor was anxious about his debts. I meant it. I'd be happy to live in this tiny house with him forever, especially if he stepped off the stellar career path that kept him and his intensely type-A personality away from home eighty-plus hours each week. For me and every other thinking, red-blooded North American woman, I'll bet, Ethan Hawke wins every time.

Money has always been more important to Trevor. In fairness, his family didn't have much, while mine did. Sure, my mom made me write a loan proposal if I needed to borrow ten dollars. But I had a car at sixteen and graduated from university without student debt. Mind you, I always had a job. Trevor didn't.

He grew up the golden boy in a working-class family. His parents and older brother, Danny, are good, solid, blue-collar people. His dad has had a big belly and a beer in his hand since I've known him. He's a kind man, though I get the impression he's almost disappointed Trevor opted for medicine instead of taking advantage of their family's pull at Dofasco, the local steel factory.

Trevor's mom, on the other hand, never misses an opportunity to gush about him. "He's always been special. Even when he was a baby I knew he would do something big." She likes to remind me that "he could've had anyone he wanted, and he chose you," which is one of those compliments you have to pretend to be grateful for while you try to ignore the not-too-deeply buried insult.

I try to convince myself that three years isn't that long. Just thirty-six months. Trevor says it's the perfect time for me to start my own publishing agency, disregarding the fact that another leading publisher folds every day. My sister says it's the perfect time to start a family. But we're still a long way from that point in Trevor's ten-year plan, and even if he changed his mind, it's hard to picture myself giving birth so far from home and everyone I know.

It doesn't seem quite reasonable that an address change would cause me to rethink motherhood, something I've wanted for so long. But the thought of having a baby in California, where I know absolutely no one, somehow feels lonelier than being alone. I'd likely take up drinking. A lot.

I lie to people when they ask me if I'm surprised at how successful Trevor has become. "Do you know Trevor? Of course, I'm not surprised," I always reply. But I didn't know. In university, we were equals. I was just starting when he was almost done, but my future was bright, too. We were both on our way to graduate school, shooting for the proverbial stars. He may have been the eerily gorgeous one, but we were both smart and driven. As it turns out, however, being a simple editor at a tiny, local publishing house pales when compared to a sought-after cardiac surgeon. He'd wrangled his way across the border to do his residency and then sweet-talked his way back to do his fellowship. Now he'd been recruited to do a stint at a private medical clinic in Newport Beach, serving the rich and famous.

We have a winner! We both win! No, no, we don't.

I'm serious—I promise I haven't always been like this. In the beginning, I was so happy. My usual outlook on life is fairly positive. Then, after Trevor sprang the move on me, I started feeling down, negative, frustrated. It was like a light switch at first: it felt like I could turn the real Ellen back on if I had to. Now it's like the fuse has blown. No matter what I do, I can't seem to get my light past dim.

For most of our relationship, I've been truly supportive of everything Trevor's done, cheering even the smallest wins, never complaining even when every step forward meant less time together.

Most of the time. The summer before he went away to New York, I ruined the last few weeks we had together because I was too upset to enjoy him, exactly as I've done this summer. I couldn't eat and lost ten pounds, worrying my family. I didn't think he would be tempted by someone else, never mind that he might be unfaithful. I just couldn't imagine being apart for so long. It was the type of love that hurts so much physically you realize "lovesick" isn't just a metaphor.

The night he left plays back in my mind now like a scene from a movie. I watch myself weeping in the shower, in agony, my tiny body crouched in the tiled corner. Not knowing if we would make it, if it would ever be the same.

We all know nothing stays the same. He eventually came home, and it got better for a long time. Those years are such a contrast to where we are now, with me almost wishing he would go to California alone.

I'm finally dressed, and my new shorter hair is swept up in a casual topknot that took me forty-five minutes. I make my way downstairs just as Trevor comes in the front door. The way he looks at me, I know he loves me. If he didn't, I'm guessing he would have given up on me a while ago. Why is it so easy to forget that?

"Someone looks particularly lovely today," he says, walking over and slipping a strong (and very valuable) arm around my waist. Most women would immediately soften. But I've been so out of it lately I almost don't notice how effortlessly attractive he looks in his cargos and old Pearl Jam tee. Even the smell of him, a sweet blend of honey and musk, just makes me angry right now. It feels like we're so far apart I can't even imagine us being intimate.

"We should go," I say, giving him an obviously fake smile.

"Guess what?" he asks. When I don't respond with the expected "What?" he spills. "I upgraded us!" He makes an awkward fist pump, lips spread tight in a Prince Charming grin, like he's just given me the moon.

"Awesome babe!" I cave, return the pump and then turn to leave.

5

As soon as we enter the back gate into my parents' skillfully maintained garden, full of people oblivious to the fact they get to return to their own houses tonight and stay there as long as they want, Audrey notices the dress and squeals with pride. "You're wearing it! I knew you would love it. Look how tiny you are! You don't eat enough. It doesn't look good, you know."

"Thanks. I've always been this size." I give my sister a hug and an acknowledging squeeze on her recently slimmed-down waist. "Look who's talking!" I throw in a couple of flirty whistles. Audrey does a victory twirl complete with a bow, attracting the attention of her three-year-old, Kate, who runs over.

"I wanna spin, Mamma," she yells, already spinning.

"Not so fast, Monkey," I tease, and scoop her up as she tries to fight me off to keep twirling. "Auntie Ellen is going to miss you!!!" I plant a big kiss on her chubby, unblemished cheek, which she immediately rubs off. "Then don't go, silly," she says with brilliant innocence.

"Then who will keep Uncle Trevor company?" I ask, looking over at him.

"I will," she yells, jumping into his arms. Like all girls, Kate loves Trevor. "Take me! We can live in Cinderella's castle!"

To Kate, the chance to visit us and go to Disneyland trumps our twice-weekly playdates. "Where's Grandma?" I ask her.

"She's putting Sami to sleep, and we're not supposed to go in there!" she says, tiptoeing mischievously toward the back door.

"Hold it," Audrey playfully shouts, running after Kate, pretending to get her. I'm not sure what happens when she's got, but Kate runs like she's terrified. Her dad Mark jumps up from his folding chair, Corona in hand, and joins the chase. They're such cute parents, so much more relaxed and playful than most of our friends with young kids.

Two children later and my sister is hotter than ever. Audrey is sweet and angelically beautiful, academically proficient but socially adorable, a combination that quickly propelled her to professional success. Her newly slim body is credit to on-demand breastfeeding and not her social hour at the gym. She has always been curvy: hips, butt and boobs, but now she's close to her dream skinny and somehow manages to keep her C-cup. Jealousy aside, she's a true beauty. People always ask us who is younger, which infuriates me as much as it thrills her. Of course, she looks older. She's been smiling, scowling and squinting for nearly three years longer than I have.

Her husband is a good guy, as well read as he is well dressed, which helps disguise his dad body, barring the glimpses of hairy belly that peek out now as he runs. It's a cruel thought, but maybe life with a husband who is just a little less, rather than so much more, would be happier. *"If you wanna be happy for the rest of your life, never make a pretty woman your wife…"*

He's quietly attractive, but apparently, he's a rocket in the bedroom. Audrey raves about their sex life in a way you know she isn't lying. She blushed when she told me about how hard he works with his hands, how his adamant fingers know no boundaries—how he knew things about her body even she didn't know.

Surprisingly, I don't get grossed out when she talks about him sexually. I'm proud of him. Go, Mark! I'm happy Audrey is taken care of that way. Maybe it's because I can nearly recite the Feminine Mystique and believe that couples should strive for mutual "infinite orgasmic bliss." Or maybe it's because our mom always told us how important it was to have satisfying sex—a solid education and a career, but also, good sex.

Audrey and I were both virgins until senior year. Mom must have known being so upfront about sex took the mystery and rebellion out of it. "Do you really want to waste your virginity on some two-second, selfish lover?" she asked me as we watched one of those wonderfully stereotypical afterschool specials they've since stopped making. I felt sort of sorry for the young man she was referring to. He was sweet and nothing like the boys in that horrifying *Kids* movie. She had a point though; the girl looked scarcely satisfied. Although, unless we planned on losing it to a thirty-year-old, I thought we were all more or less stuck with a couple of minutes of fumbling around, max.

We make our way over to the guests, and like a true gentleman, Trevor greets everyone, all seated in their BYOC ("bring your own chairs"). He shakes hands with the men, accepts a beer and is careful to make eye contact, laughing at all their jokes about plastic surgery before hugging each of the women, some holding on a bit too long. As I watch him, I can feel my resentment soften a little.

His hand moves from his strong jaw to the back of his neck, leaving it there for a minute as if to relieve some built-up stress. He must feel like shit. I haven't made any of this easy for him. And I certainly haven't let him enjoy it.

I hear him tell my dad that I'll be okay, that he will take care of me out in "LaLaLand." It's sweet, a little pathetic mind you, that he wants to take care of me—I get the idea lately he feels he needs to. When did I become someone who needs to be taken care of?

My mom finally appears, wearing a cute outfit from J. Crew. Knee-length khaki shorts and a jean shirt unbuttoned a button past grandma—likely purchased during one of their thirty- percent-off sales. She has an amazing figure for someone her age. Scratch that, she has an amazing body, period. Audrey recently let me know that "you look great for having a baby" is not a compliment; never qualify a compliment. I only wish my mom could love herself enough to enjoy it. She's having a real struggle with aging. I think it's because she was so gorgeous as a young woman and she's now in that invisible age bracket when men stop looking and women stop judging. As much as she avoids vanity, she wants to feel beautiful. Lord knows she's mastered it internally and it shines through, but as external beauty fades, it does have a way of dulling that radiance. Regardless of what Betty Friedan and every aging celebrity say, there's nothing mystical about it. It's easy to say women get more beautiful with age when you're thirty. But when your own face starts sagging, along with everything else, I think it's incredibly difficult.

"Ellen," she yells to me, "why didn't you come get me?" She's holding Sami, my new nephew. Likely claiming he wouldn't go down, which means she can't bear to put him down.

"Kate wouldn't let me," I joke. "What can I do to help?"

"Absolutely nothing, my dear, everything is all set!" This is not shocking. My mother precooks almost all her meals so there's no mess when guests arrive, even though it means it has the texture of cardboard by the time we eat. The menu is invariably a collection of last week's grocery store specials. Although there is always more than enough, it's never very good. My mother is a terrible cook and we're terrible children who tease her to no limit. She credits her lousy cooking to never having anyone around to teach her, which is sad because it's true. I, however, was surrounded by people who love me, and sadly, the outcome isn't much different. Despite her shitty upbringing and our relentless ridicule about her cooking, my mother successfully keeps our family fed with love, and I appreciate this more than ever right now. Truth be told, I loved our Alphagetti and toast nights as a kid.

After dinner is done and the paper plates are cleared, my father stands and clears his throat. "Can I grab your attention for a quick second? Lynn and I thought it was important to have you all over for this bittersweet day, to say goodbye to these two. But we just wanted to say how proud we are of you, Trevor. And you too, Ellen," he adds, perhaps sensing my back up a wee bit. "We know change has never been your strong suit, but we expect big things from you both." He smiles over at us and throws in a predictable, "And we must admit, we are looking forward to visiting Hollywood!"

It was a far cry from the speech he gave at our wedding: "Hello, my name is Peter, and I'm an alcoholic."

He'd delivered it first at Audrey's wedding, a witty account of how his dating daughters drove him to drink. Which was hilarious but couldn't have been further from the truth on my part: my entire dating history consisted of the somewhat nerdy boy down the street and then Trevor. Dad must give me credit for some of Audrey's bi-monthly suitors.

We were lucky to have him around so much growing up. He was successful at his firm, but he always managed to put us first. Since he retired, he basically plays a supporting role in the drama entitled, *My Mother*. But they're in love, lovers still. He set the bar high, almost insurmountably so. As coddled as it sounds, I think that being raised in a completely whole family with a man like my dad might be as detrimental to future happiness as the broken ones some of my friends lived through. It sets such high expectations for relationships to work, to last—to be happy.

There was nothing my father could say today that I'd receive well. But I fake a smile, stand and hug him. It's nearly sunset. All day, I've wavered between wanting to get it all over with or slow it down. Even if I could control the sun like a puppeteer, I wouldn't know whether to pull the string up or drop it with one quick cut.

Trevor thanks everyone and the goodbye hugs commence. I refuse to cry. I don't want to upset anyone who doesn't already know how grossly unexcited I am. Also, because Trevor expects me to fall apart and

I don't want to give him the satisfaction of cheering me up.

Audrey cries, wiping her tears as fast as they come so Kate doesn't catch on. My mom says a quick "be safe," and then scurries inside, pretending not to be emotional. "I love you the most, Mom!" I yell, a silly, and possibly accurate, exchange we've always made. Trevor puts a gentle hand on the small of my back and guides me down the driveway. I know if I look at him I'll give away my real feelings, so I don't, but I accept his fingers when he slips them through mine.

It's dark, but I know this neighborhood like the sound of my sister's laugh. I wonder when I'll feel this safe again. Only a few months ago, I thought this walk would be a permanent fixture in my life. Dinner at Mom and Dad's was a staple, even on the rare nights when Trevor was home in time. We would just show up, regardless of the bad food. We liked their company. We liked the easiness of this walk, the effortless romance.

This time last summer, we were so much happier. I remember it like it was yesterday: Trevor and I running out of my parents' front door as if fleeing a crime scene, which my mother's house kind of looks like after a large family dinner. The rain was coming down with punishing force, the way it does during hot Ontario summers, both of us soaked, not bothering to avoid puddles. Then, as if on cue, we stopped and started kissing. I mean really kissing, his hands on my face, his body leaning into mine so I could feel him through his soaked jeans. Water dripping into our eyes, lost in steam rising from the hot concrete road, we kissed like that for a long while, not stopping even when Mark and Audrey drove past, slowing down just long enough to yell an unoriginal chorus of, "Get a room!"

Tonight is different. I continue to keep it together even though I want to turn around and run back to my parents, back to my childhood, where everything was simple and contained.

"I thought you handled that well," Trevor says, breaking our silence. "Could've fooled me, Ellen, but at times you almost seemed happy?" I swallow hard, infuriated. How is it possible to see something that is so not there, to disregard my deep, dark hatred of what's happening and then to suggest I'm happy doing it? I twist my hand free and pretend to slap a mosquito on my neck.

"I thought it would be worse," I say cowardly.

As we get close to home, I sense Trevor is distracted. I've seen this type of behavior from him before: our engagement, the time he spilt coffee on our new ivory rug and tried to cover it with a cushion, and of course the night he told me about his new job. I cannot handle anything of significance tonight. I swear to God if I walk in to my girlfriends yelling, "Surprise!" I will turn and run.

It's worse.

I don't know how he did it, but when we walk in the door, I think the house is on fire. He has somehow lit a million tiny candles and our album, the Tragically Hip's *Road Apples*, is playing in the background. I fight my urge to flip the lights on and throw a fit about things that we still have to do tonight. But I don't. Instead, I'm able to muster a giggle when he says something about the power being shut off early. Even in the worst lighting, Trevor looks like sex personified. Right now, with flickering candlelight reflecting off his cheekbones, he is flawless. I'm angry with him, but I'm not dead.

In a bold move, because I don't want to give him time to say something encouraging like, "It'll be great," (which may make me cry), I decide to finally take the initiative he's pestered me about for years. My usual routine is more awkward, hard-to-get, but not tonight.

Without a word, I turn my back to him, place my keys on the kitchen counter, take a deep breath, unzip my dress and let it slither down my body to the floor in one movement. Unfortunately, I'm wearing my least sexy underwear, beige. I quickly improvise, slipping them off while looking over my shoulder, making eye contact with Trevor, who is now as shocked as he is aroused.

I usually keep my eyes closed tight during sex. I find it so awkward, almost like I'm looking in on someone else, as if the studious, quiet girl he married couldn't possibly be this woman, comfortable and enjoying herself.

Trevor comes up behind me and cups my breasts in his hands, breathing softly in my ear. It's a move that usually excites me, but tonight it makes me tense. I reach around and run my hands down his back, stopping just above his well-defined rear. He turns me around to face him even though I would much rather face away. He mistakes my boldness for playfulness and effortlessly picks me up, lifts me onto our counter and pulls my hips toward him. Instead of kissing him, I casually lean back on my arms and stare into his eyes, daring him to look away—as if saying, "Is this what you want? Is there anything else I can do for you?"

In his eyes, this is progress. To me, it's indifference, the way a prostitute might feel. But seeing how turned on he is fills me with confidence I haven't felt in a long time. It feels almost like power.

We finish and then there is an awkwardness between us.

"Do you want some wine?" he asks as he carefully pulls his jeans up over himself, still hard. Buzzing from my almost orgasm, I smile and nod and feel nearly happy for a second. I watch him, topless, as he grabs the two wine glasses he'd strategically set out, probably assuming I would be more of a challenge. He pours the wine we got for our anniversary last year. "Might as well drink it. Can't bring it with us," he says, clinking his glass to mine. Might as well.

Most women would thank God for the opportunity to have sex with this man. His chiseled waist is a perfect meeting point between his broad shoulders and long muscular legs. If they existed, you'd think he was one of those genetically designed science fiction babies, enhanced before they were even born. As I watch him now, glistening with sweat as he moves around our bare kitchen with athletic ease, I want to force myself to be content, like a superficial middle-aged man with a twenty-year-old wife. It's strange how you can wake up one day and feel so differently about the man you used to fall asleep dreaming of.

After we finish the wine, Trevor flicks the lights on and I blow out the last of the candles, extinguishing whatever it was that just happened between us. I head to bed alone. Trevor has to review a file on a new patient he is to see shortly after we arrive tomorrow. I promise to wait up, but as soon as my head hits the pillow, I allow myself to fall into sleep, heavy with wine and emotion.

6

Sarah has finally arrived to show us the house Trevor and Danny picked out.

One deep breath and I reach for the handle, hopping out of the car with make-believe eagerness. This woman is not sixty, by the way. I'd give her late forties at the oldest. As I approach her, I can see a refreshing streak of lines across her forehead. She's blond and attractive, of course, but more genuine than I pictured. Trevor looks panicked, like he's trying to prepare her for me as I get closer.

"Hey, Sarah," I say, tapping her on the shoulder and extending my hand. "I'm Ellen."

"Ellen! It's so nice to finally meet you."

"Yes, I'm sorry about that. This has been quite a lot harder than I expected, but I am so grateful to you for helping Trevor. It's just…"

"It's not what you expected?" she asks, though it's more like a statement.

"Well, honestly, no."

"I tried to tell Trevor that this neighborhood can be intense, but he really wanted a family feel for you, and the Port Streets are the best in Newport Beach."

Trevor is silent. His face has softened toward me, almost apologetic, but he offers no comment and lets us talk about him like he's not there.

"I understand that, and I appreciate it. I guess I'm just confused about why we need such a big house. And it's not gated."

"But very safe," she says. "You'll know all your neighbors in no time. Everyone looks out for one another here. In some of those gated communities, you'd be lucky to see your neighbors, never mind learn their names or feel you can borrow a cup of sugar."

She's annoyingly sweet and says her O's like A's. There's not a chance in hell I would ever need to borrow sugar from someone. But the quicker we go inside, the quicker she will leave, and the quicker we can make other plans.

"Let's have a look then, shall we?" I say, gesturing to the door. God, I adore this door.

"Okay. I think you'll love it once we get in."

Her hand trembles a bit as she fumbles with the lock and I realize I've turned this into an uncomfortable situation for everyone. She opens the door and allows Trevor and me to go through first. I'm welcomed by a strong wave of fresh paint and plug-in deodorizer. It floods my nose and goes right to my head, temporarily blinding me to anything but the scent. What are they trying to cover up? I think I smell dog, but I keep silent, hoping Trevor will come to his senses, or at least acknowledge them.

"I know you have some furniture coming. Trevor mentioned you might be interested in keeping the sofas and the dining table?" She glides through the foyer and down a long walkway that leads to French doors. "The place has been closed up for a while. That paint smell won't last."

As she opens the door, hot air pours into the already stuffy house, but I peek outside and fall quickly in love with a tiny, French-inspired garden: a bistro set, a brick hot tub and built-in barbecue. I can see myself here at night with a glass of wine, gazing up at twinkling stars and the faux ones wrapped in the vines that cover a solid privacy wall.

I take a deep, thoughtful breath, push my delayed teenage angst aside and look around, grinning slightly. I remove my shoes against Sarah's recommendation: "Oh, you can keep your shoes on, the floors are wood."

I almost say, "Canadians take their shoes off indoors." But given my mood, I know it will come across as harsh, and bite my tongue.

The room to the right of the front door is spacious and architecturally detailed. An archway separates a dining room and formal living area. There are plenty of bookshelves complete with the same moldings that border the walls and coffered ceilings. I wish I had moved my book collection rather than preserving them in storage for our homecoming. I keep all my school novels, texts and anthologies in great condition on the outside, but the insides are well loved, kissed with comments and brought to life with colorful highlighters. They would look absolutely at home here.

There's another set of French doors and an additional outside sitting area (another door I will have to secure). A small walkway through a butler's pantry leads into the kitchen. It's old, but the white cabinets are freshly painted and look clean. I run my hands over the cool granite island, wanting to press my hot face against it. There are a new gas range and a large two-door Sub-Zero fridge. It's not the most remarkable kitchen, but it's nicer than our kitchen at home.

The family room—ugh—is inconsistent with the rest of the house. It's gentleman-club brown and there are exposed puke-colored beams I wish would disappear. Crossing my arm, I make my opinion known, whispering, "Oh, man," just loud enough to be heard.

"Yeah, this isn't my favorite room either," Sarah agrees. "I bet I could get the owners to let you paint in here."

"Yeah, we will have to do something about this. Was this ever in style?" I ask like someone who knows about design, like someone I'm not, and then giggle in an attempt to keep it light.

Trevor is quiet, wandering by himself. I have behaved badly, and now I realize he couldn't have done a better job finding us a home. Problem is, this is the home I would want at home. Not here, not at this point.

"For a rental, this place is in great condition. All the carpets upstairs are new and the bedrooms have all been painted." She leads me up a traditional staircase. Trevor finally joins us, but refuses to make eye contact. I don't know if he's mad or just deeply disappointed. Thinking back to this summer and even the little love note, I realize Trevor wasn't only nervous in the car. He was excited to show me this house. So yes, this is another joy I have deprived him of.

"How many bedrooms?" I ask Sarah as we near the top of the stairs and see just how big this house is. The landing is lined with more bookcases, with doors on each side. "Four bedrooms up here, a laundry room, and an adorable office. It's big."

"Holy smokes, Trevor, how many visitors are we expecting?" I reach for his hand and he accepts as if acknowledging my defeat.

"I thought the room right beside the master would make a perfect nursery, eventually," he says unenthusiastically. Eventually, eh?

"Yeah, maybe we'll have triplets and justify this house!" I'm half joking, but I'm 100% an asshole. "I'm kidding!!!" I shout, laughing, but he drops my hand anyway. "I love the house. I hate the neighborhood, but the house is beautiful."

"I knew you would love it."

After we fill out some paperwork, Sarah leaves and Trevor and I collapse on a deep, slightly battered grey velvet couch. The list of to-dos in my head is overwhelming: groceries to buy, utilities to set up, luggage to unpack, movers to receive, car to get. And it's hard for me to carry on the charade of being positive when I just want to crawl out of my skin and directly out the door.

"It's way too hot in here," Trevor says. "Why velvet in this climate?? This couch has to go!"

"I love this couch," I say honestly and roll onto my side, contemplating a nap. Trevor takes off his shirt and wipes the sweat off his face with it. He lays down on the floor, his body matching its hardness. "Now I think that's the second time I've heard you say you love something. Maybe you still love someone?" He slaps the floor beside him, signaling me to join him. Regardless of the heat, the velvet provides me with all the comfort I need right now. "I'm just going to close my eyes for a few minutes." I roll in toward the couch, my back to Trevor and everything I have to get done.

I'm not sleep deprived, but for the second time today I fall asleep fast. I must be dehydrated, because my dreams overflow with images of water: I float on it, swim in it, drink it in large gulps and then start to sink, choking—drowning.

I wake up to Trevor's hand on my shoulder. "Elly, wake up, babe."

The room is dark and stale; voices and footsteps are all around me. Momentarily, I panic before reality sets in. I'm really here, in California, in this huge, hot house. "The movers are here; I can't believe you slept through all this."

I sit up and look around with a sigh. "Wow. How long have they been here?"

Boxes are stacked on the kitchen counters and scattered on the floor. Funny how our house at home seemed overcome with boxes, and in here they look so inconsequential. "Sorry, Trev!" My voice is hoarse. "I need some water. I have some in my carry-on." In times like these, his anal organizational skills come in handy; he knows exactly where everything is and is back with my bag within seconds. As he hands me my half-empty bottle of lukewarm water, I notice he is fully dressed in dress pants and a golf shirt. Tucked in, obviously. "Why are you wearing a belt, Trevor?"

I suspected he would want to check in at the practice, but it must be after seven p.m. by now. "I'll just pop over there when these guys leave. I have to consult on a patient who is supposed to have surgery this week. I'll be quick." I smile and nod, disappointed. "But," he adds, "I got our TV set up, the Wi-Fi works, and I have Five Guys' en route as we speak!"

Awesome! I darkly think to myself. "Okay, babe," I manage to say out loud.

After I splash water on my face and fake a sarcastic smile to my reflection, I finally greet our movers. I am shocked by how tiny and yet incredibly strong these two Mexican men are. The smaller of the two, who insists on calling me ma'am, throws my grandmother's 200-pound antique armoire on his back and carries it up the stairs like he's giving it a piggyback, securing it only with fingers that turn white from pressure. They work tirelessly and flash wide happy grins every time they pass me.

When our burgers arrive, all three men basically giggle with excitement. I watch the two movers turn on the hose and wash their hands before digging in, while Trevor, the doctor, takes an enormous two-handed bite. I wish I remembered what they said their names were, because I think they may be my two best friends here. They're so grateful for a couple of burgers and some fries, even though they've just worked harder than any Canadian I've ever seen.

While they eat, I walk around prepared for the worst, but every room is all set for me to start unpacking. Our bed is complete with box spring and mattress and is in the exact place I would have put it. I can't imagine this process going smoother. Sleeping through most of the work didn't hurt. Still, I had expected it to be more grueling.

Now that the heavy lifting is complete, I just want to be alone in here. I'm super appreciative and super happy when they leave, handing me a business card in exchange for a well-earned tip. I place their card on our now comparatively miniature table for safekeeping. Two down, one to go.

Before he can leave, Trevor goes through a gentleman's checklist: lock the door, don't answer the door, check your phone and make sure it's working, call 911, et cetera, et cetera. I appreciate the gesture, but truthfully, it just reminds me that I should be scared. I'm entirely alone here, I know no one, I have no car and nowhere to drive it if I did. He places a tender kiss on my forehead and waits outside for his driver, summoned with some app called Uber because cabs aren't as dependable or impressive. I'll be Ubering (if you can use it as a verb?) to the grocery store tomorrow morning.

Obediently, I lock the front door and do a quick check of all the other doors. Even with the indoor lights on and shades up, the backyard is completely black and almost exactly like the opening scene of *Scream*. I courageously open the back door and sneak across the patio to search for the outlet Sarah had pointed out earlier. Success! I find it and plug in two extension cords that transform the backyard into an elegant oasis: the mini-lights strung around tree branches overhead and around a large umbrella all twinkle on with brilliance outdone only by the summer moon, which shines so much brighter here than at home. It seems so close. So real. The lights could seem overdone, except that they're utterly charming. If I had any friends, this would be the perfect setting for a girls' night.

Despite the ambience, the sound of a car driving past sends me scurrying back indoors, careful not to step in the sprays of darkness. I lock the doors and take a deep breath. I pause for a moment and survey the lifeless scene. The stillness and silence make me feel like I might disappear if I don't move and start making noise.

I walk into the kitchen and stand there for quite a while, tapping my fingers as I press my hands together in prayer form, lips pursed. "Where do I start?"

I decide to do exactly what I would do at home: I set my phone up on Trevor's Beats speaker and Spotify myself some feel-good music. It feels like an omen when Drake's now old but never dull *Hotline Bling* kicks things off, a fellow Canadian/California import to keep me company tonight. It doesn't take long for my spirits to lift and my body to follow, twirling around far too gracefully for the song. I dance around the kitchen checking out all the cupboards and myself in the reflection of the window, Lysol wipe in hand. So far, so good.

I've tackled almost all the dishes and sung my way through half the playlist when a loud bang stops me in my tracks. I reach for my phone, quickly ending Ellie Goulding's *Burn*. What the fuck was that? I can feel my heart beat against my ribs. And then I hear it again, metal against wood.

Shit, it's the front door.

I glance at the oven clock. Who would come over at nine-thirty? I know as soon as I walk around the corner the creepy glass windows that frame the door will give me away. I wait another minute before I move, desperately wishing they'll go away. In the silence, I make my way into the foyer, fighting horrible thoughts, and then bravely peer out into darkness.

I stupidly flick on two sets of lights then realize that if whoever was here is still close, they might come back. I quickly hit the off switches. When I look out the window, I notice something small on the porch. I run into the front living room and do a scan of the street. My neighbor two doors down is watering his lawn—likely not on his watering day—but other than that, the street is undisturbed.

I've seen enough TV to know that whoever left this could be hiding around the corner. It's placed too far from the door for it to be a casual delivery, and it's far enough for me to have to step out to get it. I run into the kitchen and grab a glass vase, because a knife could be used against me and I have no idea where the knives are. If someone jumps out, I'll throw the vase and run. I slow my breathing, do a quick count to three and then inch the door open. With two long steps forward, I grab the package and reverse inside without turning my back.

Feeling stealthy, I lean against the door, let out a deep breath and finally look at the package. What I thought I saw (bomb?) was nothing like the pretty parcel in my hands. A note, *"Welcome to the Neighborhood,"* is strung onto the ribbon of an elegantly cellophane-wrapped basket. What the hell? I carry it to the counter and pull out avocado after avocado, limes, cilantro and tortilla chips. The note reads:

> *Welcome to California –*
> *Please enjoy some homegrown ingredients for*
> *some yummy guacamole.*
> *Mary and James*
> *1942 Port Charles Pl*

Wow, that was quick. Who knew such hospitality actually existed? Even though I abhor the word yummy, I feel grateful and safer knowing I've got Mary across the street. The burger I'd planned on eating now looks soggy and less than appetizing and I realize I'm starving. I roll a couple of avocados on the counter with the palm of my hand and think about Audrey, who makes the best guac. Man, I wish she were here to make it now. But she's not. I nod my head, accept that I'm on my own, then find a bowl and use a plastic Five Guys' fork to get to work.

I'm still anxious enough that it seems critical to be able to hear any more possible home invasion warning noises, so music is no longer an option. The kitchen seems like too much work to do without it, so I take my snack and head upstairs, trying not to let the little noises of the house "settling" freak me out. I quickly find our sheets and bedding, and with every piece of home I pull out of the box I feel warmer inside. Which is nice, because despite the heat, my heart's been chilly all day. The least I can do for Trevor is have the bed made when he gets home. I even consider finding some candles and sexy underwear, but ultimately I just dig out his old Queen's rowing shirt. I really need to take a shower, though the thought of being vulnerable is a bit too scary. So, I grab the shirt, clean undies, and as many toiletries as I can carry, and make my way into our new master bath.

Surprisingly for an older home, it has trendy white marble countertops and the most endearing his and hers medicine cabinets. The shades, however, are just short of offensive, gold with turquoise hummingbirds, and I make a mental note to replace them as soon as possible. For now, I just pull them up as high as they go and hope the privacy wall out back works just as well up here.

I strip down in front of the mirror and carefully assess the damage done by my depression eating. I'm not the most sexual person, but for the most part, I'm quite comfortable naked. My breasts are on the small side but their shape is great and my nipples are still a pretty shade of pink. I say still because since having her babies, Audrey's have taken on a new brownish hue. I'm willing to make the sacrifice when it's time, but for now, I turn to the side and check them out. Nice boobs. I'm lucky to have this body at my age given how little I work out, but just to be proactive, I do some squats while I brush my teeth.

I'm only ten squats deep when I hear a dog bark. I cover my chest with my arm and move closer to the window. Well, what do we have here? It's dark and I don't have the best angle, but I'm fairly sure the neighbor behind me is super-hot. My only entirely clear view is of the top of his full head of sun-bleached hair, but from what I can see, his shoulders look broad and his arms are really cut. My face is so close to the glass my breath fogs the window slightly and, feeling just a tiny bit silly, I trace a heart around him. He's on the phone with someone. It looks like he is whispering. Probably his girlfriend, and this is a family neighborhood. Cheater. For a split second, he looks up, and I think he spots me. I quickly drop down out of sight and cover my mouth as if he can also hear me breathing. There's no way he can see through the tree up here. He probably just saw the light. And what's the big deal anyway?

So, he gets a look at my awesome breasts. I stand back up, push my shoulders back and finish brushing my teeth, flushed with adrenaline as I imagine his eyes on me.

Trevor sneaks in around eleven. He sent his usual text message to let me know it was him before he came through the door. As much as I want to roll over and play dead, I am wide awake from my naps and curious about his night—curious to hear if this is all worth it.

He tiptoes into our room, careful not to wake me. In the bathroom, I have laid out fresh boxers and his toothbrush the way I always did at home. He's only in there a few minutes before he makes his way over to the bed, guided by the light of his phone.

"Hey babe," I whisper, startling him.

"You're awake? Hey, there!" He comes over to my side of the bed and sits down close to me. "Glad to see you survived your first night alone. Was it that bad?"

"Umm, it was okay," I say, sitting up. "A neighbor dropped off a welcome gift and scared the crap out of me, but it was fine. How about you, good night?"

"Yeah, it was okay. Ryan seems cool. Wants to get you and his wife together."

"Is he the guy from New York?"

"Yep, they've only been here a year or so. She probably knows what you're going through; you might like her."

"Probably not," I say immediately, absolutely meaning it. "But I'm glad it went well tonight."

He rolls his eyes and gives my leg a playful squeeze. "I know this is difficult, Ellen. Are you okay? I mean, I know you're not okay, but how bad are you?"

I breathe in deeply and consider his question. Am I okay? I don't think so, but I do know it could be much worse. Being here is a little exciting. An adventure—a new place to explore, with no one to answer to. "I'll be okay, Trevor. Really. I'm actually looking forward to seeing this place in the light tomorrow."

"That's my girl." His smile is so relieved he looks as if the whole world has just lifted off his shoulders.

"We desperately need food though, babe," I say. "First thing tomorrow…coffee and groceries."

"You must be hungry. Your dad would be so mad if he knew I left you here to starve. Thing is, I have to be back at the practice early tomorrow."

"Oh, right. Yeah. Well, I'm sure I can figure it out."

"Sorry, Elly. It won't be like this for long." He crawls over me, squishing me with his thick legs, and buries his head into his pillow. "Ahhh, this pillow smells like home."

I can tell he's exhausted. With the busy day and time change, it's understandable. Funny, tonight I wouldn't have objected to sex. Just as less than a year ago he would have insisted we christen the new place.

7

When I wake up, the room is bright. Trevor is gone, and his side is smoothed down like a hospital bed. The house feels slightly cooler, but my hair is damp from a long, sweaty night. For the first time in months, I hop out of bed immediately. Even the tornado of suitcases and boxes doesn't faze me.

Behind the curtains, I can see it's another scorcher, the heat radiating through the windows like an oven door.

Birds have made a home outside our bedroom window. The babies are up and hungry, squawking for their mother. I don't know what time it is. Other than the birds, I don't hear any family noises, no relentless basketballs or obnoxious scraping of hockey sticks. From up here, the backyard looks inviting, but I know I won't enjoy anything without coffee.

There is a certain freedom in knowing no one. In terms of maintenance, I tend to be on the low end, but here in the land of beauty I couldn't care less what I look like. I throw on some cut-offs and the same t-shirt I wore all day yesterday. I was smart to pack a few boxes of essentials like shampoo and toilet paper into the moving truck. Trying to find them now, however, doesn't interest me. I'll shower later.

My eyes dart everywhere as I make my way downstairs. Everything looks even better this morning. The light floods through the windows and makes lovely patterns on the linen-papered walls. I dodge boxes, step over them, weave around them—refusing to let them get between me and my newly optimistic outlook—on my way to adjust the thermostat.

Uber is easy to figure out, and my driver Juan is set to arrive in eight minutes. I grab a promotional notepad with Sarah's face on it, a pen, and head out front to wait. I've never been a list person like Trevor. I prefer to pretend I have it all under control and then forget everything, like a waitress who insists she's got the order but follows up with a hundred questions, ultimately fucking it all up. Today feels like the start of a new me, so I make an exception because we need so much, and grocery lists might be the closest I get to publishing while I'm here. Ideally, I would love to make this outing as bountiful as possible, because who knows what horrors await me. I may never leave the house again.

Strangely, I hadn't noticed the trees yesterday. I had pictured palm trees everywhere, but as I survey the neighbors' properties this morning I see sycamores and alders as well as a couple of lemon trees, which are cool. Then I see her: a woman on a clear mission, making shockingly swift steps for her size.

She's older, painfully cheerful, ready for the day in a too-coordinated outfit, and is headed in my direction, waving intensely. Mary, I presume. I'm torn between running away or going in for a hug.

"Hi there," she yells, while crossing the street. "Welcome!"

"Hello." I smile and walk to meet her halfway on the road. "You must be Mary?"

"Yes. I am terribly sorry if I startled you last night. Was it too late to knock? My husband said it was too late. I'm so sorry. You were probably asleep?"

She talks so fast I'm not sure if she's even noticed I haven't answered her first question. "No, not at all. I had music on, and my husband was working. I didn't hear you."

"Oh, no problem at all. Just being neighborly. Your husband…"

"Thank you!" I interrupt, not remembering if I'd said it. "What an amazing gesture."

"Anytime! We have so much back there, most of it goes to waste. Your husband, is he home now?" she asks, looking around me to peer into our windows. "I'd love to…"

"No, I'm sorry. He's not. Already back at work this morning. He's a doctor. Long hours."

"You poor thing. My husband is an attorney; I completely get it." Somehow, I doubt her husband works the hours Trevor does, but I appreciate her sympathy.

"You two have kids?"

And there it is. "No, not yet."

"Yeah, ours are grown and away at school now. In this neighborhood, as soon as your kids are old enough you get an invisible notice under the door telling you it's time to move on and make way for a young family."

I fake a laugh, infuriated with Trevor for moving me here, for breaking the Port Streets rules. When a black SUV pulls up, I am beyond relieved. Thank you, Juan!

"Fancy car!" Mary says, crossing over to the wrong side, my side, of the street. "We have a guy if you need a rental."

"I might take you up on that," I say as I turn away and step into the car. "This isn't too shabby though."

The grocery store is only a few blocks away. Juan, a charming man who likely whistles his way through life, or at least while he drives, doesn't seem to mind the short fare and even assures me he will be in the area when I'm done. So far, the people here seem friendly enough. When we pull in, I'm immediately impressed. The plaza looks nothing like grocery stores at home and everything like I expected here. Despite the heat, the palm trees and drought-friendly plants are beautifully lush and well maintained.

All summer I've secretly worried about how insecure all the custom-made women would make me feel, but the first woman I see when I enter the store is so full of fillers she looks like she's having an allergic reaction. I almost can't peel my eyes from her inflated face, which was no doubt stunning not long ago. She's still beautiful, but in a way that reminds me of the women in animated films. It's foolish to think women in Toronto don't touch themselves up. What I can't understand is why they make it so obvious here. Does this woman not have a daughter or someone to tell her that is not necessary? I chuckle and resist shaking my head, remembering there is a special place in hell for women who don't support other women. Fuck it. If they like it, I like it.

I grab a coffee at a convenient café located inside the grocery store. I stand in line watching the people come through the door, all hot and hurried. It feels nice not to be rushing anywhere. The young lady at the counter asks me if I want my coffee hot or cold. I feel like looking over my shoulder to the other people in line, pointing to her with my thumb like Jerry Seinfeld, as if to say, "Are you kidding me? Who drinks cold coffee on purpose?"

Hot, obviously.

They only have cream at the counter. As I'm waiting for some milk, a conspicuously attractive man joins the line. He's older than me, maybe forty. Tall and broad like Trevor, he has blond hair, and while his sunglasses hide his eyes, I'm guessing they're California blue. His form-fitting suit, on the other hand, doesn't leave much to the imagination, revealing a lean, muscular body. He catches me staring at him and offers me a small, coy smile that seems a combination of "Can't blame you for looking," and a Joey-style, "How you doin'?"

Women can be strange creatures. Most of my thoughts this past summer have been about how beautiful the women would be here. I hadn't even considered what the men would be like, that perhaps they'd be equally alluring. I remember Audrey telling me when I was in high school, "Don't worry about being the prettiest girl in the room." But it was easy for her to say because she was perfect, even during puberty.

I never do this, but I can't stop myself from checking for a ring.

Married.

Still, I wish I had at least washed my face this morning.

Coffee in hand, I make my way up and down aisles, filling my cart with mainly familiar brands. I'm baffled at how expensive things are, especially fruit. This is California, after all. Dairy, however, is super cheap. I load up on yogurt, ten for ten dollars. If I can't come up with a single meal from this cart, I blame Mary for distracting me from completing my list.

I'm just about to head to the checkout when I catch a glimpse of something beautiful. Wine! I completely forgot you can buy it everywhere in the States. I push my grocery cart to the side of the aisle and head too eagerly over to the only thing that makes me happier than the chocolate I just virtuously passed up on.

As I turn the corner, I see him again. He has his coffee now, hot. Strange he's taking so long to get wine, unless he has a full cart left in someone's way like I do. I feel nervous around this striking stranger. He likely won't notice me, and that's a good thing, given the way I look this morning. I want to walk away, which is silly. Wine is more important to me than feeling a little embarrassed about my hygiene!

I study the bottles, conscious of my company and thrilled at how cheap California wine is here. It may be in my head, but I swear he is looking at me, wanting to get my attention. I force myself to look in his direction. I was wrong about his eyes. They're the darkest I've ever seen. But I'm right—he is looking at me.

I play it cool and give him a mannerly smile. He smiles back, mostly with his eyes. They lock onto mine, and I can't determine if it's polite or inappropriate. It feels kind of awkward and flirty to me, but I'm flattered he thinks I'm cute enough to acknowledge at all. Mind you, we're the only two people in the aisle, so it might be more uncomfortable if we don't say hello. Rude, even.

"So, what's good?" he asks, looking back at the shelves while exaggerating a confused scratch to his chin.

"All of it," I respond, laughing.

"I'm not a wine drinker, and I need a bottle for a friend."

"Beer drinker?"

"Something like that," he says, staring into my eyes again. For a moment, I'm afraid to look away. I feel my pulse quicken, and my thoughts are drowned out by the buzz of recessed lighting and my pumping heart.

"Well," I say, breaking our gaze, "I'd go with the most expensive."

He laughs. "You don't know much about wine either, do you?"

"No, I don't." I'm about to say my husband usually chooses, but I stop myself. I spot a Mission Hill Pinot Noir and grab it. "Here, you can't go wrong with this one." I reach out to pass it to him, and he walks toward me. I want to back away, or at least put my sunglasses on.

He reaches for the wine, his eyes not faltering, not even to look at the bottle.

One finger touches mine for a brief second, and I wonder if it was intentional.

He tosses the wine up with one hand and flips it over to read the label. It looks so fragile in his strong grip, almost miniature. I lose myself for a moment and think about how easy it would be for him to toss me up like that. I feel a bit indecent picturing this unknowing man sexually. I think of my great aunt and all the perverted comments she makes, and giggle in my head as I wonder if I'm on my way to becoming an old pervert too.

"Okanagan? As in Canada?"

"Yes! Beautiful British Columbia. They'll love it."

"Sold." He tucks the bottle under his arm and gives me a nod. "Is there anything I can do for you before I go?"

I almost choke. Did he really just ask that? "Pardon?" I ask, flustered.

"You want me to get you anything down from the top shelf, maybe?" He gestures reaching up high over my head.

I laugh, impressed with his boldness. "Yes, I'm little, but you're absurdly tall! And no, I've got this, thanks."

"Absurd, huh? Okay. Well, thank you."

He extends his hand to me as a farewell. I don't want him to leave, but there's nothing else to say. I place my hand in his and notice how smooth it feels. No dryness. No calluses. The innocent touch makes me feel both guilty and more alive than I've felt for a long time. We both use our right hands even though I'm left-handed. Was he trying to hide his ring? Was I?

After he leaves and I'm sure it's safe, I consider jumping up and down and giggling like we did in high school whenever our crush spoke to us. Instead, I take a few minutes to get myself together. I stand there pretending to look at the wine, but really, I'm just standing, pulsing everywhere, unable to dig up the memory of the last time I flirted with someone.

After a few minutes, I grab a couple of bottles of Pinot and float through the checkout like I'm on uppers, perhaps like some of the women around me. How can I feel insecure when a man like that takes the time to flirt with me?

The way the whole exchange unfolded felt like I'd willed it to happen, from the moment he walked into the café to his last steps around the corner. Maybe it happened differently in his head, but the way he'd looked at me couldn't have been innocent, surely? Then again, maybe he just has insanely sexy eyes. Maybe he can't help looking at his grandma like that.

8

Juan gets me home safely, even helps carry my groceries into the house, his old-man-strength allowing him to do most of the hauling on his own. It seems like a good idea until we are alone in the kitchen, the front door blown shut behind us. Luckily, he's sensitive to my nervousness and leaves immediately. The idea of unpacking all this food is a bit overwhelming; even deciding where everything will go is a big commitment. The countertops are already full, so I have no choice but to take everything out of the bags and flagrantly line it up on the floor. Before I make another move, I decide to open a bottle of wine and do a little day drinking to celebrate a successful first outing.

I try to eject a particular face from my mind, but every few minutes I find myself thinking about my captivating encounter. I wonder if I will ever see him again. He's not perfect-looking like Trevor—his face is older and a bit more weathered, likely from the sun. His stylishly cut blond hair makes me think he is California-bred. I wouldn't say he's a surfer, though he may surf. He's clean-cut and sophisticated, not quite rugged. He's a bit of a perfect mess. Haute mess, not hot mess. Or haute mess and hot mess? Whatever. I'm insane.

If I keep my back to the rest of the house, I am quite happy with how the settling-in progress is coming along. The kitchen is clean and looks inviting. My half-empty wine bottle and picked-at cheeseboard feel homey. Like young professional, no kids (no life) kinda homey.

I was going to pick up some flowers, but I decided that I'll go back tomorrow if Trevor doesn't bring any home. Around the same time I went today. Exactly the same time I went today.

I make my way upstairs. After the kitchen, our clothes are my next priority. In our room, I give myself a short pep talk and then drag our luggage from the hallway into the closet. Of course, Trevor has already managed to hang all his suits, shirts and ties; his shoes lined up methodically: dress, loafers, sneakers, runners.

I try my best to match his side, seeing his organization and raising him an attempt at color coordination. It would seem I wear a lot of black and white. I wish the rest of my life were so simple, or perhaps more complicated. The floor-length mirror on the back of the door distracts me. Every time I pull something interesting out, I can't resist trying it on, planning future outfits with zero intention of ever wearing them. There's a strong possibility that the mirror is lying to me, or perhaps my hormones are working in my favor today, because miraculously, my "like pile" contains nearly my whole wardrobe.

I stack Trevor's t-shirts on a built-in shelf, careful not to crease them more than the travel already has. I'm always impressed and equally miffed by his folding skills. It is crucial I don't ram everything in, as I never learned how to iron, a skillset lost on my generation. Not to mention that my mother is no longer a convenient, albeit immature, option.

Pressed between his shirts and jeans, I discover a picture of me, not much older than twenty-five. I take it over to the mirror and compare the two faces. In the photo, my skin is smoother, not as thin as it looks now. My eyes have changed. They are older, maybe a little dull. At twenty-five, I knew who I was and what I wanted. I was madly in love with Trevor, and now I love him. And incidentally, I feel like I've never known less about myself.

I think about how I felt when Trevor first told me he loved me. There was no question he did, but I loved him more. My mom says it's inevitable that power will shift in relationships; at times, it will seem like it's all you and other years it will be all him.

I love he has a secret picture of me.

My phone vibrates on the marble bathroom counter. It's Trevor, I bet. He'll be home any second.

A couple of minutes later, I hear the door, which I most certainly locked behind Juan. Still in a ridiculous ensemble, I run down the stairs, excited to see my husband and his beautiful face—to thank him with a kiss for taking his turn and loving me more.

I flip the lock and throw the door open. To my surprise, it's not Trevor. "Oh!" I blurt, startled. It's a petite blond woman, looking at me with a concerned look on her face.

"I'm sorry," I finally say, shaking my head as if to excuse my confusion. "I thought you were my husband."

"No, I'm sorry to drop in on you like this, but I just wanted to say hello and give you my number in case you need anything. And I brought cookies!" Beaming, she holds up a plate full of freshly baked cookies wrapped in now-familiar cellophane. No plastic wrap or paper towel cover here on Wisteria Lane.

"Wow! How thoughtful!" I take the cookies, not knowing if I should invite her in, desperately not wanting to. "Thank you. I'm Ellen Hunter," I say, reaching for her similarly tiny hand. Then I notice my sleeve and remember my hit-and-run outfit: a see-through white blouse, black bra and track pants. Before she can even say her name, I confess: "I was just unpacking and trying stuff on, this isn't my outfit!"

"I didn't even notice," she lies. "I'm not much better." She's wearing a gray tank top perfectly front-tucked into the tightest yoga pants imaginable. She's skinny, so I have no idea why they're so tight. I feel sorry for her vagina.

"I'm Wendy Matthews. I live right behind you with my husband Ken and our three noisy boys."

Ken! Oh, I know him, the late-night whisperer, the peeping Tom. Of course, he has a name like that. All I can think of is Ken Matthews from Sweet Valley High. All-American. In fact, I don't think there are any Canadian Kens.

"Three boys? Wow, they must keep you busy!"

"Do they ever! You just have to let me know if they're too loud. Promise you will?"

"Oh, we love children, obviously. Why else would we live here?" I say, pointing up and then down the street with my best imitation of a gleeful motion.

"How many do you have?" she asks, smiling. Unaware.

"No, I mean we love other people's children. We don't have any yet. We're working on it."

She gives me a sympathetic smile. "Well, you've certainly come to the right place."

I've already decided I don't like her. If Ken Matthews and Wendy Peffercorn got married...

"Thank you, and thanks so much for the cookies," I say, ending the conversation.

She hands me a beautifully written list of phone numbers. Along with her own and Ken's names and numbers, she has written their boy's names and ages

(Kale, eight; Leighton, six; Rhys, three), all on a lovely piece of Kate Spade stationery.

I want to be Wendy when I grow up.

Right now, though, I can't handle her. God, I hope she's at least ten years older than me.

"Of course!" she says as she walks away. "We should have coffee soon. I'll invite some of the Port ladies over for you to meet. Unless you meet them first—we're a bunch of door-knockers around here!"

"Perfect. I can't wait!"

Shit.

I wait until she's off the property before I close the door. What the fuck is a door-knocker? The idea of these women constantly popping by is unnerving. Note to self: always be ready. Or never answer the door!

Where is Trevor? I run up the stairs to check my phone. I was right: he texted but hasn't left yet.

Hey sweets. Be home around six. Should I pick up dinner?

It's almost five p.m. now and I've realized I only bought yogurt and a bunch of random snack food.

Sushi would be great? I write back.

I have a long, much-needed shower and let the water pour over my head for quite a while before remembering the water shortage. Having not showered in two days, I'm surely entitled to one long one. My shamefully perfect encounter this morning inspires me to freshen up. I shave everything with my brand new twenty-dollar razor and scrub off any dry skin with an outrageously expensive exfoliating body wash. When

I get out, I lather myself in coconut oil, throw on a slightly dusty-smelling robe and feel like a new woman.

It's just about six-thirty when Trevor pulls in the driveway. Surprise, he's got flowers. Predictably charming as always. He also has sushi and wine. I feel so unworthy of the energy he puts in. Even if he can't be around often, he at least tries to be romantic. I couldn't even make dinner. I walk out to the porch in my bare feet to meet him, take the beautiful hydrangeas from him and reach up for a one-armed hug. I squeeze his shoulders tight and whisper, "Thanks, babe. These are so beautiful!" To emphasize my appreciation, I take a long inhalation of the scentless grocery store flowers.

"I should have made something, but I got wrapped up in unpacking. And neighbors kept coming by!" I say.

"More neighbors, seriously? It's like the fifties here in 'merica."

He's cute with his corny accent, but there is something about him lately that bothers me.

"Don't even worry about dinner, Elly! I don't need you to cook for me. Lord knows I'm a no-show most nights anyway."

We walk in the kitchen and he empties everything in his hands onto the counter. "Well, well, someone has been busy," he says, noticing the unpacked kitchen, ignoring the not-yet-collapsed boxes and packing paper everywhere. He wraps his arms just below my hips and picks me up as if I weigh no more than a child. He holds me close for a minute before kissing me gently. "I missed you today."

"I missed you, too." And now that he's home, I realize I mean it.

I grab some plates and he sets out dinner: take-out containers consisting of equal portions boring salmon for him and spicy tuna for me. Like I've broken some sort of rule, I hide the wine I already have open. It might make him worry if I'm drinking alone, already. I blow the dust out of two new wine glasses and open the bottle he brought home, a Mission Hill Pinot Noir. What are the odds?

"Why not get a California wine? They're so cheap here!"

"No, that's a gift from Ryan at the office, babe. There's a card there somewhere."

9

A week or so later, Trevor informs me via text that Ryan and his wife have invited us to their house for dinner. I've resisted my intense urge to Google him, bouncing between wanting Trevor's partner to be the guy I met in the wine aisle and dreading the possibility he is. What are the chances that two men are gifting Mission Hill wine to friends in Newport Beach on the same day? On the other hand, it seems unlikely that Trevor's partner would be so sexy—the combination of the two of them in one practice seems unreasonable. But this is the OC, so I guess it's feasible. Lately, I've wondered if maybe he knew it was me, I mean knew I was Trevor's wife. Perhaps he'd seen a picture? Surely, he would have said so. If he's a doctor, it explains the confidence. He did seem cooler than most doctors, though, and a little less arrogant.

It's been almost two weeks since we met. I haven't thought much about him.

Sure, I've gone back to the grocery store every day, for coffee mainly. There is a Starbucks closer, but I drive now. Trevor leased a navy-blue Land Rover for me even though I insisted I didn't need a car, certainly not the Port Streets it car. Next up, a bike with a basket. Or maybe I'll bring myself to try out the golf cart buried in our garage.

I started working out hard to clear my head and ease my loneliness. Now I can barely walk due to week three of the wildly popular Beach Body Guide, but it may be because I altered the program, skipping scheduled days off and running on walking days. I wish I had this motivation over the summer, when my exercise regime consisted of dragging my ass out of bed to the couch and shoveling food in my mouth on the way.

I'm alone most nights here, and without my folks around food has become an issue. I'm not eating particularly well, more like menstrual binges followed by guilt starvation. At least I've made it a point to stick to red wine, getting a healthy dose of antioxidants.

After wandering around the mall feeling entirely out of place, I finally buy a pair of tailored high-rise shorts and a black blouse to wear to dinner. I'm aiming for almost-sexy and subtly stylish— not desperate, dull, bowling-trophy wife. Sure, I made an appointment to get my hair blown out, mainly just to get out of the Ports. It's not like it's in an up-do or anything.

Besides, they don't know me; I easily could have done it myself. My intentions are innocent. I'm a youngish woman, and I need to make up for looking homeless at the grocery store. I do feel a bit guilty getting ready for Ryan rather than for my husband. Who knows, I may be getting ready for someone I haven't even met.

"Who's this sexy mama?" Trevor says as I come down the stairs pretending this is how I always look.

"It's me, Slater—Jessie!" I say, even though I feel more like Kelly Kapowski and wish he were Zack.

"You look amazing, Ellen—really gorgeous." I believe him, because he calls me by my proper name.

"What can I say? The California sun seems to agree with me."

"I think you're right. Turn around, let's see this outfit you've got on."

He always asks me to do this, especially in a bathing suit. Then after he whines and I finally, sheepishly, oblige, he'll say something like, "Be confident, babe. Girls are so much sexier when they're confident."

To which I reply, in my mind, they're confident because they are sexy. But today I do a little spin, trying to hang on to this new-found confidence.

"Wow, those are short," he says.

"I know, right?"

On the way over, I'm jittery, like I've had way too much coffee.

Trevor notices and asks if I'm nervous.

"Yeah, a little."

"Me too," he says, unexpectedly. "Ryan is easy to talk to though, Elly. His wife probably is, too."

"What do we know about her? Struggling actress?"

"No," he says, smirking. "I guess she was a pretty successful chef in New York."

I process this. Chefs aren't typically that attractive, are they? I feel oddly relieved. I've always been a girls' girl, but I'm glad she's not a model or editor-in-chief of *Vanity Fair.*

"Oh, wow, that's cool," I say, sincerely. "Is she working out here?"

"Who knows. Probably."

For the first time, I wish I was American, just so that I had that option. Instead, I have a P-4 visa, a classification that renders me pathetically unemployed and therefore totally uninteresting.

We pull onto their street, and I'm surprised at how dark it is. The streetlights are only set up at the entrance, so anyone could easily sneak in or out of here without being noticed. Instead of houses, we are surrounded by long, curving driveways that seem to lead down to rooftops playing peek-a-boo.

"I think this is it," Trevor says, squinting at a house number oddly printed on the curb.

My heart quickens as we get closer. From the outside, the house is modest, more like a trailer than a California beach house. When we get out, I can feel the ocean on my face, the cool salty breeze threatening my blowout. I realize that this is the first time I've felt cool in weeks. If I were alone, I would twirl around with my arms out and let the air seduce me.

I hold my breath at the door and feel foolishly disappointed when Trevor grabs my hand and runs his thumb over the back of it. In some part of my head, it's almost like I am here on a blind date.

A small Mexican woman answers, wearing a well-used apron. She has a sweet, inviting smile, and welcomes us in with exuberance rather than the typical blend-into-the-background routine most doctors' wives go for.

"Hello," I say, offering my hand to her. "I'm Ellen."

She introduces herself as Maria but turns down my hand because she's been cooking.

"Please, leave your shoes on," a voice calls from another room.

She appears, and it's like a slap across my face. She's a dark-haired angel, tall and graceful as she walks toward us with quick, elegant steps, her thick ponytail bobbing cheerfully. She's young but carries herself with self-assurance.

"Ellen," she greets me, wiping her hands on an apron that matches Maria's as she squeals, "Come in right this second!"

She reminds me of a sorority girl, one with a Southern mama.

"I won't lie, I haven't heard much about you, but Trevor did say you were just the sweetest, and he didn't lie either. Look at you; you're so tiny!" She looks at me, literally down at me, and adds, "But you know what they say, good things come in small packages!"

I am quiet except for a polite laugh, managing to resist a crazy, jealous urge to rebut with, "And penises and Adam's apples generally come in big packages."

She turns to Trevor and hugs him like they've been summering together since they were kids. I'm on the outside here, because I didn't know Trevor had even met her, whatever her name is.

I wait until she turns to call for her husband before I give Trevor a look, the look that tells him I'm pissed.

"What?" He whispers, knowing exactly what. He likely didn't tell me because he didn't want to have to lie about how stunning she is. Which makes me think he thinks she's prettier than me. And she is. I'm guessing she has a beautiful name like Charlotte.

I hear footsteps coming down the hall. The thought of solving this mystery is suddenly depressing. I've spent weeks thinking about the possibility of being around the mysterious man from the wine aisle again, feeling the intensity of his eyes. Now, after meeting the gorgeous woman who may be his wife, I'm certain that—if it was Ryan I met—he was just a friendly guy looking for a little wine advice from a disheveled girl who obviously drinks. I feel foolish, and maybe a little let down.

When he comes around the corner, I take him in from his bare feet up. Light baggy jeans worn low, no belt, and a fitted, slightly wrinkled golf shirt. I force myself to look at his face— his beautiful, entrancing face. His dark, unforgettable eyes. Of course, it's him.

"Hey, you two," he says as he approaches us. His eyes shift from me to Trevor and then quickly back to me. "I know you!" He backs up, looking me over, "You look different, but it's definitely you." He motions a straight hand up to his chest, measuring my height. Before any-one has a chance to ask, he says, "I wondered if I'd ever bump into you again." He steals a glance into my eyes before leaning down for an innocent embrace.

For a second I think my knees might buckle, but I manage to get out, "Nice to formally meet you. Thanks for the wine."

Without missing a beat, he gives me a playful wink.

"You've met Alice?" he asks, gesturing to his wife, who unsubtly clears her throat as she stands there like a gigantic tower, waiting for attention.

"Alice, yes, I met Alice. It seems like we've all met," I say, smiling. I can sense Trevor's confusion, but I don't offer an explanation, just as I don't ask when he met Ryan's wife who he said he knew nothing about.

Their house is as modern as ours is traditional. It has a coolness to it, barren almost; not a family home and not at all like it appears from the outside. There are no photos or knick-knacks, not many personal touches at all. But then no art could compete with the view provided by the Pacific Ocean and the floor-to-ceiling windows that extend along the entire property.

"Offer our guests a drink, Ry. I have a few more things to do in here."

The kitchen looks like a chef's dream, but I'm just guessing. I haven't the slightest idea why so many appliances are needed or what they do, but they look intimidating.

"Is there anything I can do to help?" I ask, nervous she'll say yes.

"You?" Trevor interjects, making a mean joke.

"Hilarious, Trev. I can cook," I say, stretching the truth. "I just have no one to cook for."

"I hear that, Ellen," Alice chimes in. "Maria and I have it all covered."

I appreciate how she treats Maria more like a friend than an employee. She looks like she'd be a good friend.

Ryan hands me a glass of wine.

"She might not like that one," Alice calls.

"I know what she likes," he deadpans, holding my eyes in his gaze.

I can't blame my face for betraying me, blushing.

"So how is it you guys know each other?" Trevor finally asks.

"We bonded over wine," Ryan answers, trying to sound mysterious.

"At the grocery store, babe. I suggested the Mission Hill, and you brought it home." I give Trevor's shoulder a squeeze, avoid his eyes, and walk away.

I saunter into the kitchen, not wanting to intrude or be antisocial. "You mind if I watch?" I ask.

"Please do," Alice says.

I can't take my eyes off her as she moves around the kitchen like a cooking ballerina, making everything look natural, effortless, not even looking as she chops celery into tiny, equal-sized pieces. We chitchat casually and exchange all the regular stuff. I put a supportive-wife spin on my side, not wanting to sound like a downer. She tells me all about life in New York, her old job as a sous chef for some well-known chef and how hard it was for her to leave. It's selfishly comforting to hear of her struggles. It makes me feel less…less.

Dinner conversation flows like the wine. The food is beyond, and the more I drink the more I think Alice might be the real catch at the table. There is a coolness in the exchanges between Ryan and his wife that makes me wonder; it's almost off-putting. He'd seemed so warm, but he's distant with her. It reminds me to make an effort to appear more loving, no matter how I feel at the moment—at the very least, Trevor deserves that.

In lieu of coffee and dessert, the consensus is more wine.

"Who wants to walk the beach?" a now drunken Alice asks as she grabs another bottle.

"I know this little one wants to," she slurs, pointing at me. It's true, it sounds wonderful, as I've yet to even go to the beach since we arrived. But I swear if she mentions my height again I'll point out how enormous she is. I squint my eyes and picture her shrinking down and falling through a hole.

Bye, Alice.

"I don't know, ladies, the tide is high tonight," Ryan warns.

"Oh, don't worry, I'll be safe with Big Ole Alice here," I tease, unable to resist.

She walks over to me, and I swear she's going to give me a nugie, but she just drapes her lean arm across my shoulders, exaggerating a hunch.

"You're a lucky man, Trevor!"

"And you're drunk, love," Ryan says, with a hint of frustration.

"Let's clean up first!" I insist.

"Can't! Promised Maria I wouldn't touch a thing." She slips off her heels, pries open the sliding glass bi-fold wall and disappears into the darkness.

"Can you guys keep an eye on her while I clean up a bit?" Ryan asks, stacking dishes.

"Trevor, you go," I quickly suggest. "I'll help in here."

He obliges almost too eagerly and follows Alice through the door without hesitation.

Ryan turns to me, raising his eyebrows, suspicious-like. "Wanna play a game?" Before responding, I take in the sterility of the house and realize it's creepy as hell. It's a perfect crime scene, nothing porous. He doesn't give me enough time to answer before he pulls out his phone and says, "We get one song. By the time it's over, the kitchen must be clean. You up for it?"

"I pick the song," I say as I reach for his phone and scan through his playlists like I'm peering into his soul. Half kidding, I select Miley's *Party in the U.S.A*, because who doesn't love that song? As soon as it starts, he laughs, rolls his eyes and darts over to the table. I follow, giggling, too comfortable with him. The two of us fumble around without any of Alice's pre-wine grace. I rinse, he loads, our hands overlapping accidentally on purpose.

I'm so distracted that I stupidly cut my finger with a steak knife. It's superficial for sure, but when Ryan sees the blood, he shuts off the music just before the song ends. "Come here," he instructs, reaching for my hand.

"It's nothing, honest. I'm just that bad in the kitchen."

"No, it's my fault," he insists. "It's a dangerous game we're playing." He's right, it is.

"That's the most fun I've ever had in the kitchen," I say, offering him a slightly buzzed, unguarded grin.

"Really? That's sad," he smirks.

"You know what I mean!" I nearly shout, now as red as the wine.

Instead of a dishtowel, he wraps my finger in the bottom of his shirt, exposing abs sparsely covered in dark hair. "It's cleaner than the towel," he says, catching my look. I'm having a hard time knowing where to look, because he's so much taller than I am. My face is inches from his body, which might be better than being this close to his eyes. His sweet, slightly sweaty scent is intoxicating, and I have to restrain myself from burying my nose in his chest.

"I think it's okay," I say, pulling away before I do something stupid. Then a thought hits me hard: this is the first time I haven't felt alone since we left my family in Ontario.

He grabs his professionally stocked first-aid kit to bandage my finger for me. He treats it like it's a vital organ and inspects it from all angles, doses it with antiseptic and then blows on it, causing it to develop a heartbeat of its own.

"All better," he says, letting my hand fall. Regrettably, he forgets to kiss it better.

We got a lot accomplished in less than four minutes. The kitchen is not yet to Maria's standards, bits of crumbs still scattered on the giant island and dishtowels thrown lazily in a pile, but it's better than leaving it all to her. I follow Ryan outside, conscious of my deceitful desire to stay inside. Trevor and Alice are sprawled out on a couple of perfectly positioned lounge chairs looking up at the sky, as the night now camouflages the dark ocean. He's likely pointing out the constellations. He's so full of knowledge that he can just pull from his mental archives in any situation—the quintessential first date. I love this about him. I don't even know the order of the planets.

When he sees me, he gives me a sobering smile and reaches out to me with both arms. I let him cradle me, snuggling into his chest. It's easy here.

"Whoa!" Trevor says, as he notices the blood on Ryan's shirt. "What happened?"

"We had a slight injury…"

"I cut myself on a knife," I say in a voice that borders on obnoxious baby-talk, holding my bandaged finger out to him.

"Babe, be careful!" He kisses it and tucks it under his arm to keep it warm. "That's a lot of blood! She need a stitch?" he asks, trusting Ryan's judgment.

"Nah, she's good." He tears off his shirt in slow motion. Even in the dark, I can see he's looking right at me. "Aren't you?"

"I am, thanks to you."

I try not to stare, but his naked upper body is glistening in the moonlight. The lingering effects of the wine still run in my blood, which might explain why I'm picturing Ryan as some sort of sex god, ready to impregnate me. His body moving in the sand, in rhythm with the moon, tide and my ovulatory cycle. His jeans are so low I don't think he's wearing boxers or briefs.

He walks toward Alice, and she spreads her long legs and arms wide, inviting him to sit with her.

Don't do it, Ryan.

Her lanky limbs make her look like a praying mantis ready to devour him. I try to look away, but I notice her long, boney feet and instantly feel more pleased about being small. I lift one adorable foot in the air, celebrating my slender ankle and perfect toes, pristinely painted in my favorite polish. (Inaptly named Eternal Optimist.) Clearly, the best feet here. It counts for something!

We stay like this for a while, just looking up at the stars. Alice passes out, and Ryan asks me about my job, says he's sorry I had to give it up. Trevor responds for me, saying they didn't deserve me. It makes me think he knew I didn't get the best farewell. I lie and say I've come to terms with it, that I've been looking into some freelance stuff. It feels so wrong to sit this close to Trevor, hearing his heartbeat, while my foot lightly touches Ryan's in the sand.

When we get home, we make love. I force Ryan's face out of my mind every time it pops in. His presence in my head makes this feel so insincere to me. I know how lucky I am to have Trevor, and I'd never cheat on him. My parents raised me better than that. But it feels so good to be seen, to feel wanted, by someone like Ryan.

Trevor whispers, "I love you, Elly," into my ear and I picture it coming from different lips. I let out a sweet moan instead of saying it back. I try to forgive myself, reasoning that a lot of couples picture other people while they have sex: Brad Pitt, his ex-wives. It's an innocent way to turn up the heat, right? How would I feel, though, if Trevor were picturing another woman, a real one? What if he's picturing Alice right now? How do they even know each other?

My mind drifts and Trevor finishes alone.

10

It's been a few weeks since our dinner with Ryan and Alice. I miss everyone at home so much, but I've settled into a nice routine. In the morning, I run or do my workout in the backyard and then as a treat, I head to the grocery store for coffee. I know he won't be there, it's been almost a month, and he hasn't been back once, but I've acquired a taste for their coffee. The baristas are starting to know my name, stopping just short of yelling, "Ellen," every time I walk in. It's nice not feeling like a stranger to all the strangers.

Wendy has invited me over for drinks this afternoon, an "introduction to the neighborhood," she calls it. With three kids, I don't know how she has time to drink and socialize in the afternoon, though I suspect a few nannies might explain it. I've never been socially awkward; I'm too smart and not quite smart enough for that. But I don't particularly like meeting new people.

I figure the occasion will be casual, so I throw on a silk tank top and linen skirt, Audrey's hand-me-down Tom Ford sunglasses tucked into my shirt and my phone in my pocket. Perhaps it's the insistent sun bleaching my hair, or maybe my toner has completely washed out, but the color is as nice as it's ever been, a perfect ombré. I keep my face bare except for a little bit of mascara and blush. I take one last look in the mirror, satisfied, yet a little bummed I don't look quite as pretty as I feel. I pause for a moment, searching my brain for a reasonable excuse that doesn't come, then unenthusiastically head out the door. On my walk over, I think about how funny it would be if I scaled the back fence and jumped into Wendy's yard instead. I picture their horrified faces as I say, "Hey everyone!" and chuckle to myself acknowledging that I've lost it.

Her house is a lot like ours, bigger and newer; more loved than our rental, but similar. The mani-cured front lawn is almost as welcoming as her bright yellow drapes. This home screams optimism. I know those drapes would piss me off most mornings: "What are *you* smiling at?!" They also have a Dutch door. I bet Wendy keeps hers open though, always welcoming a fellow door-knocker for tea. She comes to the door before I knock. "Hey, pretty lady," she says, as sweet as the invisible pie she could be holding.

"Hi Wendy. Your house is beauuuuuutiful," I say, noticing how phony my voice sounds and then how empty my hands are. Shit. Even if I tell her I forgot the flowers I picked up for her this morning, she won't believe me, like when you "forget" a birthday card. I'm Canadian, but I certainly wasn't raised in a barn (or igloo) so I tell her about the flowers so she doesn't associate the two.

"Don't you worry about that, I've got plenty of flowers in here. All we wanted was you."

She leads me through her professionally decorated home. She wasn't kidding about the flowers: real, faux, fabric—they're everywhere. I forget that it's always summer here. At home, this décor would get old with the snow, but Wendy likely has seasonal throw pillows, not tacky snowman ones, but the fancy ones from Pottery Barn.

"The kitchen," she points out unnecessarily as we walk by it. "Always help yourself. The powder room is here, or go upstairs if you prefer." She is so welcoming, charming even, that I find it difficult to hate her. Unexpectedly, I feel incredibly comfortable.

I don't think I would go into her fridge or take a pee in her en suite, but the offer is nice. "Okay," she says, stopping and putting both of her hands firmly on my shoulders. "They can be a little intense, but they're a lot of fun…"

Then, she pauses strangely, as if she is looking through me, and yells, "Those little shits!" She storms toward a once-white wall now covered with suggestive stickmen.

"Oh man," I say, trying not to laugh. "Is that what I think it is?"

"Yes, our stickmen have penises over here." She's laughing now.

"Impressive ones, too!" I add, patting her back in sympathy.

"You just wait, Ellen."

The naked men settle my nerves. This woman is perfect but her kids are little perverts, and she calls them "shits" behind their backs. We could be friends.

"Shall we?" She gestures for me to go out first, exactly as Trevor insists on, politely feeding me to the wolves.

The backyard is stunning. Apart from a sunken, separate area paved for bikes and basketballs, it looks like a Restoration Hardware catalog. The gazebo is insane: sheer white curtains, deep chairs and what looks like a custom stone table. Above the gorgeous built-in fireplace is a huge, suspended TV (and a partridge in a pear tree).

The table on a separate patio is also elegant, but it's the four women sitting around it who are spectacular. Not exact clones, but all perfectly manicured, just like the lawn: pretty nails and waxed brows. I know they sense me come out, but they don't break conversation until Wendy announces me. "Ladies, this is Ellen!" I can feel their judgmental eyes on me. I make my way closer and shake hands with each of them, clearly catching some of them off guard with the formality. With all the formal dinners I've had to attend with Trevor, obligatory trips around tables shaking hands doesn't faze me.

"You're so young!" one says, as if she expected another version of herself. "What are you doing living here?"

"Good question!" I laugh. "I'm not that young, mostly just short."

"You're not short," another says. "You're perfect."

They've all said their names, but I don't even try to remember them. I've tried all sorts of tricks: repetition, association, listening (hahaha). Still, after I've said my name, I don't hear much of anything. There are two pitchers of sangria on the table, each full of an impressive variety of fruit. When offered, I guess I sound too eager because they all laugh at me. "Get her a bigger glass, Wen!"

We chat for hours. I am relieved and shocked at how hilariously vulgar they are. It's like discovering Danny Tanner's dark side all over again. It's clear they've been friends a long time. They tease each other completely offside yet compulsively have each other's back. As when I said I was short, putting yourself down is not allowed here.

For the first time since I learned we were moving, I feel like I might be okay—like this might work. I learn they all have at least two children, except for one who must be younger than me. But she has teenage stepsons who she purposely cock-teases with her swimsuits. No one asks if I have children, which I suspect is Wendy's doing (loving her), but I'd like to think they assume I'm too young.

What I find the most reassuring is they all had professional careers before they moved here. They humorously reject the term housewives or stay-at-home moms in favor of 'women of leisure.' It's all in good fun. These women are clearly impressively educated. Aside from Ken, who I know to be gorgeous, I picture the rest of their husbands with dark, hairy, fat faces for some reason. I'm sure it has something to do with a nineties sitcom.

The conversation shifts at one point, and I can feel that they're all thinking the same thing, as if in unison. "So, you're miserable," is at the tips of their wine-purple tongues. I guess my use of "a fucking nightmare" and my answers to their questions about adjusting to life in California didn't come out as cheerful as the yellow drapes. It's likely the wine and the fact I feel so comfortable. I just lie back on an invisible couch and confess to them like I'm in therapy. Of course, I don't mention the insane chemistry I have with my husband's colleague. I can tell they want more, but I feel loyal to Trevor and do my best to keep him out of my rants. I do tell them I'm bored and intensely understimulated. They all nod almost as if they're pleased in a way, hesitantly sympathetic. After I've shared, I let out a huge, exaggerated sigh that feels amazing. Wendy, of all people, tells me they get it, like really get it. The rest concur, with "Completely!" and "Totally!" Then they hilariously, shockingly, take turns poking fun at each other's children.

I feel like I'm hallucinating a bit, because the closer I look at these wonderful creatures the more I see similarly high, plump cheeks and lips that look subtly bee-stung and cherry Kool-Aid stained. Definitely filled by the same hands. Suddenly, I feel self-conscious about my comparatively thin lips, which aren't full at all until they're stretched out in a smile. I bite my top lip, which is noticeably smaller than my bottom, trying to plump it up, certainly not trying to be sexy. I'm not going to make Christian Grey do backflips.

I excuse myself to use the bathroom. When I stand, I know I've had too much sangria. It's not until I'm safe behind a locked door that I realize how drunk I am. I wash my hands, staring at myself in a trance, not blinking, as the sink fills, the drain not able to keep up with the relentless water. My face looks strange. The longer I look at it, the more distorted it becomes. Have I always had that bump on my nose? Someone knocks at the door and snaps me out of it.

"You all right?" asks a woman with a faint British accent.

"Yeah, I'm good," I call back.

"Open the door; you've been in there for a while."

I don't want to open the door, and I think it's rude that she's even asked, but I turn the water off and open it anyway.

"Hi, darling. You okay?"

"I'm for sure drunk," I say, wiping my hands on my shirt as she hands me a towel. I stare intensely at her face, but I can't figure it out. "How old are you?" I ask, surprising myself. "And what's your name again?"

She laughs and says, "I'm as old as you will be someday soon, my friend—I'm Scarlet."

"Yes, you're definitely a Scarlet!" I laugh, looking at the deep V of her impeccably fitted linen tank, and then go quiet when I realize she's not.

"You are quite pissed, aren't you?"

"I am," I concede, returning my eyes back to the mirror. "Hey, do you think I should get my lips done?"

She makes a hmmm noise like she's considering it, then reaches out and grabs my face with a heavily jeweled hand, inspecting me. Finally, she says, "No, I like small lips."

I somehow find my way home and crash on the couch. When I wake up, it's dark, and I have a well-deserved headache. It's true I've been drinking quite a bit lately, but I'm not in the habit of getting drunk in the afternoon. Just enough to take the edge off, not fall completely over the edge. But I feel that way now, literally, as half of my limbs are lifelessly hanging off the couch. If Trevor came home and snapped a picture of me, I imagine I would look like the millions of Instagram babes caught asleep without a care in the world or a thought about how they look sprawled out drunk. Or how their shriveled lips look to their new friends. I take a couple of Advil and almost drown in the shower, feeling too cold and sick to get out. I have mascara streaks running down my face, and it reminds me of Annie in university—it was rare she didn't end a good night out with ugly tears. I miss her so much. Instead of washing my face properly, I just throw on my glasses to disguise it.

I feel awkward about this afternoon, but I feel sober enough now to text Wendy:

> *I'm really sorry. Can't remember if I thanked you? Hope I didn't embarrass you…or myself. Ellen.*

When I don't hear back from her right away, I get nervous. In my mind, I run over all the things I'd said. Nothing was that bad. Mind you, I can't remember much after my third glass of sangria. I hope I haven't completely humiliated myself and Trevor. Which reminds me, it's dark, and I haven't heard from him all day, so I also send him a quick text to let him know I'm still alive.

I knew when he took this job that his ridiculous hours would get worse. I swear, though, even during his residency he texted me all the time, and I was safe at home then. Not here alone. Or getting into mischief.

The next few hours are torture as I don't hear back from either of them. I'm not too worried about Trevor, but with Wendy, I go through something like the stages of grief people talk about, completely mind-screwing myself. Why hasn't she texted me back? She hates me. I embarrassed myself! You know what, maybe they're just better drinkers—drunks even!! I should walk over those flowers and leave them on the porch, maybe? They shouldn't be so judgmental!

This all while not checking my phone, because I don't care. I fold the laundry. Check my phone. Fine, screw you. I don't even care! I empty the dishwasher, a pathetic few yogurt spoons and wine glasses, then promise myself this is the last check for one hour. I'm on my way up the stairs when I hear a *ping!*

I run to the phone and pause briefly, hoping it's not Trevor. My life here in Wisteria Lane may depend on it.

It's Wendy.

> *Don't be silly! I fell asleep and woke up panicked I'd forgotten to get my kids. Sitter had them at the pool! Phew. We all agree we would love to see you again! Soon. I'll be in touch.*
> *xo Peffercorn*

Fuck, had I called her Wendy Peffercorn? If she'd seen *The Sandlot* she certainly wouldn't find the comparison insulting. What else did I say to them? I scratch my head, feeling almost like I've been drugged. Regardless, I feel reassured. Yay, I have friends! It's not until I'm back in the kitchen eating a chunk of cheese that I reread the message. Her wording seems a little peculiar. "We all agree." Did they wait for me to leave and then vote? It could just be an auto-correction. She probably intended to write something normal like, "We all agree you're awesome!" Even the "I'll be in touch" is a little strange, maybe an American thing? So, what now? I just wait for them to contact me? I feel oddly like I've just had a job interview. At least the feedback seems positive.

Despite being out all day, I'm now disturbingly bored. It would be so nice to have a family to come home to. Or a dog. Anything would be better than this deafening silence. I look at the clock. Shit, Trevor. What the hell!

I could use this time to call my mom and Audrey back, but I'll save that for tomorrow's excitement, plus it's way too late in Ontario. Like a slob, I open a bag of Doritos, grab a Pellegrino and flop onto the couch. I think about reading, although I'm not sure I'm sober enough. Plus, I've boycotted anything that reminds me of work. It's shocking how many bestsellers are riddled with errors. At times, I can't commit to a story because I'm too busy underlining and celebrating errors with exclamation marks—the publishing world does need me! I resolve myself to killing an hour looking for something to watch on Netflix.

I decide on *Random Hearts,* a nineties movie about infidelity, double lives and heartbreak. Watching Harrison Ford expressing complete shock at his wife's affair kind of pisses me off. Why wouldn't a neglected wife find love with another person? (Mind you, would anyone cheat on him?)

It's funny how, when you're in a certain frame of mind, you see things everywhere that support it. For instance, when you think you find a lump (okay, so it was a mole) it just happens to be Breast Cancer Awareness month.

People are always appalled when women cheat, almost as appalled as I am that Harrison Ford continues to get hotter as he ages. And then there is Kristin Scott Thomas, who is a classic, old-fashioned, honest beauty, which should be applauded. Though, I guarantee aging has been much rougher on her and her nonfiction lips than it has been on Hottie Harrison. Around here, natural beauty seems to be baby Botox and mini facelifts. Remember when women only had to compete with genetics and bad life choices? Now it's Coolsculpt, fillers and who knows what else. I resist the urge to throw a chip at the TV.

My lips are my mother's. I guess they're Trevor's, too. I should be happy with them. They're fine. But I can't watch Kristin's lips move without imagining what they would look like with just a little more volume. I'm certain I could go from cute to sexy with a fuller top lip. Audrey says women with full top lips look like they want to give blowjobs all the time. Regardless, I decide I want to get my lips done.

I am in a strange, coma-type sleep when I hear Trevor finally come home. I smell him before I see him: a combination of antiseptic, latex and a faint boozy smell. (Actually, that might be me.) Before I open my eyes, it dawns on me why I didn't hear from him all day. Trevor had a sixteen-year-old boy on the table, a surgery he'd been worried about all week. The boy collapsed during a high school basketball game and went into complete heart failure. Hypertrophic cardiomyopathy, a condition I never forget because the stories are always so sad and the sufferers are often so young. Luckily (and unluckily), because of its severity, the boy was pushed to the top of the transplant list. Today was the surgery.

Even in the quiet darkness, I sense it didn't go well. I feel oddly uncomfortable, so I force my eyes open. When I do, I scramble straight up, hugging my knees to my chest like a frightened animal.

"Oh, my God, Ryan! What are you doing?" I yell as I jump up to turn the lamp on and then, remembering my mascara-stained face, abruptly sit back down.

"I'm sorry! Relax!" He laughs quietly while shushing me with one finger to his sensational mouth. "Trevor had a few too many after surgery, so I brought him home."

"Really?" I ask, shocked. "Did it not go well?"

"No, it was great. He was a rock star in there. The kid was in bad shape, Ellen, but he's good as new."

I'm genuinely happy. But my mind is now preoccupied with the Doritos I'd wolfed down before barbarically throwing the empty bag on the floor. Orange fingers. My breath! Oh, my God.

"He's on the couch in the front."

"What? He is?" I'm so confused. I'm worried I might be dreaming. "How long have you been here?"

"Just a minute or two—I wasn't going to wake you, but then I figured you were probably worried, and his phone..."

"No, I was really worried," I interrupt. (Despite sleeping like the dead.) "Thanks, Ryan."

"I should have your number," he says, pulling out his phone.

"Yes!" I almost shout, sounding way too eager. "In case this happens again," I add to cut the over-enthusiasm.

We exchange numbers, my voice shaking a bit as I say mine. It makes me feel safer knowing I'll have another connection to Trevor, but also a little defenseless: having Ryan at my fingertips, knowing that I could reach out at any time. Maybe accidentally pocket dial him on purpose.

"You look cute," he says, likely noticing I'm a disaster.

"I'm disgusting!" I laugh, pulling Trevor's t-shirt over my naked knees and tucking it in under my toes. "But this is how I roll these days!"

"Well, we can't all save lives..."

"Very true," I agree, nodding in defeat.

"You must be so bored here," he sighs and leans into the couch beside me, settling in as he hugs a throw pillow tight to his chest. He seems so comfortable with me, like we've sat this way a million times before. I can so easily picture myself crawling over to rest my head on his lap.

"It's not the beach," I say, trying not to fidget. "I'm in transition, I guess." I feel embarrassed, but I can tell he is being empathetic rather than insulting. "I spend some of my time exploring and most of my time feeling sorry for myself."

"I know how capable you are, Ellen. I hope Trevor realizes how much you've given up. He is lucky to have you here." He looks at me intently, like he really means it, but I feel like I'm missing something, like I don't quite understand what he's telling me.

"And you're lucky to have Alice," I reply.

"I am," he says, rubbing his eyes. "But it's completely different."

"It's exactly the same. She was a successful chef. She gave it up, just as…"

"You're right, I'm lucky to have Alice," he says, but there is something in his tone that tells me he is just saying what he must to end the conversation. He smiles and stands, running his hands down the front of his thighs, stretching.

"I'm not this person," I blurt out of nowhere, desperate to explain myself and desperate to keep him here.

"What person is that?"

"I'm not the type of woman that sits around waiting to be taken care of, eating shit and not showering." I shift my lips to the side of my mouth and exhale, ashamed that I've now stooped low enough I have to make excuses for myself.

"Stand up," he says, standing in front of me.

"Why?" I ask, looking up at him.

"Just do it, k?"

Unusually for me, I don't push for a reason. Absurdly, I just stand up on the couch, careful not to show him my underwear, not knowing and strangely not caring what he's about to do.

From this vantage point, our eyes are almost level, and I feel ridiculous and intrigued and embarrassed. "K," I answer.

I tremble as he brushes my hair behind my ears, then puts one hand firmly on my shoulder, the other on my waist. "You got this, Ellen. You're going to be great."

I nod at him, feeling a sincere connection, my attraction to him instantly transforming from pure lust to something deeper.

He must talk to his patients like this.

"I know. I'm just a bit lost right now," I reply.

"Well, I've got my eyes on you."

My heart and head compete for attention, but I stand frozen, defying them both.

"I've got to go," he says, breaking our gaze.

"Yeah, I know. Thanks, Ryan."

"Of course! He's gonna feel it tomorrow." He chuckles sympathetically, gesturing with his chin to the front room where Trevor sleeps, oblivious.

"And thanks for the talk," I say. I give him a goofy smile, the opposite of romantic, but then catch his shoulder as he turns and run my hand down his arm.

"Anything you need, Ellen. You're not alone here," he assures me. "And there is nothing pathetic about Doritos, either."

11

I wake up the next morning to the smell of coffee and sneak downstairs to find Trevor in the kitchen being thoughtful. Before I say good morning, I take a moment just to watch him; the meticulous way he cooks, putting every ingredient and dish away before moving on. He hums a made-up song to himself, and I can easily picture him with a baby on his well-defined hip: the two of them making breakfast for Mom in bed. Despite his almost compulsive kitchen routine, he looks a bit disheveled with his messy hair and scruffy, unshaven face as he moves around the kitchen in last night's underwear. It's rare to see Trevor relaxed. He even has his glasses on instead of his contacts. Probably letting his eyes breathe after last night. Sleep deprivation he can handle, but the aftereffects of shocking his system with alcohol can't be easy.

"Morning, Dr. Hangover," I say, knowingly corny, and walk over to give him a kiss.

"Morning, beautiful." He puts down the bowl and whisk and gives me a big hug. "I feel horrible about last night."

"Why? Don't. It was a big night for you."

"My phone died, and I was only planning to have one drink…"

"Honestly, I wasn't that worried, babe. I spend a lot of nights alone."

"I know you do, but I should have called you. You could have joined us. And then Ryan coming here like that, with no warning. It must have been awkward for you."

Truthfully, I hadn't even thought enough about Trevor last night to be mad at him, although I did have a reason. As I think about it now, though, I feel an actual stab of pain in my chest. When did I stop being the person he wants to celebrate with? Then I feel guilty for not being mad at him, guilty that I snuck past him on my way upstairs last night, under the influence of someone else. And the experience certainly was not awkward in a bad way.

"Nah, I was fine," I say. "It would've been nice to go out with you though."

We spend the afternoon together, walking around Fashion Island holding hands.

After a month or so of living here, I realize this is the culture: The Orange County Museum of Fashion

Island. It's well done, with large outdoor walkways, cafés and fish ponds. We're mostly quiet, aside from trivial chat. It seems that both of us are scared to talk about how we're really feeling. His hand feels comfortable in mine, but it doesn't feel like home anymore. The harder I work at being the woman he married, the less I feel like her. If Ellen was a Jane when we met, Newport Jane is a Virginia, resentful and unstable.

Trevor takes a call, so I wander up and down rows of stores we could only dream of in small-town Canada: Nordstrom, Bloomingdales, Neiman Marcus. I feel a sense of freedom having a moment to myself, to breathe and not feel judged by all the women looking at Trevor and then at me. You get used to your own company after a while.

I've been here before, so it's no surprise I find myself indirectly, directly heading to a MediSpa I saw last week. I walk past it a few times and stop to read the advertisements in the window, pretending to be intrigued by the information even though I have Googled the place at least four times. I pace in front of the store, biting at my nail. I know Trevor's call will end at some point, so I take the plunge and dive in, rationalizing that I can always cancel the appointment.

The woman behind the counter, whose nametag says Lydia, could be anywhere from fifty to one hundred years old. She's welcoming, but stares critically at my face, not hiding her unsatisfactory assessment. So she can stop inspecting the lines on my forehead, I tell her that I'm just interested in having my lips done. She is surprised, but assures me I'll "absolutely love it." I know it's her job, but a little "you've got great lips," would have been nice. There is so much competition here I'm able to get an appointment the next day. I exit the store in the complete opposite state in which I came in, now 100% committed.

I find Trevor in the same spot. He puts the phone down as soon as he sees me, almost suspiciously. I don't bother to ask, and I pretend not to be jealous. Knowing him, he's just trying to be present today because he ditched me last night. That's the thing about Trevor— he says and does all the right, romantic things, but I'm never sure if it's because he loves me or because he just wants to be the kind of person who says and does all the right, romantic things.

"So, should we go?" I smile, feeling sneaky.

"Sure, babe. I've got to swing by the office. You mind coming?"

Shit. What? I wasn't expecting this. I'm certainly not dressed for it, but I don't want to be difficult. "Okay, sure."

I've only been to the practice once, and so far I've just met the receptionist Crystal. She is insanely gorgeous but is a lesbian, thankfully, so I really like her. I'm wearing a cute-enough skirt and t-shirt, tucked in. Sounds bad, but with my frame, I think I pull this look off reasonably well. I should have put make-up on, though. Even with this tan, I'm too old to leave the house without mascara at least. I clutch at the sunglasses tucked into my shirt. Thank God for you!

Between making the appointment, which I keep reassuring myself is nothing, and now off to potentially see Ryan, I am full of adrenaline. I like being around him. It doesn't mean anything. It's just fun for me and keeps my otherwise bored mind active. My second year at university, I used my lit professor, young Elliot Duffy, to help me stay focused. I dressed up for his class and never missed it, but it never went further than an occasional inappropriate, extended glance. This is sort of like that.

As we drive along the coast, Trevor flips through the radio channels and stops when he hears Ben E. King's *Stand by Me*. He grabs my hand and belts out the lyrics: "*Just as long as you stand, stand by me....*"

The windows are down, and the relentless seventy-five-degree air fills the space between us. I want to feel romantic and sincere, but I'm stuck in a fog and my head is in the clouds. I turn my face to the window, unable to resist the song, and sing, "*If the sky that we look upon should tumble and fall...*" as we drive along curves, teetering close to the edge.

From the outside, it's like any other medical building, but inside, Trevor's new clinic almost feels like a modern luxury hotel lobby in the sky. The ocean view is distant but breathtaking, distracting enough to drown out the anxious thoughts of patients and families in the waiting room. And if the view doesn't make their experiences less dismal, the good-looking staff will.

Ever the gentleman, Trevor opens the door and stands aside so I can uncomfortably enter first. Crystal is at her desk, placed in the middle of the office like a throne reigning over an empty court. She stands to greet us, and I uncharacteristically give her a hug. She was wisely named: beautiful as a jewel. Even if his fantasies are unrequited, I know her porcelain skin and perky, uncaged breasts are unquestionably on Trevor's mind when we have sex.

After we exchange pleasantries, she says, "No patients coming in today. Ryan just left and I'm about to go too. You guys good?"

All I hear is "Ryan just left."

She walks across the office with easy poise, watering plants and flipping lights off as I stand there, deflated, taking in the scene. Though the Port Streets are lovely, they could exist in Ontario. Up here, in this exquisitely decorated high-rise, overlooking the little people with big dreams who live in the postcard below—this is California. I wonder if Trevor pinches himself every day? It must feel amazing to walk in here to his beautiful receptionist and dazzling office, knowing everyone is admiring his striking good looks and brilliant mind, too.

"You okay? I'm just going to grab a couple of things from my office," he says.

"Yeah, of course. Take your time," I say, still mesmerized with the scenery.

Once he's gone, I do some predictable snooping. I sit in Crystal's chair, which is more comfortable than my velvet one at home. I take an innocent peek in her drawer, but it's all the usual stuff apart from a package of Sour Patch Kids, which automatically makes her awesome. There's a picture of her with her girlfriend on the desk, at Coachella maybe. They're both uncommonly feminine for a lesbian couple, two pretty women smiling at each other instead of the camera. I can't help but beam at the picture before placing it back on the desk. The idea of having a female partner doesn't bother me one bit. For whatever reason this makes me think of Wendy. Huh? (Which seems to be the American version of Eh?) Does this mean I'm bi, I wonder?

Two other doctors work out of this practice, but I haven't met them yet and certainly am not tempted to look in their offices as I am Ryan's. I find his name on a door, followed by a bunch of hard-earned abbreviations. I run my fingers over his nameplate, *Dr. Ryan Ashford,* and childishly think about writing Ellen Ashford all over my notebooks. With my back to the door, I reach back and give the doorknob a slight turn. It's unlocked. I check over each shoulder; it's dark and motionless in both directions. I push the door open a crack and peer in like I expect someone to be in there. It's empty. Cold, like his house. He has a surfboard on the wall, but that is standard décor here. Aside from that, there is a bookshelf full of medical books and a copy of Melville's *Moby Dick.* I pick it up and check behind the cover. It's a first edition, given to him by his father, inscribed: *"For all men tragically great are made so through a certain morbidness.... All mortal greatness is but disease."* His father must be well read. I wonder why he would inscribe this particular quote and what it might say about Ryan? A shiver runs down my arm as I carefully place the book back the exact way I found it.

I wonder if Ryan is like Trevor, who makes little time for literature and reads only nonfiction, mostly medical journals, and an occasional historical account of something. I consider the quote, Trevor's ambition and the dedication he's had as long as I've known him, all the sacrifices and isolation. *O young ambition*, in extreme, is a bit like an illness. I read a study once that likened surgeons to serial killers in that they can both separate the person from the body. I picture Ryan as Dexter and it doesn't turn me off, just leaves me a little shocked at how morbid I'm being.

His desk is messy, like his hair. Piles of paper, a half-eaten blueberry muffin; a few open journals wait to be returned to their home on the shelf. There are also two framed pictures. One is an older photo of a young boy, likely Ryan, fishing with a man who is presumably his father.

The other is of Alice. I can't resist picking it up. It's strangely old-fashioned to have a picture like this. It's not a selfie, just Alice sitting on a swing, her long legs dangling gracefully over cement, probably in New York. I lose myself in the photo, so I'm startled and almost drop the frame when I look up to see Crystal watching me from the doorway.

"Sorry, Ellen!" she says, walking toward me, grabbing an old coffee cup off the desk. "I forgot I said I would tidy up in here. He's got a patient early Monday."

"Oh, my God, Crystal," I say, catching my breath. "I'm sorry, the door was open," I lie. "I was bored. I just wandered in."

"Who cares?" she says coolly. "Is that Alice?"

"What?" Oh, the photo. "Yeah, it's a good picture. Like she could take a bad one."

"She gave that to him a couple of months ago. Before that, it was like she didn't exist."

"Really? What do you mean?"

"Well, between us, I think they had separated for a while..."

"Oh, really? They seem to have worked it out, I guess." I place the photo back on his desk.

"I guess, but the word in the office is that she's a real piece of work. Had something going on with her boss in New York. It's like she goes back and forth between the two of them." Crystal tidies while she talks.

"That's awful."

"Yeah, well, he's no angel, I'm sure."

"Really?"

"Men like him never are. It made me like Alice more, but she tries wayyyy too hard now. Always showing up with lunch, bringing pictures of herself," she says with a dry laugh.

I don't know what to think. Am I naïve in thinking Trevor, a guy like Ryan, is a straight shooter? Funny, I liked Ryan more when I thought he was an American Psycho.

She reads my mind, or likely my face, and backpedals. "Not Trevor, though, he's a keeper. Always talking about Ellen. He worries about you."

"Ha. Well, he shouldn't. I'm doing okay. It's just a big change."

"He brags about you, too. Not obnoxiously, but about how brilliant you are—the smartest girl in the world," she says, mimicking him quite well.

I smile and take a breath before saying, "I don't know about that, but I'm smart enough not to deal with that horseshit," referring to Ryan and Alice.

We leave his office together. Crystal locks the door behind her, and I try not to take it personally.

Once she's left for good, as if I'm someone completely different (and maybe that's my goal), I decide to strip down to my mismatched bra and panties and thank Trevor for telling everyone that I, unemployed plain Jane, am, in fact, the smartest.

We've barely made love since we've been here, and even though this makes me extremely uncomfortable, the bigger picture is we need to have sex. I step into his office and linger in the doorway, waiting for him to notice me.

He's reading through three files at once, tapping his pen to an inaudible beat. He looks incredibly sexy behind his desk in his casual t-shirt and vintage Blue Jays cap. I'm sure I'm not the first woman to picture herself sprawled out on top of those files. He's seen me in my underwear countless times, getting changed, walking to the bathroom after sex, but he's never seen me like this: on display, tanned and toned.

But it takes him so long to look up that I lose my nerve. I know if I try to leave now I will get caught and look foolish. Ugh. It's frustrating, because the longer I stand here, the more awkward I feel. Where do I put my hands? Where do I even look?

Finally, I clear my throat. (Even that sounds forced.) He looks up to say hello, but rather than the delighted smile I expect, the expression on his face is pure panic and horror. He drops the file in his hand and runs toward me like he's trying to save me from falling.

"Ellen, what are you doing?!" He pushes past me, his head darting back and forth, looking for someone who isn't there.

"Relax. Crystal is gone!" Trevor is my husband. I've farted in front of him. But right now, I am utterly, totally humiliated.

"Are you crazy?" Breathing deeply, he shuts his office door.

I must be, and I might be. My clothes are in the hallway, so I have no moves. I just stand there, exposed, trying to play it cool.

"Wow, Ellen," he says finally, his face strangely blank.

"I was bored," I explain, as he crosses the room toward me.

I stand still, waiting for him to take me like on the cover of a supermarket paperback.

"You look amazing, babe," he pauses, looking me over, "and if we were at home, I would be all over you. But this makes me nervous."

I'm stunned.

"We're in your office, Trevor."

"I know, but what if someone comes in? These guys pop in and out all the time."

"But we're in your office, Trevor!" I repeat, annoyed.

"There are cameras in the hallway, Ellen. And how will it look if someone comes in and your clothes are scattered around the office?"

"Like you've had a good afternoon."

Then, mortified, past defending myself, I say, "You're right."

I brush past him and head into the hallway, awkwardly doing my best to strut for the cameras. I can feel my face burning, but I refuse to turn around or even acknowledge Trevor calling my name. On the outside I keep it together and manage the walk of shame without hesitation. On the inside, I'm a mix of waterworks and rage. The person watching this surveillance footage will probably be as torn as I am, not knowing if they should feel bad that I've been caught in my underwear or that my husband rejected me. Plus, they'll have witnessed me feeling up Ryan's nameplate before breaking into his office.

Right now, I don't care about that. Oddly, I feel I can trust Ryan with my emotions more than Trevor right now. I grab my clothes and run into the restroom, frantically, clumsily dressing while hyperventilating.

Do not cry, Ellen. I swear to God, Ellen, if you cry.

I splash water on my face to camouflage my disloyal tears and drown out Trevor's pathetic tapping on the door. I didn't think it was possible to feel lower than I have lately, but remembering the way he looked at me in his doorway makes me realize it's possible to feel a lot worse.

"I'm good, babe," I say, trying to salvage a little pride.

"I'm stupid, Ellen, I'm sorry." I can hear a thud on the door, which I hope is his head.

"Honest, Trev, I'm good." I know I didn't do anything wrong. I put myself out there, and he knows how shy I am, but he didn't want me. I can't feel bad about that. I wish I could cross my arms, blink, and magically be transported home to Canada.

A sad thing about getting older is knowing that feverish, all-consuming young love is behind you, possibly forever. I know it's an entirely pessimistic outlook. But right now, all I can think of is the way my high school boyfriend Nathan would run to me in the halls and wrap his arm around me, marking his territory even in front of his friends. He'd pick me up from work, drive me wherever I needed to go, and buy me cheap jewelry that I proudly showed off along with the many teddy bears I still have tucked away in the hope chest my grandfather built me. He looked at me like I was the only girl he would ever love. Nathan would have made love to me in the middle of the street if I'd given him the green light.

Sure, like everything he does, the first time with Trevor was perfect. He was gentle and sensuous and oh-so-in-control. His body was already a man's body, filled out in all the right places. He was so confident it made me feel even less skilled than I was. He'd slipped my panties off, not breaking eye contact with me the whole time; lasting so long I started to feel self-conscious and wonder if I was doing something wrong, that I might not be enough for him.

It was nothing like that with Nathan, who snuck me downstairs to his basement bedroom our first time. It was chilly, and his sheets smelled of damp and his deodorant. I'd worn a skirt that afternoon, not planning on going all the way, but it felt better when I straddled him, our clothed bodies rubbing up against each other as we made out. I still remember how passionate our kissing was, his soft, wet lips and his active tongue imitating what he wanted to do to me. (The thought reminds me that Trevor and I barely even kiss anymore during sex.) When Nathan put on the condom, his hands were so shaky I had to help him, trying not to freak out, or worse, laugh. I didn't have much experience at that point, but I knew enough to know he wasn't that skilled. Yet he was so grateful and excited that I felt like a goddess. I know men learn to control themselves, slow things down, change positions and so forth, but it turned me on knowing how much Nathan wanted me.

He's a teacher now, Nathan. Things never really ended between us, mostly just fizzled out after I left for school. We gradually talked less, then not at all. Now he tortures me with his resistance to social media. I don't know much about him. I don't think he's married, but he'd be an amazing husband. Unless they all change as they get older. I wonder if I would be happier with him. I'd certainly be happier than I am right now.

12

We had a quiet evening of me pretending not to be upset and Trevor pretending to believe me. He fell asleep immediately after we turned the light out. Now I'm stuck here listening to the sound of his breathing, smooth and regulated like his personality. I either fall asleep or my mind goes completely blank, because when my phone vibrates, I'm disoriented. I feel around on my night table, careful not to knock over my water.

It's Wendy.

It's too dark over there. Tell me you're not sleeping?

I'm awake.

You need to get your Canadian ass over here.

It's eleven p.m., which to me is extremely late. I've also had a lousy day, and I don't know if I can handle Wendy tonight. Then again, I've had a lousy day and the idea of sneaking out to drink with girlfriends, even new ones, makes me feel a bit better. I slip out of the sheets, feeling excited for my callback interview, careful not to wake the human white noise machine beside me.

I throw on jeans and a tank top and creep out the front door like I'm a teenager leaving by the bedroom window, holding my breath until I've safely escaped. The night air feels good on my skin. I don't feel scared at all, even though it's just me and the sound of my flip-flops in the dark.

I can't let Trevor make me feel numb, regardless of what's going on with him or with us. Staying strong will be crucial to us surviving this slump. I refuse to let him strut around our house like he's the king of the castle and I'm the help.

As Wendy instructed, I use the side gate and join the five of them in the backyard a measly forty feet from where Trevor is sound asleep. I wonder why I'm only getting an invite now, as the empty wine bottles on the table make it clear they didn't just get together. I might be an afterthought here, like maybe the conversation got boring so they invited the Canadian to make fun of? Whatever. Had this been high school, the idea that I was initially excluded would be forefront the entire evening, but now I'm quite satisfied to be invited at all.

"You came," Wendy says, standing to hug me, her hair wild and frizzy from the late-night humidity.

"I wasn't sure I had a choice," I joke.

"You always have a choice, my dear!" She pulls a chair out and throws a cashmere blanket at me. "Sit," she instructs.

Everyone reintroduces themselves to me, laughing that there's no chance the drunk woman remembered anything from the last time we were together. So, there's Wendy, my neighbor. British Scarlet, who doesn't live in the Ports anymore. She's a tad hard, doesn't smile as much as the others, but she's probably the most beautiful of the beautiful. An athletic woman named Jen, who doesn't say much but is very agreeable; she nods in support of everything Wendy says. Maria, who may be in her mid-forties but is not admitting it, and her body and Botox keep the secret well. She has olive skin, green eyes, long incredibly dark hair and a voice that's as low as mine is high, almost suspiciously low. And the baby of the group, who smartly sets herself up to be the always-younger woman with her friends and husband, every ex-wife's nightmare and stepson's dream, Laura.

We chat for some time, hitting on topics like the currency market (Canadian dollar troubles and how rich we'll be when we move back); Maria's son's teacher, who moonlights as a Disney princess; and Wendy's neighbor, who gives her the creeps. (We dissect his Facebook and somehow decide he has erectile dysfunction.)

It's after midnight, but they don't seem to be running out of steam or wine as they take turns telling stories, chiming in here and there. Listening to each other, not just waiting to talk.

Then, out of nowhere, Wendy says, "Okeeee, it's late, so we need to get on with the evening." She takes an awkward breath. I almost expect some sort of performer to pop out of the bushes until I realize everyone at the table is looking at me.

"So, we brought you over at this risible hour because we have a proposition for you," she says, turning toward me. Everyone nods and leans in, scanning me for a reaction. Wendy pauses, maybe waiting for me to say something, and when I don't, Scarlet takes over. (I knew she was in charge!)

"We want you to consider joining our little group." The way she says it makes it clear she isn't talking about a book club, but she pauses without offering any more information.

"I don't know. I sort of thought I already was." I lean back in my chair to give myself a little space from their crowding eyes. "What kind of group is it?" I ask. I can feel Scarlet's impatience, but I also know that, whatever this is, I'm just not a group person. "You guys in a band?"

"Just tell her, Scarlet," Maria nudges.

"Okay. So, hear us out. We're not swingers or anything like that…"

"Yeah, we don't fuck each other's husbands, Ellen!" Laura says, taking a long sip of wine.

"Well, that's a disappointment, 'cause I had dibs on Ken!" I laugh, looking at Wendy.

"I hear that!" Laura agrees, tapping my glass with hers.

"Hey! You ladies haven't seen Ellen's hubby yet!" Wendy teases, not fazed.

"But we do occasionally screw other men," Scarlet says flatly, her accent only marginally tempering the sordidness.

I'm stunned. I wait for them to say they're kidding, but they don't. All I can hear is the sound of sprinkler water hitting leaves. I've heard of these quiet suburban sex clubs, usually swingers, but I'd thought they were male-driven. Audrey even once told me about Kate's private preschool parents getting super-inappropriate at welcome parties. I have so many questions. It's intriguing in the same uncomfortable way the addiction intervention shows on TV are.

My mind is swirling. All I can come up with is, "Like, together?"

"No, Ellen," Wendy says, topping up my glass, hopefully feeling responsible for putting me in this bizarre situation. "Not together."

"Ew," Laura adds, eloquently.

"I'm confused," I say, leaving out uncomfortable, disappointed, put off…

"It's pretty simple," Scarlet continues, still holding the talking torch. "We go out two Fridays a month, rain or shine. It's not that we look to cheat, but if it happens, they're just indiscretions." She looks around for support, playing with her bracelets, and then elbows Maria.

She seems the least likely of the four to be a part of this, but pitches in. "We like to go out and feel young again. Sometimes stuff happens, and it's no big deal to us." She shrugs, watching for my reaction, her eyes wide and intensely green.

"But—but what about your husbands? Don't you love them?" I almost whisper. I hear the innocence in my voice and realize I am utterly shocked at how nonchalant this all is.

"Of course we do! It's not like that," says Laura.

I turn to Wendy, looking for some reasonable explanation. Not that they owe me one, but hey, they brought it up!

"Have you never considered that Trevor might hook up with someone just for sex?" she asks, looking at me sympathetically.

"Why? Does Ken?" I shoot back, shocked and betrayed, before I remember his late-night call from right here in this backyard.

"Yeah, he probably does, sweetie."

It scares me. I think of Trevor's complete disinterest in me this afternoon. "Well, he better not fucking cheat on me," I say, actually considering it for the first time.

When I think about it, Trevor and I have spent most of our relationship apart. How much do I really know about him? If he cheated on me once, he could do it a million times. He certainly has many opportunities.

"Well, hopefully he doesn't, Ellen," Jen says, speaking for the first time, startling me. I've forgotten she was even there, sitting quietly in the dark corner beside me. "But let's just say it was only once or twice, when he was away at school, maybe. Would that change the way you feel about him?"

"Of course it would! I don't know, guys—this is so depressing."

"It's actually normal, natural even," says Scarlet, as if it's not open for discussion. "Expecting successful people to be monogamous is unrealistic these days. I'll never forget the moment I realized Mark was cheating on me. I passed them on the street—on the way to pick up our children! His hand was on her flat ass; he didn't even care who saw them, didn't even care enough to save me from the humiliation. It was cruel."

"And you didn't leave him?" I blurt, horrified, still stinging from the way they'd clumped Trevor in with their cheating loser husbands.

"I considered it. I even kicked him out for a while. But otherwise, we had a good thing." She pauses and looks up at the stars like she's beckoning the memories and certainly not bothering to make any wishes. "He thinks I moved past it, like I'm naïve enough to think it won't happen again." She pauses, gives a small, disturbing laugh as if trying to give me the impression she is over it, and smiles bitterly. "I just got wise. Now we're both happier, and our children have two parents who guiltily treat each other like gold."

She might mean what she says, but it makes me incredibly sad for her, for all of them. I decide to keep my judgment to myself and steer the conversation in another direction.

"So why tell me this? Do I need to know to be in your group, promise to keep my mouth shut?" I smile and look around the table, meeting each of their eyes.

"Not that simple, girl!" Laura says, pointing at Scarlet like she's the enforcer. "No rush, but if you want to be part of our little group we'll eventually need some dirt on you."

Is this really happening? Are these words really coming from this Oxford-educated woman? Is it the wine? She's slurring her words but still manages to sound credible. It's almost like listening to a 1980s feminist argue that women shouldn't be limited to traditional forms of relationships, which confine them to patriarchal ideas of normalcy. (Husbands fuck their secretaries and wives wash their boxers.) Even though I may be going through a superficial stage, I am a feminist. But I've also always believed in marriage, gay or straight, first or second, makes no difference—likely because of my parents.

I suppose I understand where these women are coming from. They're strong, they're independent, and they're behaving like their husbands behave.

I don't know what to think or say, but I know I feel exposed, so I stand up and check the neighboring houses for open windows. I peek over the three fences that cage us back here to make sure we're alone. As much as I'm disappointed and super-uncomfortable that the first women I met here have turned out to be mostly middle-aged trollops trying to manipulate me into adultery, I'm a little bit excited they trust me with this, too.

I'm also angry with Trevor. And, surprise, I've had a lot to drink, so I tell them I'm heading home. I make a point to keep it light on my way out. They're going out Friday, which gives me five days to decide if I want to tag along. If I go with them, I'm agreeing that I am open to the possibility and won't be all judgey. Mercifully, I don't need to sign any perverted contracts. But I leave Wendy's yard thinking I've probably just lost my only California friends, my own group of Heathers.

13

I sleep better than I have in a long time, possibly because I've been reminded there are people far worse off than Trevor and I. He doesn't wake me before he leaves, but I find a hand-written note downstairs telling me to have a great day and that he loves me. So much nicer than a text, I think, as I scrunch it up in a ball.

A lot about yesterday seems surreal, including making the appointment for my lips, which is in two hours. I usually don't do things like this, obviously. What I mean is I'm not spontaneous. Generally, I give big steps giant thought. A few years back I considered getting a tattoo to match Audrey's, just our initials. I had a consultation and a design plan, but ultimately, I backed out. It's shocking how set I now am on doing something so unbelievably vain, how I've rationalized it as just for fun, no biggie.

I don't have anyone to talk to about it with either. I could call Audrey, but there's not a chance I could explain over her laughter and harsh judgment. I'm fairly sure Trevor would divorce me—he's made more than a few comments about touched-up faces since we've been here. "Never do that, Ellen!"

I want to call Wendy, or maybe Scarlet, but I don't know what the rules are. If I don't join their group, are we not friends anymore? No more freshly baked cookie deliveries? As light as I tried to keep it last night, today it all just seems bizarre.

I eat two yogurts to make up for skipping dinner last night and then throw the vacuum around, limiting my cleaning to two songs. (It's a lot less enjoyable than cleaning with Ryan.) The house doesn't get that messy with just me and my imaginary cats. If the house was my husband, I wonder if it would be happy with just me, or if it would sneak other people in when I wasn't home.

Running short on time, I skip the dishes and shower quickly. As I dry off in front of the mirror, I notice the newly defined line down the side of my leg and the soft yet surprisingly lean curve of my hips. I muster the courage to turn around to take in a rear view, and unexpectedly, I'm not entirely disappointed. My ample cheeks are unquestionably higher, which takes some pressure off my short legs and smooths out the skin I'd resolved to accept as "genetically" dimpled. I could sense my body tightening up this past month but seeing confirmation of the transformation lifts my spirits.

Next, I move on to my face. I zoom in on the undeniable lines on my forehead and around my eyes, which is a bad sign because it's only ten a.m. and I haven't been particularly expressive. I try aggressively to rub them off, with no luck. I promised myself no botulism until I'm at least forty, so I apply some firming cream and give myself a smile, thinking it might be the last time my smile is actually my smile.

As if I'm sleepwalking (which is how the extremely anxious function, I think), I manage to make it to my appointment on time. I have a mountain of paperwork to fill out, which is a good distraction for my nerves. I breeze through it, feeling grateful I can check no on all the boxes. Only one other woman is waiting, and she's much younger than I am. Maybe twenty-five, I suspect, or even younger. She doesn't have any wrinkles, which makes sense, but the extreme tightness and shine on her forehead suggest she's as afraid of aging as I am of fading away. She's drinking something so green it's almost black—Botox plus detox?

I haven't completely lost touch, because I feel ridiculous sitting beside this tormented little girl. And yet I feel so different from her, too. At her age, I was defending my thesis in front of women who made me feel silly because I wore lip gloss. What would Dr. Keen, my women's studies professor, think if she saw me here now, wading in self-justification like a would-be, soon-to-be duck lips?

Nope, I've lost my mind. This is not me, not any of it. I've been with Trevor nearly my whole adult life, and although I've always been aware of our looks I was accepting of mine, happy even. I'm going through a shallow stage, perhaps because I'm also going through a my-life-has-no-point stage. This place is changing me. Will the real Ellen Hunter please stand up! I decide to forgive myself, and I'm about to walk out when my name is called. I spinelessly turn around.

My nerves seem to be breaking down, and I feel tingles like a sleeping foot throughout my body. The nurse who shows me to the room is a good advertisement: filled but not overstuffed. She's quite cavalier, though, and does not appreciate my hesitation or my rambling, unintelligible explanation for it.

She tries to keep it light as I blurt unintentionally insulting things like, "I'm not the type of person," and "I know it's shallow, but…"

"Okay. So, are we doing it?"

When I don't answer, she lowers her eyes to look at my chart instead of the clock, probably counting the seconds before the doctor shows up to save her from me.

He's young and calming. He walks in like it's his scene on General Hospital, with his lines prepared. Wisely, he is supportive, "completely understanding" my hesitations while he reassures me, with his hand on my shoulder, that the procedure "is as safe and easy as routine teeth cleaning."

I don't take the bait until he lures me with his client list: doctors, lawyers, teachers; even men. I feel relieved but also stuck, not brave enough to excuse myself. Then it happens: he sticks his hook in me.

I was so caught up in the mental aspects of this I hadn't even considered the pain. Initially, it's just a little pinch, like losing your virginity, but when the filler is injected my whole mouth starts to sting and burn. It's more like peeing with a bladder infection than teeth cleaning. He starts to massage with his latex fingers. He is so close to my face, looking at my lips like they're his masterpiece, completely forgetting they're attached to a real live woman. He nods to himself, and I gather he is pleased. He passes me a handheld mirror. I feel the weight of it in my shaking hand and bring it to my face in what seems like slow motion. When I see myself, everything speeds up: my heart races and the thoughts in my head seem to implode.

What have you done, Ellen? How am I going to get to my car?

I'm too distraught to be sentimental, even though it hits me that I've just betrayed my parents, my first kiss, even my resemblance to my future children! I can see the doctor's completely natural lips move, but all I hear is a faint buzzing sound that seems to get louder and more intrusive. Then the room goes black.

"You're finnnnne," an almost amused voice reassures me. "I think you've had a panic attack."

I have an ice pack on my face and a cool cloth on my forehead. The pain is gone aside from a quiet throbbing.

"I fainted?" I've never done that before, but I have witnessed Audrey faint on many occasions, starting when our puppy mistook her finger for a stick when she was six and I was three. The tiniest drop of her own blood, and bam, she's out.

"You sure did! But don't worry, you're not the first!" She leaves to get the doctor.

I'm queasy and lightheaded. I feel like he should have come back right away, but I sit for at least ten minutes. I'm too scared to look at my lips, which feel like a balloon must right before it pops. There's a large advertisement for Botox on the wall in front of me. The woman is young: not "wow, Botox really works!" young, but about twenty years old. I don't even know how Americans can brave getting the injections when television here is riddled with medical commercials that end with "may spread days to weeks after" and then something about death. Besides, wrinkles don't make you look old; being old makes you look old.

Who am I to talk, sitting here like a porn star.

When the doctor does show up he assures me that the swelling is completely normal and will subside in twenty-four hours. His face is close to mine again, inspecting, looking less pleased. He makes a strange sound, scratches his pointy chin and then tells me that if it doesn't, he can reverse the procedure with some eraser enzyme.

I bob my head like I understand, but I'm freaked right out. All I can think about is grabbing a medical mask and running to my car like my friend Shirley does during flu season.

He makes me sit there for another twenty minutes. I sip the nauseatingly warm water he gave me and wonder why I thought having this done in an outdoor mall was a good idea. On my way out, I see the same young girl still sitting there. I want to give her a good look at my fucked-up face, but I'm ashamed and embarrassed, so I cover my mouth with my hand and keep my head down.

As soon as I'm safely in the car, the panic and frustration that's been mounting releases an avalanche of emotions. Tears pour down my face, stinging my mouth and trailing black mascara down my flushed cheeks. I fight with my oversized bag and throw the contents on the seat beside me, desperately searching for my phone, a lifeline to someone for help. When I find it, I lean back, barely able to text with my shaking hands. I don't know who to call. I'm congested because I'm sobbing, but I start to feel like I really can't breathe. I drop the phone in my lap, look in the mirror, and scream wildly inside, knowing this can't be normal. My top lip is so swollen it's nearly obstructing my nostrils.

Get it together, Ellen. I swallow hard and drive home, feeling out of control.

Mary is out front when I pull into the driveway. Of course. She calls me as I dart to the front door and fumble with my keys.

"Hey, Mary," I call back over my shoulder, with no idea of what she has just said. I sprint up the stairs two at a time, praying the whole way: please be okay, please be okay. I pause before looking in the mirror, touching my lips lightly with my fingers. I know how bad it is, but I can't help hoping for a miracle.

It's worse than I could have ever imagined, hard and bumpy double Ds. I feel like I might faint again. I text Wendy to please come over, not caring about the rules, then fly back downstairs for ice. I'm startled by a knock at the door. It's too quick for it to be Wendy. It must be Mary.

"You okay, Ellen?" she asks through the door.

Shit, I have to answer it. I open it a tiny crack and tell her not to worry. "I'm just having an allergic reaction. I've got it under control."

She's concerned, like a mom would be. She says something about Benadryl, and that she'll check on me later. I thank her, feeling genuinely comforted. I consider telling her the truth, and I will if I don't hear back from Wendy soon. I don't even know where the hospital is, and the prospect of walking in there like this is out of the question.

Finally, Wendy texts back, saying she'll be right over and that she's bringing her three-year-old. That poor child will be traumatized. I almost stop her but instead text, *thanks, please hurry, door is open.* Not knowing what else to do, I grab the ice and lie down on the couch, my whole face pulsing. It's like a self-inflicted nightmare.

Minutes later Wendy and her son explode through the front door. I feel like I should get up and be hospitable but I can't move, I can't worry about my ugly furniture or the breakfast dishes still on the counter from yesterday. "In here," I moan. "It's not pretty."

I hear her walk in and feel her eyes on me. "Oh shit, Ellen!" she says, immediately noticing the damage despite the huge bag of ice.

"Mom, don't say SHIT," a little voice echoes, sounding happy to have an excuse to say the word.

"Rhys, iPad, now!" she barks in an unrecognizable tone.

"Okay, Ellen," she says with concern as she sits on the table in front of me. "What happened? Who did this to you?" Her voice is gentle.

"I did it to myself."

She lifts the ice off my face, and from the look on hers, I know it's bad.

"Ellen!!! Does it hurt?"

"It throbs. I think they're getting bigger!" Tears roll down my burning cheeks. I sit up, ice tight against my mouth. "I got lip injections."

"What!? What did you inject them with?" She holds her hand over her mouth and tries not to laugh.

I tell her the story, watching her face while she tries to process my stupidity. She insists I call Trevor; she's surprised I haven't already. Calling him didn't even dawn on me as an option. I can picture the disappointment in his eyes.

"Then I'm taking you to the hospital," she says, collecting her things.

"This is so embarrassing. I can't walk in there like this!"

"It's California, Ellen. People get botched here every day."

"Not people like me, Wendy. Is it getting better?" I say, lifting the ice.

"It's not worse."

"Fuck me," I whisper, shaking my head in disbelief.

I don't know what to do, but I hear Wendy's warning about permanent damage and I'm not going back to the mall. I call Trevor. His phone rings, one, two, three times—straight to voicemail. I listen to his message: he'll get back to me as soon as possible; if it's an emergency, call 911. No option for, "If this is my wife, desperate for my attention..."

I call twice more, texting in between. In the meantime, Wendy takes Rhys home and tries to reach Scarlet. I realize I've handled this situation like a forlorn pregnant teenager who doesn't know where to turn. My actions are completely illogical.

I've overthought every possible option while my lips continue to swell, pound and change color, turning bluish-purple.

I stand up and call Trevor's office. I need to solve this like a grown-up. I try to disguise the panic in my voice, and since I don't know what panic sounds like, I just come across as abrupt and cold. Crystal puts me on hold, trying to figure out where my husband is. How does she not know? Look at the schedule, Crystal! My knees feel weak, and I think that if I stop shifting my weight from foot to foot, heel to toe, they might give out. I sit to be safe, not needing a broken bone to go with my shattered pride.

"Ellen, hi. We think he's in surgery."

"You think?" I say, my tone bitchy.

"Well, it's not on the schedule, but Ryan says…"

"Ryan's there now?"

"Yes. Ellen, are you okay?"

Before I have a chance to answer, I hear fumbling and then his voice. "Ellen, what's up? You okay?"

"Ummm, do you know when Trevor will be done?" I fight back tears and fix my hair.

"Not really, he got called into surgery after lunch. What's up?" His voice is comforting.

As much as I don't want him to see me like this, or even think of me like this, I need help, and strangely, I trust him.

"I did something stupid, Ryan." It's too embarrassing to put into words.

"Ellen, you're scaring me. Did you take something?" Oh, my God, he thinks I tried to kill myself! How pathetic does he think I am?

"No, nothing like that! Can you just come over?"

"I'm leaving now."

Running into the kitchen, I suddenly don't feel any pain and hope the swelling has plateaued. I throw the dishes in the washer, spray Lysol on the counters and start scrubbing. I cannot allow him to think I am also lazy. Satisfied, I light a Bath and Body Works candle to diffuse any old food smell and open and close the back door wildly, fanning the stuffy house with some fresh air.

There is absolutely no use looking in the mirror. No makeup in the world could cover this up. I reapply deodorant, spritz some perfume and attempt to gargle, spilling mouthwash from my mouth like I'm a fountain. There's no way I can get out of this by hiding. I have to take this dose of humiliation like the strong, capable woman I used to be.

14

His knock on the door stops me in my tracks. I stand there for a minute gathering myself, aware of my heart racing, not feeling or thinking of the calamity on my face. I grab fresh ice and walk to the door, hoping not to have to explain myself.

"Hi," is all I can get out.

"Hey," he replies, looking confused. He slips in the door, drops his keys on the table, and turns to me, saying nothing, offering a small, sympathetic smile. He comes toward me and touches my chin with his warm hand, tilting it up gently, subtly moving it side to side, like a father inspecting his son's black eye. "Oh man, I'm sorry. It hurts, doesn't it?"

I nod yes, feeling so safe but vulnerable, my chest visibly moving up and down with each breath.

"Restalyne?"

I nod again.

"Okay. I can help. Do you want to come back to the office with me?"

I shake my head no. He understands and wraps his strong arms around me, holding me tight for just a moment.

"You're too much, Ellen," he says, releasing me. "Go sit down, okay? I need to get a few things, and then I'll be back. Will you be okay alone?"

"I'll be okay," I whisper and give him my best, "I'm pitiful but hopefully still cute," smile before realizing that any movement of these lips is probably disturbing.

He sighs heavily, leans into me and boldly kisses my forehead with soft, seductive lips. He's only the third man to ever kiss me there, after my father and Trevor, and the sensation lingers long after he's gone.

I follow his orders and head to the couch. I'm exhausted, but I feel so much better knowing he's going to fix this, like a modern-day hero in a screwed-up fairy tale. I can't imagine what Crystal is thinking as she sits there in the center of Trevor's office, not knowing anything but also knowing way too much. I didn't say it, but I'm certain Ryan knows I wouldn't want this to get out. I check my phone for a missed call from Trevor, this time hoping I don't hear from him; for one, because there's a small chance he never has to know about this, and two, because Ryan has been the only bright spot in what has to my morally darkest day.

Just as I let my eyes close for a moment, I hear Wendy and Scarlet come in. I completely forgot to intercept them.

"Ellen," Scarlet whispers, coming to my side.

I sit up, taking in her successfully altered lips and suspiciously flawless nose, her eyes a mix of horror and amusement.

"What on earth happened here? Someone really cocked this up!" She reaches out her delicate hand almost like she's going to touch my swollen lips, then retracts it abruptly. She stands and pulls her phone from the back pocket of her incredibly well-fitting jeans, taking charge of this god-awful situation.

I stop her, speaking for the first time. "It's okay. I called Trevor, and someone's on their way over to try and deal with this mess."

"Thank God, Ellen," she replaces her phone. "It's hard to even look at you like this. It looks like someone beat the shit out of you."

"I told you it was bad!" Wendy adds.

"I can't even look in the mirror. I'm such an idiot. But you guys should go. I'll text you later." I stand up, attempting to corral them to the door.

"I'm staying," Scarlet announces. "Someone has to be here to make sure you're okay!"

Oh, no, you're not.

"No, no seriously, Trevor will probably come home, too. I'm fine. I'd like to limit the embarrassment and drama as much as possible. But thanks so much for checking on me. You two are the best, really. Thank you."

Scarlet purses her lips together (showing off?) and then nods. She tells me she has a plastic surgeon friend who will help if I need someone. I thank her again, truly meaning it. But now I'm worried I could need surgery to fix what was perfectly fine to begin with.

Like children, it takes them forever to get moving and they find a million distractions on the way out. They comment on the kitchen and the old-fashioned, thin-planked maple floors before reminiscing about the hot hag who used to live here…

As politely as possible, I open the door and stand waiting.

"Wow, she really wants us out of here," Wendy jokes. "We're going, we're going!"

They're halfway across the patio when Ryan pulls up. I hope he will take a few minutes before getting out, check his messages maybe. But no such luck, he hops out immediately. I hold my breath and try not to smile or look guilty.

Wendy whips around. "Who is that?" she mouths dramatically, looking impressed.

I watch them introduce themselves, both perking up their posture, fixing themselves as they speak with him. Likely playing nurses, filling him in on how helpful they've been. Nothing about the way Ryan looks says doctor. As he walks up the steps to me with his doctor bag, he looks more like a well-costumed stripper or a deeply committed husband trying to spice things up with a dirty pretend house call.

Scarlet gives me the thumbs up, and I give her a "What's wrong with you?!" wave goodbye.

When I let him back in, he gives my face a long inspection.

"You look beautiful," he says, chuckling to himself.

"It must be my hair."

"There is so much I want to say to you, Ellen, but let's get you fixed up first." He grabs my hand and takes me into the living room. "Lie down; this might hurt," he says with a suggestive smirk. (No foreplay, I guess?)

He leaves the room, and I can hear the water running in the kitchen as he washes his hands. I think about his ungloved finger on my mouth, and I feel nervous like it's my first time. I wonder what he's thinking, if he likes being alone with me the way I do with him, if he thinks inappropriate thoughts about me or if he thinks of me at all. Perhaps he's just showing me some kindness, sensing I need support. Maybe he's afraid his colleague's wife is unstable and feels obligated to help him out.

"Okay. I'm going to numb your lips first, then I'll inject a second needle that will dissolve the Restalyne. It shouldn't take long to work. But I've never done this before."

I try to make a worried face, but my mouth doesn't move the way I want it to and he starts laughing.

"I don't know what that means," he says, mimicking me.

I laugh with him, holding my hand over my mouth, knowing how hideous I must look.

"Do you trust me?"

"I trust you," I say, closing my eyes and trying to be calm.

"Great. I got you," he says, and angles my head back on the pillow, smoothing my hair back from my face. "You know, you'd make a beautiful clown."

I open my eyes, and he's smiling. "Seriously, Ellen, what were you thinking?"

I try to sit up to explain the unexplainable, but he puts his hand on my shoulder, guiding me back down. "I'm sorry. Okay, try to relax again."

"Ryan!" I laugh and then close my eyes.

His body hovers over mine, his arm across me, his hand beside my hip holding his weight up. He touches two latex-free fingers to my lips, pressing softly, lighting me up inside despite his tenderness.

"Can you feel that?"

"Yes," I say, a little too breathy.

"Okay, just a little pinch."

It hurts, but I deserve this pain. I flinch a little, and he lowers his face closer to mine, wiping a tear from my eye. A few minutes later he presses my lips again, and this time I can't feel them. He injects the second needle, and I feel only some pressure.

"I think that will do it." He carefully pulls me up. "Let's go see my handiwork."

Without letting go of my hand, he takes me into the powder room. We stand in front of the mirror staring back at our reflections. They're judging us, I think, especially her. We watch as my lips slowly contract, tiny bits at a time. I've never done this before, looked in a mirror side by side with someone, seeing what the other person sees. We don't break eye contact as we look at ourselves in awe, like we're watching fireworks.

"They're blue," I finally say.

"They're frozen, Ellen!" He laughs. "You can lay off the ice now."

He leaves the bathroom first but stops in the doorway and waits for me as I get a closer look.

"I'm really embarrassed, Ryan," I say, turning to face him. "But I'm so grateful to you."

"I'd be embarrassed, too," he says, straight-faced.

I hold my breath, knowing I can't escape this without a lecture.

"Not because of what happened," he continues, staring intently at my mouth, "but because your natural lips are so small."

I take a fake swing at him as I shout his name like a teenager, "Ryyyyyan!" and then cover my lips as he fakes going down from my punch.

"Don't be embarrassed; I get it. That shit is everywhere around here. It's normal to be curious, but you're at least ten years away from even thinking about it. Hell, I've even thought about it." He makes an angry face, exposing some sexy wrinkles between his brows.

"Yeah, but those are hot on guys."

"Oh yeah, you think they're hot?"

"I meant in general," I say, giving his a second look. "But, yes, they're kinda hot."

"You should see them after sex," he says, laughing.

"What!?!" I gasp, hilariously shocked.

"Yeah, I guess I really concentrate, because after, they're super-deep."

"Oh, my God, Ryan! That's horrifying!"

When I offer him a drink and he accepts only after checking his watch, I'm reminded he has important stuff to get to. I should give him an out, but instead, I make coffee. I do my best to keep my battered face looking pretty, my eyes nearly bugging out in an attempt to maintain eye contact.

"I'm glad you're all right. You scared me, Ellen." He places his cup on the counter and walks over to me, touching my lips gently. Maybe to check my progress, maybe just to touch me.

"I'm sorry. You don't know how ridiculous I feel."

"Shhhhh," he says, leaving his finger over my lips. "I'm glad you let me help you."

He must go, get back to the working world, leave me and my yearnings inside this house that feels more and more like a cage. Maybe I should be locked up. After today, I seriously question my sanity. I said I would go crazy if I wasn't busy, and recent events suggest I was right.

Ryan told me to call him tonight. "Even if I have to sneak it," he'd said, to keep this afternoon a secret.

I want this person in my life. As I watch him drive away, I feel like I might not see him again, at least not like this. He didn't cross any lines, all t's remain l's, but I wonder if he feels guilty like I do. Guilty but inspired.

I spend the rest of the day thinking about his touch, his playfulness. The way he talks to me like I'm his buddy but looks at me like I'm capable of being the kind of woman I loathe. The kind of woman I may need to be before the fantasy is gone and I'm left empty.

Trevor is a gentleman: brilliant, successful, generous. I love the way he looks, the way his body feels against mine when we're together, how he encourages me to be better even if I am happy being where I am. I hate that I will never live up to his expectations and that my best day would be nothing for him. I hate that being with him means being alone ninety percent of the time and invisible a hundred percent of the time. And I hate that I can't stop comparing him to Ryan.

I tell Trevor the same lie I told Mary: it was something I ate. He seemed hardly sympathetic, dismissing my tragic afternoon with a condescending hug that might as well have been a pat on the head.

I didn't press about where he was when I was trying to reach him, not wanting to sound suspicious. But I could barely look at him without wanting to pinch his cheeks and demand, "Where have you been, Trevor?"

It seems awfully unfair to question my straight-arrow husband while omitting answers to questions he hasn't thought to ask. He wouldn't recognize me if he knew what was going on in my mind: how cruel my thoughts are to him, how consumed they've been with Ryan.

If he was with another woman this afternoon, am I so much better?

Is having sex with someone who isn't your wife worse than being totally emotionally obsessed with someone who isn't your husband?

15

The next day, I wake up with slightly sore lips and five missed calls from Audrey last night. There are no text messages, so it's not an emergency. We're close, but since her kids were born we've fallen into the mostly texting category; every time Audrey even thinks about taking a call, someone starts bleeding.

The three-hour difference buys me a little time, so I splash some water on my now mended face and dash out the door for coffee before I call her back.

On my drive out of the Port Streets, I see Mary and a friend in their matching underwear-lined black yoga pants, walking their dogs. They're deep in conversation but acknowledge me with a friendly wave.

"Feeling better?" Mary yells a bit too late.

I've already passed them, so I throw my hand out the window and give her a thumbs-up.

Before I turn off our street, a boy runs in front of my car, chasing a runaway ball, oblivious to his mom's shouted warning. I'm driving slow enough that my stop isn't abrupt and I'm able to exchange knowing smiles with his mother.

I feel light today, thrilled to see Mary and her cheerful face. Even the scare with the careless kid doesn't upset me the way it would have a month ago.

Feeling settled into a new place is a funny thing. You can't ever imagine it happening. You plan to have a wall up forever and then one day, without warning, you notice it's gone. After the hell I put everyone through this summer, I almost feel guilty about being happy here. It was only a matter of time before all that sunshine sunk in, turning my white skin golden and my black heart light.

In the line at the café, a young mom plays a game of "which pastry would I choose?" with her son. She seems legitimately happy, lovingly squishing his little tummy when he guesses right. I fight the urge to smile, as the sight of her reminds me I'm failing in every aspect of my life right now. I imagine her social media, likely full of perfectly filtered shots all displaying her maternal bliss, making all her childless friends cringe or cry. She might be thirty; around the age Audrey was when she had Kate. She seems happier than Audrey did, though, possibly because I knew all of Audrey's worries, how she itched to get back to work after only two weeks and her insecurities about her changed body. And I know Audrey's mother-in-law: SUFFOCATING.

It dawns on me that this mom is likely as fucked up as the rest of us, despite how lovely and carefree she appears, her photos unquestionably filtering out more than crow's feet and spit-up.

It's still only nine a.m. by the time I'm back home, coffee in hand, seated comfortably in the backyard. Audrey will assume I've just woken up, which would be a huge luxury for a mother and lawyer, but is not late enough to raise any depression flags on my part.

She answers on the first ring. Her voice is a mix of adrenaline and annoyance. "Ellen! Finally!"

"I'm sorry. It's early here!"

"I know, I know, but Mom is losing it."

"What? Why?"

"She says you never call her back. I told her you're busy but she insists something's wrong."

"Oh, man! Tell her I'm fine! Tell her to get a cell-phone so I can text her like a normal person."

"Like that will happen. And tell her yourself. Just call her and make her feel better. She's your mom, Elly, she worries."

Right. I wouldn't understand that, not being a mom. I bite my tongue and agree to call her straight away, because I'm not looking for a fight and it's not Audrey's fault my husband doesn't love me enough to want to start a family. Truly, I'm only days away from using Pinterest to figure out how to turn a mason jar into my own Bell Jar.

She tells me Trevor has been talking to Mark, planning a secret visit to cheer me up, though it looks like it will only be Audrey, which is not a bad thing. I know the kids would love it here, escaping a cold Canadian fall and seeing Mickey in the off-season, without the holiday crowds. But honestly, I'm just wrapping my head around this place. I'm not quite ready to play tour guide. I've put off my parents so far, but there is no way Audrey would understand if I told her I'd rather be alone.

She tells me to get the guest room "prettied up," and I try my best to fake excitement. I miss her so much, I do, but I don't want her to see how messed up I am here.

She doesn't come out and specifically ask how I am, but the long pauses she takes suggest she hopes I will fill the void. Staying fairly quiet, I just keep her talking, out of both selfishness and love, asking questions about kindergarten plans and first words. I want to keep my marriage problems and my new crush to myself, and hearing all about the munchkins also makes me feel that I'm not quite so far away.

When we hang up, I realize why I don't call or return calls. It makes me feel like shit. I miss them all, and talking makes it worse. One last long swig of my cool coffee, the coffee that I carry around like company until it's time for wine, and I start to feel even more lonely than usual. I get up and stretch, reaching up high with two hands and let out a deep, strangled breath. Walking around the garden, mostly succulents, I smell flowers and run my fingers through the lavender bushes, trying to be present. But even this seems forced; fake. Like I'm in an Austen novel, romanticizing my struggles with a stroll through the garden. I dip my toes into the stone hot tub and twirl them around in circles, watching the water imitate the motion with fading ripples, eventually disappearing only to be replaced by another, and another.

Unable to resist the soothing heat, I slip off my shorts and t-shirt and tiptoe across the yard to flick on the jets, then lower myself into the water in my now see-through bra and thong. The water holds me close in all the right places, kneading the tension in my shoulders. I unfasten my bra and throw it behind me, feeling the rough current on my breasts, my nipples tingling as they float just on top of the water. Tiny bubbles cling to my skin, forming and popping, like little creatures crawling all over me. The idea that anyone could come over and catch me exposed, floating here on display for the birds and squirrels, is strangely erotic. I must be ovulating, because I rarely feel this sexual alone and almost never at ten in the morning.

My eyes close and I imagine our ruggedly good-looking, older UPS man finding me here like a gift. Not hesitating, he strips off his uniform and climbs in beside me. His eager hands, clumsy on my breasts, taking me all in, afraid I might disappear; grateful to touch my young, wanting body. He puts his mouth over my nipple, gently nibbling as his hands reach around and grab my ass, slipping his fingers inside me. His face becomes Ryan's, his dark eyes locked onto mine. My breath quickens and my hips rise toward the jets, which excite me as much as the fantasy. I don't have an orgasm or anything, never having been able to pleasure myself, shy even with my own body. But I do realize how much I want Ryan.

When I open my eyes, I'm startled by how bright it is. I don't have a towel and surprisingly, I don't feel inhibited. Now feeling more like a character in a Henry Miller novel, I step out of the tub, my breasts shocked by the cool air, looking fabulous in the reflection of the window. I shake my head at myself, feeling silly about the UPS man. It's unlikely I'll ever be able to look at him again.

I collect my bra from the bushes and notice how tattered it is: it's put in some long hours. Annie would be disgusted with me, standing here in my purple thong, holding my old, used-to-be-white bra. Even when money was tight, Annie insisted on always matching her bras to her panties. "Looking good has to start under your clothes."

I make a note to improve my underthings, not for Trevor or Ryan, but for myself. And perhaps the squirrels. Back inside, I turn on some music, not

caring that it blasts out the windows on its way upstairs with me.

Strangely, it's only when I'm in the privacy of our
room that I feel the need to cover up. I throw on the
robe I brought home from the Four Seasons in Maui
last year. It's basic waffle cotton, but it's fancy to me.
Trevor and I took a twelve-hour flight from Toronto
for a four-day trip, and it was worth every minute. We
had a blast hiking in the mornings and collecting
complimentary treats at the pools in the afternoons.
Frozen pineapple? Yes, please! It was one of our few
non-working vacations together. I left my laptop at
home, and aside from an occasional check-in at the
hospital, Trevor was all mine. Not in a million years
would 'Ellen 2016' picture us here, both physically and
emotionally, only twelve months later.

There is a mountain of laundry building up in our
closet, and I just can't put it off any longer. After I've
danced around the room, pretending not to check myself out in the mirror, I grab our giant basket of last
week's outfits and head to the laundry room, defeated.

I sort to Adele's *Hello*, listening to the lyrics and
dedicating it to high-school Nathan, finding it ironic
that I live in California now. I find a pair of Trevor's
suit pants, accidentally thrown in the middle of everything. I give them a swift shake and something flies
out of a pocket, sliding across the wood floor as if it
were ice. As soon as I see it, a knot forms in the pit of
my stomach. I approach the object in slow motion. It's

a little, plastic rectangle and I pray it's a Starbucks gift card. But I know better as I can read it from four feet away: Newport Beach Marriott.

That son of a bitch!

My knees tremble as I crouch down low, not wanting to believe what's in front of me. I spin the card around with my finger, my thoughts going around in circles with it.

Trevor is my husband! We're married—I love him! My family loves him!

This can't be happening to me. The idea of Trevor cheating on me, me fantasizing about Ryan...until now, it was all in my head, just the stress of moving across the continent.

This is real. I couldn't have imagined feeling this betrayed or this physically sick. It all comes back to me along with the rising nausea: the way he hasn't reached for me in weeks, even when I threw myself at him; all the hushed phone calls; the many all-nighters he's spent "at the hospital."

My stomach and throat switch places and I run to the bathroom. I throw up this morning's yogurt and coffee, and I'm left heaving and sobbing. Exhausted, I lean against the toilet, rest my face in my hands, and somehow resist banging my head on the wall.

Despite my misery and the violent anger brewing, I'm overcome with images of Trevor at his best. Of us at our best. The way he always opens the car door for me and almost tucks me into my seat before closing it. Even when I've left him waiting outside stores for hours, coming out with nothing. It's a big deal to me, but I never tell him how important it makes me feel. Sometimes I don't even say thank you. At parties, he's the only husband who leaves the guys to check on his wife, making sure I'm comfortable, that I have a glass of wine. Tears sting the corners of my eyes and little squeaks escape my mouth as I try to contain myself. I think of how he whispers, "I love you, Ellen," every single night, even when he thinks I'm asleep, and I completely lose it, turning to the bowl again.

After what seems like hours, I let myself collapse on the floor. I feel foolish, like my life is a sham. How long has he been cheating on me? No wonder it feels like we're completely disconnected. No wonder the like-it-or-lump-it move. Does he love this woman? Or is she just a better fuck than me? It hits me that this can't be his first offence. Once a cheater always a cheater, and he spends so little time at home he could have six of us waiting for his phone calls at once. He probably screwed his way through med school. No wonder he never admitted to masturbating: he had more than patients on rotation. Why did he even want to marry me? Why get married to some average woman when he obviously wants nothing to do with me? Maybe I'm his beard, his excuse to keep the others at arm's length and the complications at a minimum.

Did I have to leave my friends and family and career because of her?

How could he look me in the eye, shake my father's trusting hand?

I open my eyes but feel almost paralyzed, like I've been hit by a car and I'm lying on the road. I'm stuck between grief and rage, the loss pinning me to the floor, rage urging me to do something, now.

I hear children yelling outside and it snaps me out of the spell.

Full of adrenaline, I jump up but I have no idea what to do first. As if I'm in hyper-speed mode, I fly around the house, pulling out luggage, rummaging through drawers, collecting little parts of myself. I'm only half-committed, because when I hear the dryer buzz I stop what I'm doing and fold the laundry.

I'm on the third pair of Trevor's underwear when it dawns on me: Wendy and her group of rogues are right. I keep folding, quicker and a bit messier with each new thought.

Can I blame him? I've become uninteresting. Even cranky. How much do I contribute in response to his polite, "how was your day?" and "what's new?" If a woman as beautiful and accomplished as Scarlet gets openly cheated on, why wouldn't I?

I don't know what I'm going to do, but a part of me feels almost grateful for his oversight, grateful to the Marriott for freeing me from my naïve delusions.

Slamming the dryer shut, I consider sweeping the folded clothes onto the floor, but without an audience it seems a wasted effort.

I head back into the washroom to collect my phone—to send a text that now seems way overdue.

Wendy, what time Friday?

16

Do you have any idea how hard it is to keep something like this to yourself? My perfect husband is cheating on me. I'm too embarrassed to tell Audrey, I have too much pride to tell Annie, my mother would castrate him, and I'm afraid to confront Trevor. If he admits it, I will have to divorce him. Or I'll have to have an affair myself to even things out, and I'm sure I'm not the casual-affair type.

But the idea of hooking up with Trevor's partner does have its appeal. Not in a million years would Trevor suspect his emotional (short) wife might be involved with his mentor. Our conversation would go something like, "Ellen, I'm sorry! It meant nothing to me…" and I'd be all, "Don't sweat it, babe. I've been fucking Ryan for weeks now, and his paycheck isn't the only thing that's bigger than yours…"

Ouch.

Over the next few days, I swing between grief—blaming myself, wondering if I can win Trevor back, disbelief that our marriage has come to this—and rage. When the anger comes, I think about those spurned spouses who kill their cheating mates or set their cars on fire. It doesn't seem quite as crazy now. I would never hurt Trevor or his entirely innocent SUV, but I do fantasize about grinding up Viagra in his coffee so he has to walk around with an erection all week.

I won't lie. Watching Trevor fake love for me distresses me so much I can't sleep. Instead, I close my eyes and pretend when he comes in. I try to picture him as he looked to me even last week, before I realized this devastatingly handsome man is also devastatingly deceptive. Not my Trevor anymore. I find myself revisiting memories in which he is loving, strong and so sexy doing everyday things—even the way he takes the garbage out, spraying the cans clean with the hose before he brings them in. Small, tender acts I didn't even acknowledge at the time.

It wasn't long ago Trevor would have disregarded my sleep, his fingers between my thighs interrupting my dreams, never making love to me until I was wide awake and wanting him. Now he sneaks in, as quiet as I am, neither of us wanting to give the other any reason to initiate. He still kisses my forehead before he leaves in the morning, but he doesn't linger anymore and wait for me to peek up at him.

I always wipe his kiss away before the tears come. The tears at least are real.

I had coffee with Wendy this morning at a little café in Corona Del Mar. Being out of the Port Streets and closer to the ocean makes me feel better. Mary suggested I take a drive along the coast every day, get my coffee down there maybe, just to remind myself that I live in California. The beautiful and desperate people I see along the way also remind me that I'm not special in any way, that I'm not more protected than anyone else.

I've spent too much of my life trapped inside my mind, overthinking and freaking out. Out there, on the busy, palm-treed streets, I could be anyone. Anyone else, that is—certainly not this fragile woman consumed with equal parts betrayal and fantasy.

It's interesting when you sit back and watch and listen to the people around you, observing them in relation to yourself. Like the young man behind the counter who smiles at me but keeps his eyes on the younger woman seated to the right of us. They are certainly closer in age, they may even know each other, but he couldn't give me my change any faster to clear away his obstructed view. Then there are the older men and the even older men who attempt to make themselves noticeable, their voices loud as they talk about their portfolios and expensive cars.

With my painful recent insights into the male psyche, I have no doubt I could have an affair with most of the men over forty-five in here if that's what I wanted. I'm sure getting them to leave their wives would be a bigger challenge. Why not have it all, right?

In my thirty-two years, I have never taken in the world with such a dark perspective. I can't help feeling bad for the premenopausal wives who I'm fucking with in my head. The nerve of a younger woman assuming she could destroy their lives based on youth and a pretty face alone.

I'm curious how men like the ones trolling the café today can sleep with other women regardless of how much they love their wives, perhaps their best friends. Is it libido, or fear of a diminishing one? It baffles me how people can just block such an important person from their minds while they penetrate someone else. True, I don't believe that all men who cheat are deplorable. Some, like Trevor, must be good people—who maybe can't be good all the time.

Wendy shows up after me. When she walks in it is like time stops for a moment. She's so subtly beautiful I hadn't found her that attractive the first time I saw her on my doorstep, but as I watch her today she beams confidence that is almost brighter than the sun shining through the windows. Maybe it's how happy she is, how free she is from obsessing over a philandering husband. I guess Trevor is right: confident girls are the prettiest. She moves her tiny body through the crowded café without thought or self-consciousness. When a fifty-something man smiles at her, she simply smiles back. Not flirting; not worried about seeming flirty. A happy response from a happy woman.

On the drive over, I promised myself I wouldn't say anything to Wendy about the hotel key. Alone, it's just a key—he could have found it on the sidewalk and decided to pick it up to put it in the recycling bin later. But combined with his complete lack of sexual interest in me and the fact that he is mentally absent whether he's home or not, it reads like a *Three Signs Your Partner is Cheating* article.

As soon as she sits down, she tucks her perfectly highlighted hair behind her ears as if begging to hear all about it, and I can't resist.

She is mostly quiet while I talk, touching my hand and nodding a lot. She doesn't say she knows how I feel, the way I thought she would. I appreciate this, because how could she possibly? She doesn't know our past, how we've shared loss and family and laughter, along with many thousands of hours binge-watching Netflix. As the words come out of my mouth, I don't recognize the sound of my voice. It is the closest thing I've had to an out-of-body experience, like I am listening to some sad stranger at the table next to us. I've gone over it in my head again and again, but to hear it out loud makes it sound like a lie. Trevor is cheating on me?

What. The. Fuck.

Somehow, I manage not to cry. As confused as I am, I've decided to ignore Wendy's suggestion that I go back to Canada for a bit. Instead, I'll go out with them on Friday to get drunk and have some fun for once.

Wendy assures me it's way more innocent than Scarlet let on. In fact, she only admits (with a straight face!) to casually making out with a couple of younger guys, all in one day, as if that made it better.

"Zero pressure," she says.

According to her, they mostly just wanted me to know, so I didn't freak if I saw something on a night out—and to enlighten me about a third option: married, divorced, and whatever this is.

An overpriced French lingerie shop waved at me on my way into the café, so I make a point to swing by after Wendy leaves. I open the door to roses and antiques. It's interesting how an atmosphere can transport you. Five minutes ago, I was sitting in a room full of aging hipsters and Barbie dolls on the corner of MacArthur and Pacific Coast Highway, and just like that, I am in a boutique in Paris.

Until this afternoon, I thought this kind of lingerie was limited to honeymooners and Victoria Secret models. The full-figured salesperson, who introduces herself as Joanne, is unusually helpful. Not pushy, just encouraging. News flash! According to Joanne, who is superbly sexy, a lot of women wear this sort of stuff every day. Half playing, I have her select some options for me. I wait in the dressing room, seeing my body from three angles all at once—appreciating how clever the lighting is, with shadows in all the right places.

(Completely the opposite experience of my lifelong battle with swimsuit shopping).

At this point, even though my self-esteem is at an all-time low, my body is as good as it could possibly be. Eating less and exercising more, plus not having kids—that's the secret.

The first piece I try on looks and feels amazing, a L'Agent bustier complete with suspenders. I run my hands down the sides of my body and think about what Trevor's reaction would be if I walked out of the bathroom wearing this. How I would tempt him with it and then pull away.

There isn't a chance I could leave the store without it. I feel like Clark Kent must have, knowing that under his clothes, he was Superman. I didn't want to take it off and even thought about showing Joanne when she asked. I bought it and several other pricey pieces and walked to my car feeling like my version of a superhero. Ellen on top; Annie underneath.

When I pull into our driveway, Trevor's car is already there. I can't say it's something I've seen many times since we've been here. It looks lonely parked there all by itself.

If I were a betting woman, I would say he's sleeping, oblivious to my troubled heart. But I'm not taking any chances, so I pull up to the curb, roll the windows down to let the cool California air on my face and then check the same emails over and over. I sit in the car for a long while, stretching out the time he spends in there alone—wanting him to know what it feels like to wait on someone, to feel the walls closing in.

17

Once I get the nerve, and when I've felt enough pressure from Mary's concerned glances, I roll the windows up and lock the car. I open the door to a quiet house, but a strong cross-breeze makes an upstairs door slam and startles me to a standstill. So here I am, not moving, just listening for sounds of movement. After a few moments, the house still, I make my way to the kitchen. It's clean, with no sign of Trevor. Even though I expected him to be asleep, part of me hoped he would be sitting at the table waiting to have a "talk" like my father used to. But Trevor is turning out to be less and less like my father. I take a hopeful peek into the backyard, but it too is empty. I don't know why, but I'd rather him be at work than upstairs asleep. I know he's tired, but we so rarely see each other. My impatience increases when I think about foolishly wasting time in the car, avoiding him. But it feels much worse now, being avoided.

It's awkward being down here, knowing he's up there. I want to be doing something useful when he comes downstairs, but I have nothing to do. The house is clean, cooking would be a complete waste of effort (plus, we have virtually no food) and my workout was done by nine a.m. I want to have a nap, but how pathetic would that look? I give him another ten minutes, and then I make my way upstairs, slowly and with extremely light feet. I stop just short of our bedroom door, frozen like an animal, waiting for the slightest noise, trying to figure out if I'll enter or flee when I do.

The house is completely silent, even with the windows open. All I can hear is the sound of my own breath, and it gets louder the more I try to quiet it. With a delicate touch, I reach out, turn the knob and carefully push open our door. I take one tiny step into the room. It's completely untouched, no sleeping Trevor. I would've been less shocked to find Goldilocks in my bed. Where is he? My body relaxes, and I let out the breath I've been holding. I turn to leave the room when I hear a familiar thud.

Someone just came into the house.

As casually as possible, I go downstairs and find Trevor in the foyer, dripping with sweat. He's completely spent, bent over at the waist. His hands rest on his knees, bracing his weight as he pants. I used to love this look, especially after we'd had particularly good sex and he hovered over me, exhausted. His hair is stuck to his head. I don't think I have ever been that sweaty. I know I've never looked so sexy after a workout.

I will absolutely not have sex with him right now.

"You decided to come in?" he asks, surprising me, because he hasn't yet looked in my direction. Something in his tone throws me.

"Hello to you, Trevor." I come down the rest of the stairs with conviction. "What's your problem?"

"I just think it's funny you see my car..." he's trying to catch his breath as he talks, "and decide not to come in to see me." He stands up and walks past me into the kitchen.

He's got a lot of nerve talking to me like this. He hooks up with some California marriage-wrecker, and now he can't even be nice to me? I'm so angry I don't even want to fight, and I have zero excuses for hiding in the car, so I just ask, "Why are you home?"

"I thought it would be nice to grab lunch together."

"Well, babe, I don't just sit around all day."

"No one expects you to. I do however expect my wife to prefer seeing me to sitting in her car for an hour."

I finally think of a comeback: "I thought you'd be asleep."

"Thanks for letting me sleep, Ellen. And don't worry, I'm leaving now."

"Trevor?!" I shout as he storms up the stairs.

What the heck was that all about? He must have had a bad day and decided to take it out on me to spare the mistress the foul mood. I can't remember the last time he treated me so coldly. I suppose being caught in the car is a bit embarrassing, but he should be happy he got to dodge me and my possible questions a little longer. I know I have nothing to be sorry for. He's the one deceiving me and destroying our marriage. But there was something in his face that made him look genuinely hurt. I suppose that's narcissism at its finest—he expects to have two cakes and eat them, too.

I'm sitting at the landlord's old wood table, lost in thought and the sound of mourning doves calling when Trevor comes down. I straighten my back, trying to look bigger, more intimidating I guess, and prepare for round two. I can tell by his long stride he's still angry, or late. "I have a surgery scheduled for five. Then I'll be home."

"Okay. So, I won't make dinner?" I ask sarcastically, knowing I'll be eating alone again.

"Look, I know this hasn't been easy. The whole thing was probably a very bad idea. But your attitude is killing me, Ellen."

"My attitude? When are you around to even witness my attitude?" I yell as my animal instincts kick in and all the hair on my arms stands up.

"I'm not trying to fight with you. It's just…we're here now. So could you try and make the best of it?"

"What the hell do you think I've been doing?"

"You've been completely shutting me out! You barely talk to me. You're asleep all the time…"

"Are you fucking serious, Trevor? You have no clue what I do!"

"Because you don't tell me anything. You don't even respond to my texts." He walks toward me, but there is no chance I will let this attack go. He puts his hand on my shoulder and I throw it off.

"Just go to work, Trevor."

"Ellen, relax!"

"You fucking relax. You know what? I was having a fairly nice day before you came home. Just leave already!!"

"This isn't what I wanted, Elly."

"Yeah, well, I'm sorry to ruin your plan."

He drops his arms to the side of his body in defeat. It almost looks like he's going to cry. He stares at me with pleading eyes as if willing me to understand his side, but I just stare back, challenging him. He sighs loudly and turns to leave.

As he passes me, I get a quick glimpse at his pants and see that his fly is undone. It's like a sign from the gods that I'm right! I fight the desire to let him leave like that. My mind goes back and forth while he walks to the door. Letting him go through the humiliation of noticing it at the end of the day would be gratifying but not as immediately fulfilling as calling to him now as he gets into his car.

"And Trevor," I yell, ignoring the hopeful look on his face as he turns around, surprised to see me on the doorstep, "your zipper is undone."

I slam the door and let out a scream that starts out as a girly shriek and ends with a low growl. How am I the bad guy here? I'm so full of rage and nervous energy I march upstairs and throw on some yoga pants, not even bothering to change my shirt or bra, dig out my runners and head furiously out the front door to hit the pavement, each step heavy and aggressive. I surely look like a lunatic running in this getup, even more so because I didn't take the time to grab my headphones and so my music blares from my iPhone for all to hear.

Shit! I hit the green space just as the elementary school in the middle of the park lets out. Little kids everywhere, darting toward their moms with artwork in their proud, dirty-finger-nailed hands. It's hard not to acknowledge the genuine happiness these small people bring to their parents, even the distracted ones who are looking at their phones. I wonder if I'll ever have that kind of happiness. If I'll ever spend the moments before three p.m. counting down the seconds, excited to add another masterpiece to my already full fridge door. This thought and the bodies of these forty-something moms encourage my feet to move faster. I fly past them all, ignoring annoyed glances in my direction as questionable lyrics escape from my pocket.

When I reach the end of the path, I dart up to the main road. Cars pass me in both directions as I catch my breath at a red light. I decide to cross and take on the hill behind Pavilions. I'm gearing up, moving my feet in a standstill jog, not wanting my heartbeat to slow too much. My eyes scan everything without seeing anything of real interest—until I spot Trevor coming out of the grocery store holding a tray with two Grande Starbucks. He's on the phone, no longer looking upset. It's probably innocent enough, but the idea of him doing everyday things without me makes me feel a million miles away from him.

Is that second coffee for her?

This happens every day. He's out there participating in life, doing all sorts of things I have no idea about. I suppose I've always pictured him at work, in his office with patients or the car driving home to me. Not stopping at Go, or for coffees for someone else. It's the strangest thing to watch the man I thought was my partner for life living his life without me.

Just like that, it's as if someone put a pin in me: all my air and energy escape, leaving me slumped and deflated. The image of him driving out of the parking lot, away from me and down the street to God knows where is gut-wrenching. I almost shout out, "Come back!" but instead I turn my back to the hill and walk home like an exhausted toddler, desperately wanting my mom to be here to carry me.

I'm only home ten minutes when Trevor calls me. Seeing his name light up feels reassuring—he still loves me! As much as I want to pick up to ask him who the second coffee is for, I wait until it stops vibrating, as if it is taking its last breaths. Afterwards, I just stare at it, as if he would somehow know I was there if I move. When it vibrates once more, it startles me and even makes me jump a little. This time I snatch the phone quickly, feeling so much safer with a text. He says we need to talk, that he has a conference this weekend in San Jose and wants me to come.

I go over his wording carefully before I text back, which I will do because he accused me of ignoring him (not total bullshit) and I refuse to let him wave his "told ya" finger at me.

So, I have two pieces of information to work with.

1. We need to talk. This could go ugly, like a re-run of this afternoon, with him scolding me again and making himself feel better about his cheating. Or he could be so guilt-ridden he needs to confess. A confession at a conference? It seems like the ultimate in bad taste, even for a busy surgeon.

I don't particularly like either option, which directly affects:

2. Attending a surgery conference in San Jose. If his behavior at his office was any indication, I can expect to spend the weekend hidden away in his room, ordering room service or eating takeaway leftovers from his dinner meetings. I didn't much enjoy feeling

unwanted at the practice, so anything to do with work does not appeal to me right now. Plus, what if he asked me second because she couldn't make it? Or what if he asks her now because I say no? My brain might explode. Everything is suddenly so complicated.

I must play this right. I type: *You're right, we do need to talk… but when you're back.*

A little resistance would be appreciated, but he texts back almost immediately with a simple *ok*. I don't want to keep fighting, but I figured he would at least insist I come, or better still, say he'll skip the conference.

I gather he is too important and mature for my silly games. Which they are, aren't they? He likely typed his insulting "ok" and then returned the phone to his desk to get back to his coffee date. He won this round, I guess, because I now feel even worse.

I'm the one who said no, but I get the feeling that's exactly what he wanted.

18

When Trevor gets home, it's still before nine and I'm curled up on the velvet sofa watching the Canadian version of *Love it or List it*. I force myself to look up at him and say a quiet, "Hi."

"Nice to see you up," he says, equally emotionless.

"Nice to see you home before eleven," I reply, his slight not unnoticed

"Ha!" He says and plops down on the coffee table in front of me, completely blocking the TV and ruining the last five minutes of a show I only watch for the last five minutes.

"Wanna watch a movie?"

I show restraint and stop myself from saying I'm already watching something. "Sure."

"Okay, great. Let me shower quick and I'll be right down."

"Do you want some tea?" I ask, still using my monotone voice, not sure if we're still fighting or not.

"Love some."

After he goes upstairs, I quickly rewind my show just far enough to see the big reveal. Jillian wins. I knew it!

I put on some hot water, select two teabags, his English Breakfast, mine green, and place them in our Good Morning Handsome and Good Morning Gorgeous mugs. As if it's our first date or something, my stomach feels nervous, and I can't tell if it's butterflies or disgust at my cowardly avoidance of certain topics. I just stand there and tap my fingers on my legs while I wait for the whistle so I can move on to the next step. When it boils, I pour the water and then scan the kitchen for something to go with our tea. There is banana bread hidden in the fridge that Mary brought over earlier this week. It's delicious banana bread, no walnuts and a lot of chocolate chips, and I've sort of been saving it. Perhaps it would be too nice (he deserves nothing!), but Trevor would really like it. Maybe I could even take credit for it. Against my better judgment, I slice three generous pieces and then cut them in half. I shove one in my mouth, remove the teabags and carry everything into the TV room.

Not wasting any time, because I'm exhausted and I'm guessing he is too, I line up *Daddy's Home* on Netflix just as he comes down the stairs, unintentionally pounding his heels into the wood as he walks.

"Looks good," he says as he scans the TV, and then adds, "real good," when he notices the bread. "You make this?"

"What do you think?" I laugh.

"Mary?"

"Yep! And it's so good." I grab another piece and he sits on the couch beside me, but not close enough for any part of us to touch.

Before either of us feels pressured to get into anything serious, I start the movie. I make sure to keep my feet curled under me and don't share any of my blanket. When my head gets heavy, I lean it on the back of the couch instead of its regular spot on Trevor's shoulder. I don't know if it's intentional, but Trevor keeps his distance too. At one point he stretches out, but he puts his head on the other side of the couch instead of on my lap. He also curls his legs up. It's hard to concentrate on the movie because I'm too busy analyzing our every move. Mark Wahlberg is as hot as Will Ferrell is funny, so it is a great combo, and we've planned to watch this movie for over a year. But tonight, neither one of them do it for me.

Close to the end, and just after one of the funniest parts, I realize Trevor is sleeping. He's been silent through the entire senseless scene, and his foot keeps flexing out like dogs do when they're dreaming. I don't wake him. He looks peaceful with his angelic face smushed against the armrest, his hands between his knees. Like this, Trevor doesn't look like he could hurt a fly. Sure, he's beautiful and strong, but he also seems sad. More likely, he's just tired, dog-tired. I used to get mad at him when he'd fall asleep during our movie dates, because they were so rare and I was also tired. But how could I be mad at this hardworking man-boy, asleep in the fetal position? I have to give him credit for making the effort. But he should make the effort! I'm not luggage. He doesn't get to bring me along because he owns me and then leave me to wilt like a neglected houseplant.

He's sleeping hard. Waking him seems mean, so I grab a pillow and give it a few shakes, then carefully lift his head and place it underneath. Selflessly, I unwrap the exceptionally comfy throw I'm wearing like a dress, and cover him up from his giant shoulders to his hairy toes. I stare at him for a few more minutes and watch his eyes twitch. I hope he's dreaming of me—maybe how I was when we were first married, or even yesterday. Either way, I just hope I'm still there, somewhere in his unconscious thoughts.

I'm a little sad to go to bed alone again, but it feels good not to be afraid at all, and I'm not sure how I'd feel undressing together while thinking about him recently undressing with someone else. As soon as I enter our room, I spot Trevor's Tumi carry-on by the door. Such an efficient guy; he'd somehow found time to pack and shower while I made tea. I'm pathetically tempted to go through it, to check his toiletry bag for condoms, but I don't. He really is leaving in the morning. Off to some hotel, possibly to cheat on me again. But this time I could have prevented it had I been able to put our relationship before my pride and hurt.

Throughout our marriage, our bed has often been one-sided, but lately I've been waking up in the middle night panicked about it. Panicked that him not being here is a sign. That he's not been called away to surgery, he's just not come home, and he's truly over me and my complications. I'd even gotten out of bed a few times, hoping that he might be downstairs having a snack, or called out to him thinking he's changing in the bathroom, putting on the boxer shorts I still never forget to leave out for him. Each time, I end up disappointed and then, predictably, scared.

My alarm is set for six, as I am desperate not to miss seeing him off. I want to get a good look in his eyes before he leaves, and let him look in mine, maybe to remind us both that underneath all the resentment it's still us, Trevor and Ellen. 'Til death do us part.

As tired as I was downstairs, once I'm cuddled down in bed, my mind refuses to be still. I try to lie on my side, to mimic Trevor's total relaxation. But pushed against the pillow, all I can hear is the sound of my heartbeat in my ear. I flip around for a while and try sleep strategies like counting backwards and flexing my butt cheeks, one and then the other, but it's no use. Finally, I grab my phone, defeated. I go through my photo album, starting way back over a year ago. My finger swipes the pictures quickly, not allowing myself time to get too sentimental, but I'm not able to resist the good memories, and small smiles escape me. Eventually, I drift off to sleep.

When I wake up, I can tell it's late, the sun's warmth invading an otherwise cool room. At first, I'm almost euphoric, and then the panic sets in—Trevor's gone. I pick my phone up and realize I'd stupidly set my alarm to p.m. I throw it across the room like it's to blame, and then hurry out of bed. His luggage is gone, but just to be sure, I run downstairs and open the front door. His car is gone too. I let out a frustrated "UGH," and run back up the stairs to check the phone I threw, hoping for a message from Trevor.

Nothing.

I cross my arms for a contemplative moment, and then it dawns on me he probably left a note on the island. One last hopeful trip down the stairs to check, walking slowly, as if buying the note more time to present itself. When it's clear there is nothing there, I feel a blow to my stomach, to my heart. But worse, in the living room, the blanket Trevor slept with is folded and placed neatly on top of the pillow. He left like a departing houseguest, not my husband.

I spend the morning wondering if he's somehow mad at me. Perhaps he thought I should have woken him last night, although the same could be said for him not waking me today. I resist the urge to text him, even though I know it's the grown-up thing to do, to be the bigger person. Beyond our fight and barely speaking, last night seemed like progress to me.

Only a few months ago he wouldn't leave the house for an hour without giving me a pep talk, and now he leaves me overnight without a word. It's just further proof that he's reprioritized. I'm no longer at the top of his list or even just below his work and his ten-year plan.

The realization is potent. I'm more than down. I feel like someone has died. Until this minute, I felt like I had choices about how I responded to his cheating. Now I'm not sure. Maybe he just doesn't care at all anymore. I keep hoping for him to barge through the front door with coffees and announce the conference is off, that we are going to spend the weekend together doing all the tourist things people keep asking me if I've done. (Which I haven't, because you don't do those things alone.)

After maybe an hour of sitting, staring into space, I realize he's not coming home. Before I start to cry, I run to the shower, as if it conceals my tears so I can pretend they're not happening.

A good cry is always a good idea. When I'm sure the last tear is out, I give myself a quick shake like a wet dog and grab my towel. I wrap my hair up tight and dry myself with swift, rough pressure. Now I feel angry. Shocking, I know! Once I realize why, it's like an epiphany: I haven't been mad at Trevor this whole time, I've been mad at myself. Mad that I'm not more successful, mad that I've been so selfish, guilty about everything! But now, now I'm not heartbroken anymore—I forgive myself, but I DO NOT FORGIVE HIM.

The lingerie bag is hidden behind my luggage in the closet. I dig it out and dump the contents onto my bed, tear open the tissue and scatter black lace across our bed, making it look like the set of a noir film. I grab a bustier and its matching thong and put them on. The image of myself in the mirror is shocking, but I immediately feel a million times better. I sit on the floor across from the mirror, my knees up to my chin. I stare at myself, with yesterday's makeup and an imaginary cigarette. Not at my body or the lingerie, but at my eyes. They're no longer sad. They seem animated again, almost wild.

Wendy texted last night to confirm our plans, but I had put off my reply, secretly hoping I wouldn't need to go. Not thinking that today I might want to.

19

The girls should be here to pick me up in fifteen minutes. I don't want to admit that I'm nervous, but I keep picking at my nails. As soon as I stop myself, my knee starts shaking. The wait is killing me, so I grab a magazine and flip through the pages, too distracted to focus. I can't remember the last time I got this dressed up to go out with girlfriends. At home, a girls' night is a movie and coffee. The dress code is, "what's a dress code?"

Since trying it on this morning, I haven't taken the lingerie off. I wore it under my tracksuit when I got my hair blown out earlier and felt like I had a secret the whole time. Annie was so right. Who cares what your outfit looks like when you've got this going on underneath! To the stylist and everyone else, I was just an unfortunate lady in gym clothes, but I knew the truth, and it was hot.

I'm also wearing my first ever Herve Leger bandage dress—in champagne, which seems less desperate than red or black. It might even make me look too small, but Wendy says that's impossible. My heels add a welcome four inches, minus the fact that I feel wobbly in them. There is nothing worse than a woman stumbling around in heels, but I've practiced on all kinds of different flooring, preparing myself for the worst possibility, tile!! I've made that mistake more than once: try them on at the store, do the test walk on carpet and then never wear them again.

It feels strange leaving the house alone knowing I will remain alone all night. Knowing I will be coming home to a dark, empty house, which is so much worse than the darkness gradually settling in while I'm safe inside. My only hope is that after a few glasses of wine and maybe a confidence-shot of tequila, I won't even notice.

When the large black SUV pulls up, I feel a punch of adrenaline. I'm frantic, like I don't know what to do next. After a final mental debate, I open the door to climb into the vehicle and then realize I stupidly still have the magazine in my hand. As coolly as possible, I head back to the porch. I look at the chair, then the table, back to the chair and then just throw it on the ground. What is wrong with me? I shake my head on the way back just in case anyone was watching. Wendy hops out to greet me. She's wearing a black jumpsuit with a fitted top and pants that flare almost to a bell at the bottom. Her hair is in a simple high pony, making her look about twenty-five. She lets me climb in first and then the driver closes the door behind us.

"You look so much better than the last time I saw you!" Scarlet shouts from the back.

"Ha! You still remember that, eh?"

"It's burned into my retinas!"

"I've completely forgotten about it," I lie. "Though I must admit, I have a new fondness for my natural pout!" I turn my head and give her my best duck lips, and notice how stunning she looks. "Whoa! Scarlett, you look insane!"

"Really? I usually hide it better!"

Her hair is long and full, with subtle waves, and I'm fairly certain I've only seen it up before. "Seriously, is that your real hair?" I ask, always too bold.

"Are those your real breasts?"

I take a quick peek at my chest. "Obviously!"

"Well this is obviously not all my hair!" She laughs. "But tonight, I'm JLo!"

"You're gorgeous!" I say, turning to the front. "Who else are we picking up?"

"Just Maria. The rest will meet us."

Maria's house is the most European-style in the Port Streets. It's square and flat and has two Juliet balconies with vines spilling over. She gets in with a wide, happy grin, surprising me in simple jeans and a white linen tank top, and then we're off. I didn't ask where we're going because I wouldn't recognize anything by name anyway. Clearly, it can't be too dressy because out of the four of us, I border on overdressed, which is nearly if not actually impossible in Newport Beach.

The ride isn't too bad. They talk about some guy named Tom and make failed attempts to fill me in. (He's "this loser," and "from work.") I don't mind not knowing all the details; I'm just happy they don't completely ignore me. In fact, I don't remember a time I've clicked with people so effortlessly. For a moment, I just take them in, their beautiful clothing and made-up faces, their sweet-smelling perfumes and fruity shampoos. Their excellent vocabularies and proper English, which makes total nonsense sound impressive. Maybe it's part of being an adult, or maybe it's because these women aren't the jealous type, like super not jealous at all, not of me or each other. Not even of their husbands.

We drive along the coast and when Wendy announces, "This is it!" I'm not totally blown away. Like many of the fancier beach houses, at first it doesn't appear to be much more than a bungalow, but as we get closer and enter a typical valet roundabout, I can see that it extends down and back toward the ocean. I can hear waves even before we get out. A young man offers his hand to me and I accept, feeling shaky.

The foyer is fully exposed to the elements; the walls pushed to the side as if admitting that no décor or music could compete with this natural setting: blowing palm trees, tiny stars and crushing sprays of seafoam. The surf and breeze seem to eat up every other sound.

Everyone is ahead of me, waiting for an elevator, but I hang back a moment to gather myself. It's hard to believe that a few months ago I was content, even thrilled, to live my whole life in Ontario. Now that I'm here, at least in this moment, I can't imagine ever wanting to go back. I do a slow-motion twirl, seeing the dazzling women in front of me, then the ocean through a glass window, the charming greeters and valet drivers, a few modern chairs and the sleek reception area, and then the women again. It must be the air, because every part of me, even the nervous parts, feel wildly alive. Like Orphan Annie must have felt getting settled into Sir Oliver Warbucks' mansion: *"Yes, I think I'm gonna like it here!"*

Aside from the staff, the foyer was empty, so I'm surprised when the elevator door opens onto a busy lounge. Scarlet gives a young woman at the door a hug and elegant kisses on both cheeks, before heading into the room as if she owns the place. We follow her like she's the popular girl at school. She stops every few feet to acknowledge people she knows, mostly women but also a few impressively handsome, surprisingly not old, men. She's proper enough to introduce the rest of us each time, but I'd much rather she would keep walking, because although the place isn't tiny I feel on display standing in the middle of everything.

Even though I don't recognize the song that is playing, my hips haven't forgotten how to move, and suddenly I'm strutting. I catch some stares from a few people, but no one lingers once they're caught, making it seem more judgey than curious. I try not to let it intimidate me. Besides, stares from women are often a disguised compliment. We tend to check out pretty women, to size up our competition or at least be inspired by them. Tonight, I don't care. I'm just happy to be here, not at home being angry and pitifully hurt. Or with Trevor, pretending I'm not.

When we reach our table, I don't immediately recognize the people sitting there. For a second I'm not sure how comfortable I'll be, but then the one who I think might be Jen shimmies over and pats the seat next to her. Before I know it, I have a glass of wine in my hand and I'm laughing as Jen points over to Laura, who is taking shots with a group of men. It's an adult lounge, not a club, so the music is not so loud you can't have a conversation.

I don't know exactly when it happened, but out of nowhere I'm giggly, relaxed and my seat dancing game is strong. Wendy, who sits a few people down, wedged in between Maria and some guy she knows from college, takes care of me like a big sister, keeping my glass full and checking in on me every few minutes with a questioning look. Not entirely lying, I answer with a thumbs-up or give her what I hope is a convincing nod. A few men come and go, but there is certainly nothing going on that makes me uncomfortable. I scan our table, and aside from one hand on one thigh (closer to the knee end), I can't see anything wrong with this picture.

Then again, this is likely why you stop going out like this once you're married. If I picture Trevor in this exact scenario, him in my place at the end of the booth, would I be uncomfortable with it? Him drinking drinks paid for by a couple of beautiful women, sitting with friends who he knows cheat on their spouses. Would that be okay? No, it wouldn't be, but that doesn't mean he doesn't do it. And given the status of our relationship, I have absolutely nothing to feel bad about. So just to be social, I accept a tequila shot from Laura and some guy who looks like Billy Blanks (you know, *Tae Bo*).

It goes right to my head, and I feel like I will probably throw up later. I can't sit here any longer. The music now has no words, just an intrusive base that thuds in my ears and makes it hard to concentrate on the conversations around me. One guy, who could be my age, has been stalking our table all night. Sizing us up, he finally zeros in on Maria. She seems happy enough to talk to him, so I get up and give him my seat. I make my way through the crowd, people passing me on both sides like blurs as I try to find the restroom. Even when I'm sober, finding the restroom has never been easy. After a few dizzying laps, I break down and ask a bartender who looks a lot like I think Ryan must have ten years ago. He makes a point to personally escort me; the whole way I'm paranoid he's going to attack me, but instead, when we get there, he just gives the door a half-ass point and pushes through the men's, cleverly marked with a giant M.

I soak a towel in cold water and dab it over my face, careful not to ruin my eye makeup. The last time I was drunk in public, sometime in the final few months of university, the bathroom looked a lot different. Rather than fighting for an inch of mirror in a crowded and dirty room, I'm now standing alone at a large, spotless quartz counter blotting my furnace face with a luxurious Turkish towel instead of a paper towel or toilet paper. When someone comes in, I duck inside a stall and flip the lock. The toilet looks clean enough, and luckily, it's not automatic, so I take a seat on the tiniest edge, careful not to ruin my dress.

I've avoided my phone all day, but I decide to pull it out, hoping for some word from Trevor. My heart sinks when I see there are no new messages. It's one a.m., and he hasn't even checked in on me. My mood plummets with my heart, the night crashing with them. Suddenly I feel superficial and old.

I think about sneaking out and texting later to say I was sick, but I refuse to go home this early. I give myself a little more time in my hiding place and scroll through my texts, remembering I haven't answered a few from Audrey. But instead of clicking on her name, my buzzed finger hovers over Ryan's. With one quick, intoxicated movement, I press down and my finger, as if it's out of my control, types a solitary *Hi*, before I've given it any proper thought.

"Holy shit, Ellen," I whisper. I feel nervous and give him sixty seconds to respond before I backpedal with an "oops! That was for my sister!" I'm only at thirty-Mississippi when I see the three moving dots that signal he's awake and has read my text.

He responds right away, not playing any games, and he doesn't just give me a coy little hi, either. Word for word, he writes: *Hi... I've been thinking about you...*

I could use some sober advice right now. I don't know what my next text should be, but after a few attempts and erases I decide to relax and go with:

> *me too...what are you doing?*
> *Sleeping...you?*
> *Don't ask...*
> *What sort of trouble have you gotten yourself into now?*
> *Out with some new friends...hiding in the bathroom*
> *Drunk?*
> *A little...*
> *Having fun?*
> *I'm in a bathroom stall...lol*
> *Right...want me to come get you?*
> *I can't leave yet...it would be rude*
> *Want me to come join you?*
> *...yes*
> *Where are you?*
> *Laguna?*
> *Lol you're too much! Where in Laguna? Ask someone in the restroom...*

I'm alone
Really? Are you in the women's?
Ha ha
Take a picture…
????
Of the restroom…you'll have to leave the stall
Why do you know so much about women's
bathrooms?
Just do it… ;)

I take the picture and he somehow knows exactly where I am. He tells me he's on his way and I make zero objections. After giving my face some serious attention and thanking God I didn't destroy my makeup, I attempt to check myself out by dangerously climbing onto the toilet seat directly in front of the mirror, careful not to let my feet fall into the bowl. I feel sort of stupid in this dress. It's not something Jane would wear, but then thinking of myself as Jane may be my biggest problem. Satisfied enough, I climb down and finally leave the bathroom, passing a full-length mirror and shaking my head, but feeling so much better than when I came in. A quick stop at the bar for an outrageously expensive glass of champagne and I make my way back to our table, light-headed and full of enigmatic smiles.

Wendy spots me right away and stands up abruptly, remembering me as if remembering she'd left something in the oven. She scrambles over an obstacle course of legs and gives me a hug. "There you are," she says loudly, then whispers, "you okay?"

"I'm great," I answer honestly. I sit down, this time beside Scarlet. She is in a too-serious conversation with a woman I've never seen before, but gives my leg an acknowledging squeeze without pausing in her sentence.

Not much has changed since I left. Maria is still chatting up the same man and throws her head back to laugh every few minutes. Laura has calmed down a bit and sweetly rests her head on Jen's shoulder, I'm guessing more out of necessity than endearment. "Champagne!" she yells when she notices my glass. "What a fabulous idea!" She quickly snaps her arm up and gives our server a wave. It probably would have been cooler to order a bottle to share, or at the very least ask my friends if they wanted a glass. But I needed a quick fix, as if the elegance of the bubbles would somehow lessen the knots and seediness in my stomach.

I pretend to listen to Laura as she prattles on about how her tennis instructor is pressuring her to join a team. She would much rather practice just for fun. "Serving, serving, serving. That's all he has me do now." I smile, nod and try to look her in the eye. Not that she would notice. The way she is jumbling her words, I imagine her eyesight can't be much clearer. But I'm heavily distracted as, for the first time in my life, I search the crowd for a tall blond that isn't Annie.

It's probably only been twenty minutes or so, but with every second that passes, I'm both more worried he won't show up and more worried he will. Another thought hits me: I've been here all night and I can't say any one guy has given me much attention. Ryan will probably get one look at Laura's smooth peach skin and spilling breasts and forget all about me.

Someone sends a tray of shots over to our table. I've already had far too much to drink but the pressure is on as Scarlet passes out glasses and everyone accepts. Most of the women at the table can't weigh much more than I do, despite a height span of at least five inches.

If they can do it…

I've just finished a pre-shot cheers when Ryan walks up beside me.

"You sure you want to do that?" he asks, taking my free hand and pulling me up to my feet. I look him straight in the eye and bring the glass to my mouth, tilt my head back, swallow, and then wipe my slightly open mouth with the back of my hand. Not my classiest move. But he doesn't take his eyes off me, doesn't explore the table for a better option, and says, "Well, all right."

He's wearing a basic white fitted t-shirt tucked loosely into summer-wash jeans. I throw my arms around his neck and hug him like he's the quarterback and I'm his cheerleader. When we part, I let him run his fingers down my arms and hold onto my hands for a moment or two past friendship.

"Umm, what's this little dress you've got on?" he says, stepping back and looking me up and down.

I can feel everyone's eyes on us. Everything about our exchange is wrong. There is no way I can pass him off as a buddy. His eyes are all over me, and the way I respond to them leaves no mystery about where this relationship is likely headed. But even if they don't believe me, I introduce Ryan as my friend and he gives them a nod and a sly half-smile as he runs a hand through his hair, not pretending to be more proper than he is.

"Who needs a drink?" he asks before tracking down the server.

As he leaves, Wendy scoots over and we sit back and watch him walk away. She tells me to be careful and Scarlet yells, "I knew it!" in the background, distracting us from our view as she shows her age and pretends to fan herself.

A few minutes later, Ryan slides into the booth beside us with a Guinness. He slaps his hand on my leg playfully and raises his brows. "I'm glad you called. This is much better than what I was doing."

"What, sleeping? And I texted you," I laugh. "And it was meant to be for my sister…"

"Yeah, sure it was…n't." He leans over and whispers so close to my ear that the tiny hairs on the back of my neck stand up. "You look hot."

Even though they're compressed under excessively tight fabric, I swear I feel my nipples get hard.

"I feel strange being this dressed up and not, like, at a wedding, or something," I say, trying my best not to sound drunk. I keep my head straight when I talk because he hasn't moved his away from my ear and if I were to turn ever so slightly, our mouths would be too close, too soon.

"I think you should wear this sort of thing all the time. Definitely one of your better looks." He snickers a silly, "tee-hee," and finally leans back in the booth and takes a long, manly swig of his manly, black drink.

"Well, you've seen some doozies," I admit before thinking about how much it rhymes with boozy and instantly regret the word choice.

"Nah, you're hot in just about everything you wear. Even the Orange County lip works for you."

I let out an extreme, Julia Roberts-type laugh and then rest my head right beside his. "Ahhhh, it's been an interesting few months."

"You're definitely putting yourself out there," he says and nods slightly toward the group at our table. "Who are all these people?"

"Well," I say, as both of us lean forward, our shoulders, arms and legs touching. "I really only know a couple of them. But here's what I've figured out…"

I start with Maria and say things like "exotic" and "Manhattan rich." He fills in some blanks, making things up like, "her third husband died in a boating accident." We go around the table until we're satisfied with our fictional character descriptions. We keep it light, throwing

in only a few offside remarks, but when we move on to the
men at the table, and we've each finished another drink,
things get vicious. Neither of us have any attachment to
them, so we don't hesitate: loser in high school, wife so fat
she can't get out of bed, boss' bitch…

It's not until we're at the young man clinging to
Scarlet and Ryan throws out, "gold-digger," that I stop
laughing.

"So he only talks to her because he thinks she's
rich? She's beautiful, Ryan. Just because she's older…?"

I don't know where this protective instinct comes
from, but for whatever reason, coupled with the idea
men could only want an older woman for money, it is
unnerving. I wait for an apology or explanation, but
instead, he just says, "Who knows, Ellen. And who
cares. You're not old and I've got way more money than
you." He gives me the goofiest smile and the little lines
around his eyes crinkle as if they're laughing at me.

"Now, do me!" he says.

"Ummmm, excuse me?" I laugh, pretending to be
offended.

"Hey…I'm happy either way," he says, laughing as
he realizes how that sounded. He swirls the ice around
in his rum and cola and uses his other hand to gesture,
I'm waiting…

"Okay." I lean back and try to come up with something clever but can't decide if I should be funny or
truthful. Everything that comes to mind sounds dirty,
like he has big, skillful hands. I'm quite drunk, so the

more thought I put into it the more confused I become. I want to say, "you first," or decline altogether. But that's what Jane would do (refusing her turn at karaoke and Guitar Hero), so I woman-up.

"The fellow at the end is Ryan. He's the type of guy who would take really good care of you. First you think maybe he's like your big brother, but the way he rubs his leg up against yours and doesn't take his eyes off you…" I don't know what to say after that, so I add, "he drinks beer and surfs, though he's better suited to reading classics like Moby Dick and sipping brandy."

I'm done, instantly regretting the book reference and hoping he doesn't notice. I know it wasn't the best, so I scrunch my nose up and scratch my head. "Ta-da!"

"You noticed the leg, huh?" he laughs, not moving it. "Not terrible, not great either."

"I'm drunk, Ryan. That was good considering. My turn," I say, nervously enthusiastic.

"Wait one second here, you've been in my office, haven't you?"

I laugh it off, hoping it will go away, and then admit, "Yeah, I followed a line of mice in there!"

"What are you saying?" he asks, pretending to be offended, poking my side.

"Messiest office ever. Repulsive really! Okay, stop stalling!"

He takes no time at all, runs his hands along his thighs as if gearing up and starts. "The prettiest girl at the table, well most tables, is Ellen. She can't take a compliment so don't tell her I said that. She's smarter than most people but is still endearing, partly because she hasn't figured out how great she is yet. It would take forever to make her happy, so it's best not to try. If you're smart, you'll let her get there on her own. If you push too hard or leave her too long, you'll ruin her. If you're lucky and patient enough, she might just surprise you and send you a text from a bathroom stall in the middle of the night."

I give him a big smile. I feel grateful for his words and a little embarrassed that he already knows how crazy I am. But I'm also a bit sad, because my first thought is, I wish Trevor could get me this way. He leans his body over to me like he's slowly falling, closer, closer, closer and then, bam! He plants a quick kiss on my cheek.

"You're pretty impressed with yourself, aren't you?"

"I am," he says.

"You forgot Canadian…"

"Yeah, no, I purposely left that out…"

"Whatever, that's why you like me."

"Actually, that's why I don't really like you…"

I shove his arm. "Please, everyone loves Canadians."

"Not me," he laughs. "Too cold, and too many Democrats!"

"If you voted for Donald Trump, you can leave right now." I point toward the door.

"I'm kidding. We're the same me and you. East Coast," he says like Biggie, making an E with his fingers.

"Oh, myyyyy Goddd, Vanilla Ice loves hip hop!"

The deejay picks up the pace and all around us, people start to dance. It's entertaining—no one seems to take themselves seriously. Scarlet tries to spin Wendy, but she's wasted and keeps going in the wrong direction. Laura does some strange dance that's not quite as embarrassing as the robot, but is not cool either. In fact, the way she tries so hard not to be sexy is hilarious, her arms swaying against the beat. There may even be a little sexy in its total lack of sexiness. I guess I figured these women would either two-step and snap, do the YMCA maybe, or alarmingly full-on grind each other. But five years into the future doesn't seem to change that much on the dance floor.

Ryan stands and I wonder if he is about to start dancing. What would that look like?? Would it be as terrible as when men who aren't Dierks Bently think it's hot to sing to you? I think about Annie breaking up with her boyfriend a few years ago because he insisted on serenading her before sex, which totally had the opposite of its intended effect on her. "I swear to God, Ellen, it was the most awkward thing ever. Where am I even supposed to look?"

Luckily, Ryan just stretches and says he's going to the bathroom. He looks at me and asks, 'wanna come?" all cheekily before he leaves alone.

Once he's gone, I pull out my phone, hoping to hear from Trevor. But even drunk, I know if he hasn't texted by now, he won't. It's not that I even want to talk to him, it just hurts my heart, and maybe my pride, that he hasn't even checked in.

Is it strange we haven't even mentioned Trevor or Alice all night? Does Ryan know Trevor is away? And where is Alice? I guess this is exactly how people cheat. They just compartmentalize their lives, lock parts of themselves up in order to do what they want. No surprise, it's all crickets on my cell. I shrug my shoulders to myself, and bury my phone deep in my bag and throw a bunch of junk on top of it, as if trying to keep thoughts of my crumbling life as far away from me as possible.

I climb up on my knees and lean over the top of the booth flirtatiously to watch for Ryan, try to sneak a peek at him when he thinks no one's watching. It seems like he's been gone a long time, but I'm so caught up in the spectacles on the dance floor I've probably missed him coming out of the washroom. I stay perched and survey the crowds, the dance floor, the bar, and a few sunken tables with club chairs currently all occupied with overdressed suits who look much too serious. I've almost given up, but then I spot him at the bottom of the steps talking to some woman.

He has his arm on the railing and from here it almost looks like it's around her, but when he spots me watching him and doesn't move it, I decide it's just his effortless sex appeal. The woman is talking without a break, even while his eyes stay locked on mine. Neither of us is smiling; we just gaze intensely at each other from across a busy room that seems to have been put on pause. It's as if the music stops, and all the people out enjoying themselves fade away, like they're inconsequential extras in our life.

Laura climbs up beside me, throwing her blond hair around while she dances with her shoulders, and asks, "Whatcha lookin' at?"

Abruptly, I pull my eyes away from Ryan's like a needle across a record, like we've just been walked in on. Feeling warm and shaky all over, I take a quick peek back in his direction but he's gone and the woman who was just shot down makes her way back over to her friends, which means I won.

A few seconds later he comes up behind me and braces his arms on both sides of my shoulders, caging me in. He moves my hair to one side and brushes his slightly prickly face against my cheek for a minute.

"Jealous?" he asks and then runs his hands down my shoulders, waist and hips.

This is our first borderline real sexual encounter. It's a clear step over the line, crossing over into cheating territory. Even with our clothing in place, it ranks among my top hottest sexual experiences. I feel frozen and wonder if sex with Ryan would always be so exciting. Something about him and the way he toys with me makes me think he would always want to be in control.

I whisper, "a little," and shimmy around, still within his arms, to sit down facing him.

My head is completely, wonderfully hazy. I feel like I did when I was younger, sneaking into clubs feeling high on adrenaline and the joints we passed around, not worrying about germs. A worry-free life. Suddenly everyone around me looks like a professional dancer and the once twilight room is now shadowy with sprays of light. No one looks like themselves. Even I don't feel real, like a dream version of myself. Which means anything we do in the shadows doesn't count. When my focus returns, Ryan is still standing over me, smiling his sexy smirk. Taking his cue from my Woodstockesque head swaying, Ryan reverses and lifts me up from my seat. Our bodies begin to move together in rhythm, like we were made for each other. He clenches my hips and I swing my head back in slow motion, my hair flying as if gravity, like clarity, is gone. When he pulls me back up I see his eyes first, dark and dangerous, like I'm dancing with the devil. Then I hear it: the music that was just sound has words again, a remix of Tracy Chapman's *Fast Car*. For the first time, it's like it was written for me. *I had a feeling I could be someone, be someone, be someone…*

I run my hands through Ryan's tousled blond hair and sing along. "*You got a fast car, is it fast enough that we can fly away?*"

Ryan spins me out and I feel almost like I'm flying, twirling and twirling, lost in the music and the moment, and then I'm back in his arms. Before I'm fully committed, his mouth is on my neck, kissing me with full lips. I want to turn away and even though I know I can, I don't, and then, like it was inevitable, we're kissing and our chemistry is volatile, like mixing hydrogen sulfide and nitric acid.

But instead of exploding, I suddenly feel like I'm melting, slowing down and heavy all over. Ryan is now physically holding me up.

"Time to go, I think," he says as he helps me back to our seats.

Now Wendy is talking to Ryan, but I can't make out any of her words. Time speeds, and out of nowhere, he hands me a cold glass of water. I take it in my unstable hand and when I swallow, it's like heaven. It's enough to wake me up and allow me to answer Wendy when she asks, "Are you sure you're okay to go home with him?"

I only slur a bit when I say that I am.

20

We stop at the washroom, and I insist to Ryan that I can handle it alone.

Once inside I stand at the same counter I was at a couple of hours ago, now feeling very different. I fill my hands with water and splash it over my face, again and again, trying to stop the swirling feeling that is no longer fun. When I finally lift my head, the makeup I was trying to preserve earlier is everywhere it shouldn't be and three lines of mascara drip from each bloodshot eye. I look like a scary clown. I force an exaggerated grin at myself, and the image is terrifying. But it is either smile or cry, and I do not want to cry.

Ryan peeks his head in and I turn my startling face to him. He laughs loudly and shakes his head. "Surprisingly, this isn't the worst I've seen you!" I give him the same creepy smile, and he holds his hand out, blocking me. "Knock it off, you!"

He walks over to the sink, not seeming to care that he's in the ladies' room, and runs warm water over a cloth. He dabs the makeup off under my eyes. "One too many?" he asks.

I give him a pathetic nod and ask in a defeated voice, "Will you take me home?"

"You got it, babe."

"Trevor calls me babe," I mumble, the mood completely killed anyway.

"You got it… weirdo?" He laughs and puts his arm around me while holding the door for us both.

"He calls me that, too."

"Makes sense," he chuckles and then defends his kidneys from my playful jab.

I can't remember my address, so Ryan gives the driver directions, and I'm more lost than ever. Even sober, my sense of direction is terrible, but I can't help but laugh when I say, "Turn right," and Ryan corrects with a "left," and vice versa the entire drive.

"What would you do without me?" he asks.

I give it some serious thought and eventually come up with an articulate, "I'd be totally fucked!"

I lean into him and let my head slide down until it's on his lap. As if he knows how shitty I feel, he doesn't make the obvious joke and just strokes my hair, making sure it's out of my eyes.

I've fantasized about having an affair. I've even given real thought to sleeping with Ryan, like actually doing it, but never in a million years have I thought about developing feelings for someone other than Trevor. I barely know Ryan and yet I feel so safe, despite being drunk and uncharacteristically vulnerable, pressed up against him. I breathe in his scents: his cologne, his soap maybe, the laundry detergent Alice might have bought.

I must drift off, because when the car stops I wake up with a small stream of drool on my cheek and a drop or two on his incredibly flattering jeans.

"Is this your house?" Ryan asks, joking.

"Ha-ha," I snicker, and then try to get myself together.

"Give me a sec," Ryan says to the driver and then gets out first. He offers me a chivalrous hand, out of absolute necessity, and walks me up to the door, holding my arm.

Even though I feel a bit better, I fumble, searching my bag for something. It's not until I try to open the locked door that I realize I can't find my keys. I kneel close to the ground and then dump out my entire purse to sift through the contents, even though it's clear my keys aren't here.

"You okay down there?"

"I lost my keys," I say looking up at him, like "uh-oh."

"Is this the feminine version of 'I'm out of gas'?"

He goes to look in the car and with no luck, scales the side fence, far too easily, to check the back door. I watch him dodge planters and lawn furniture like he's a ninja, before I realize the stupid motion sensors haven't come on. I forget the bigger picture and feel angry at Trevor for screwing with the timer, for carelessly promising me they'd work. Obviously, the doors are all locked, and thanks to my sober diligence there's not a chance a ground-level window is open.

Seconds later, Ryan startles me by coming back from the other side of the house. "Get your stuff, we're havin' a sleepover."

We cannot have a sleepover.

"Just drop me off at a hotel." I sit down on the grass, stretching my legs out and crossing my arms.

"Not a chance. You're coming home with me."

"What about Alice?"

He laughs a single, "Ha," and then mutters under his breath. "She's with her boyfriend."

"What?" I ask, not sure if I heard him right.

"Don't worry about it. She's definitely not home."

"Ryan," I call out as he walks ahead of me, but he either doesn't hear me or ignores me. Shivering and feeling an intense empathetic connection, I follow him to the car. I already knew a little bit about their troubles from Crystal, but I only half believed it. In the car, he holds his arm up and signals for me to scooch under it, which I do because I'm freezing and I want to be near him as much as possible until this is over. He tells the driver his address, and for a moment I wish this were a different, simpler life, and it was *our* address.

My head feels less drunk, but my stomach is still tipsy. When we pull up to his house I can't get out of the car quick enough. There's a rush of saliva in my mouth, and I know I'm going to throw up. But I plead to myself, please don't throw up, please don't throw up and hope all my body parts cooperate. Unfortunately, my feet don't listen, and I stumble violently down the sloped driveway. I can hear Ryan running up behind me, but he's too slow. My foot hits something and I'm falling. It seems like forever before I hit the ground.

The next thing I know, I wake up to the hot sun on my face, the hypnotic sound of waves, a deep throbbing in my head and an even sorer sensation on my forehead. Too shocked to even move, I just let out a pathetic moan that sounds like I've got minutes to live, which is exactly how I feel. As if it were a bell, Ryan comes in wearing nothing but a towel around his waist, with tiny beads of water clinging to his shoulders.

"Hey there," he says, placing a damp cloth on my forehead. The coolness almost stings at first, so I foolishly sit up too fast and the room starts spinning. Pressing the cloth hard against my skin, I lean back into the pillow until I feel normal enough to open my eyes again. When I do, it finally registers where I am and the night comes flooding back.

"Is this your room?" I sit up again, slower this time. His back is to me and I almost feel like I'm in one of those nightmares where my hands are bound and he's a crazy scientist about to turn around with a giant needle and an evil grin.

Instead, he turns around, as handsome as ever, and gives me a couple of ibuprofen and some water. "Easy," he says as I try to drink it all at once. "Drink slowly."

"What happened?" I say, moaning again.

"What do you remember?" He sits beside me, putting his arm over my legs and leaning on his hand beside me.

"I remember..." What do I remember? I look around the lovely, simple, all-white room and relax my arms on the giant cushions Ryan must have placed around me like safety bars, likely scared I would roll off the bed. The room is devoid of anything personal, so I gather it's only the spare room. At least I'm not in Alice's bed.

"I remember losing my keys," I blurt out, more like a question.

"Good. Okay. So, you remember the good stuff." He gives me a look, and I know exactly what stuff he is referring to. I don't think I'll ever forget kissing Ryan—how his tongue felt touching mine, not lingering too long—making me want more. Much more.

I nod, and he continues. "Well, you fell pretty hard getting out of the car. I'm sorry, Ellen. I should have been beside you, but I honestly thought you were okay."

"Oh, my God, Ryan. It's not your fault." I lift the cloth and can almost hear my skin crying out. "I hit my head, eh?"

He gets up and brings back a little mirror and holds it up for me.

"Oh man!" My forehead is bruised and already scabbed. "I'm a monster," I laugh.

"Impossible. Yeah, you didn't hit too hard, but you slid, so there is quite a scrape," he says, taking the mirror from my hand and replacing it with more water. "Maria made coffee and waffles."

"What???" I whisper-yell, "She's here?"

"Relax, Ellen. She knows everything that's going on with Alice and me. I told her you lost your keys. And, unfortunately, nothing happened anyway."

"Ryan! Oh, my God, she knows I'm married…"

I throw the down comforter back and try to get up, then almost die when I see what I'm wearing. "Oh, my God," I yell again, diving back under the covers.

"Oh, that!" he teases. Yes, I am wearing this outrageous lingerie. I try to be serious because I'm humiliated, but I'm still muddled, so instead I just start laughing.

"You're full of surprises," he says, laughing, and throws a robe at me.

"Did you…?"

"Did I what? Umm no, I did not assault you!"

I try to stop laughing, but it's as if I'm delirious. "I know. God. I mean, did you take my dress off?"

"Well, yeah, I did that, but you were disgusting." He holds up my dress and it's covered in dirt and what I hope are just wine stains.

"I didn't plan on looking, but wow. Ellen! I had no idea."

I cover my face with a pillow and roll onto my side. "I'll have you know women wear this stuff all the time."

"Ummm no, no they don't, Ellen!" He's laughing with me now.

"Well, Joanne lied to me then."

"Who the hell is Joanne?"

"She works at the lingerie store. I thought it would make me feel better."

He's dipped into the washroom now, buying some time for the redness to disappear from my cheeks. He calls out, "I'll tell you one thing. It didn't make me feel better!"

"What?" I ask, peeking out from behind the pillow. He sticks his head out of the door and mouths, "Blue. Balls."

"Seriously!!" I throw the pillow at him.

"You'll have to give me a proper look at you this morning when you're not all sloppy."

He suggests I grab some clothes from Alice's closet, but I refuse even to look. He has truly saved my butt and being difficult probably isn't the best thank you. But I've totally made out with him, her husband, and I'm not also going to borrow (well steal, because I'd never return them) her clothes.

"Can't I just wear one of your smaller t-shirts and maybe some workout shorts?" I beg.

He shakes his head at me like it's a big deal and I tell him he doesn't share well. He leaves me to shower and I try my best not to look in the mirror, for so many reasons. For starters, I look like a beat-up call girl, but worse, I'm not sure I'm ready to face myself, to ask myself what the hell I'm doing right now.

The shower, a tranquil waterfall, punishes and soothes, helping to calm thoughts that were otherwise building to a panic. Oddly, I don't feel that bad about kissing Ryan, but I do feel bad being in Alice's guest room, lathering myself in her expensive L'Occitane body wash. It's safe to assume she bought it for a different sort of guest. Even though I know she's not fully in, toweling off with their monogrammed towels makes me feel like an asshole.

At some point, Ryan snuck in and left some clothes on the counter for me: his well-loved Rochester School of Medicine t-shirt and a huge pair of navy blue Under Armor shorts that I'll have to roll down a few times like my kilt in high school. At first, I don't think much about it—I just put on his shirt and feel like he's all over me, but then I pause and give myself a good looking at. I used to love wearing Trevor's Queens t-shirt. It meant something to me, like wearing your steady boyfriend's letterman jacket. Alice probably loves wearing this. When he knocks, I can't help but ask if he has a different shirt.

"Yeah, for sure. You didn't ruin it, did you?" He chuckles.

"No!" I snap. "This is a special shirt, Ry."

"You're a special girl, Ell," he says like a smartass, exaggerating the short-form.

I don't think I would ever get tired of our banter. Always laughing, this guy.

"Please...?"

"You're a lot of work. Hold on."

Not long after, we're walking on the beach with some of Maria's French-pressed coffee, totally worth the humiliation, in our hands. Ryan put a huge bandage on my head, and I'm now wearing a bright red Quicksilver shirt, the color bringing out every pigment in my skin I want to hide. But I didn't even think about complaining. The warm sand under my feet and squishing in between my toes, the sound of his voice as he tells me he wants to get a dog to throw a stick for, and the crisp fresh air makes me feel fully awake. Like maybe I could be happy again.

Completely sober, I stop, and when Ryan turns to me I stretch up on my tiptoes, place my hands on either side of his face and kiss him softly on the lips. I pull away for a moment to look at his expression, to reaffirm that I'm someone he still wants. He runs a free hand through his hair and then takes me by the waist, pulls me close and kisses me back. It's even better than the drunk version that until now was the best version of kissing ever.

We kiss for a while, our passion intensifying and then calming, over and over, as if mimicking the tide that comes in and splashes at our feet, cooling us off with unwelcome reminders that we're married to other people.

It's nearly nine a.m., and because Trevor hasn't been in touch I have no idea what time he plans to make an appearance. At some point, Ryan and I stop kissing and I tell him I have to get home. I plan on calling an Uber, but he insists on driving me. I don't object, even though I understand the risk involved: Trevor possibly being home or Mary seeing us (if she somehow didn't hear us fumbling around last night). We clean our feet in the outdoor shower and Ryan brushes sand off me. I repeatedly flinch because it scratches; he calls me a wimp and then runs his hand too far up my leg. I keep my eyes on his as he smiles and goes higher and higher like we're playing chicken. And then I lose, predictably swatting his hand.

We head to the driveway, and as the garage door opens Ryan stands there with raised eyebrows. I'm a bit lost until I see it: a shiny black Maserati. "Like it?" he says as he opens my door. I can't help but smile at how excited he is. Had he been pretentious about it I likely would have hated it, but he's like a teenager showing off his dad's car.

"Love it," I laugh.

"It's hot, right?" He shuts my door with comical joy. And for just a minute, sitting in the quiet car alone, I think about Trevor.

As we drive along the coast, the windows are down to dry my still damp hair. An explicit version of a Weeknd song plays a tad too loud for my hangover, yet it all feels blissful. Despite my aching head, my conflicted heart and my horrible outfit, driving with Ryan in this car on this beautiful day is paradise. Like Milton, I know that in a few short miles this feeling will be lost, but I've tasted the forbidden fruit. There's no turning back.

We approach the Port Streets, and I wish I could slow down time or stop it altogether, just to look at him without the pressure of conscience or reality. To be with him inside this moment without the fear of it unraveling. To rewind this morning, not to take anything back (certainly not the kiss), but to relive the whole thing again and maybe, again.

I try to stop focusing on how many minutes we have left together, how many blocks we have left to pass, to just be present. But the more I try, the less present I am and so I try harder. And as if we drove through a time warp, we're already pulling onto my street: six houses left to go, five, four, three, two, and it's over. But we're not alone.

21

"Looks like you've got company," Ryan says, slowing the car as we pull up. I carefully lean forward in my seat to see around him while I try to stay hidden.

"Shit," I say, processing everything with jumbled thoughts.

"Who is that?" he asks, looking at me like he doesn't know if he should stop or speed away.

"It's my sister. It's Audrey." Reality can be harsh, like getting a bucket of ice water dumped on your head. Her face is a cold reminder of who I really am, and the person in someone else's t-shirt and shorts is not who she expected to see.

She saw us; she's looking right at us right now. We can't drive off and leave her to wait here longer, sitting on the steps like a little girl whose mom forgot to pick her up from school. How long has she been here?

From here, I can see her reading the situation in her mind. Her scandalous little sister being dropped off by some strange guy in a sports car at ten in the morning while her husband is away working. I can't imagine stooping low enough to say, "It's not what it looks like." I'll have to tell her everything, and somehow, I feel like I want to.

"You gonna be okay?" Ryan says, touching my hand, realizing the gravity of the situation.

"I've got some explaining to do." I give him a nervous smile and resist the urge to lean over to kiss him. "Gotta go."

He tells me to call him later, and I nod that I will. I grip the door and take a deep breath before opening it, keeping my head down as I step out, knowing there is only one explanation for these oversized shorts.

"Audrey!!" I call out, running toward her, trying to look more excited than guilty. She stands up and gives me a long hug and over her shoulder I see Ryan pull away. She's beautiful as always with her blond hair swept up in a perfect messy bun, trendy drop-crotch track pants and a t-shirt that says, *I used to be punk rock and other lies.* It all makes her look less intimidating than her regular attorney attire, but it doesn't fool me. "You look gooood," I say, meaning it, and knowing how much Audrey loves compliments.

"Ummm, Ellen." She says, looking agitated.

I try to grab her luggage and head to the door, but she stops me, takes the bag from my hands and gestures for me to sit with a forceful mom point. I can't remember a time I've ever felt so uncomfortable with Audrey, not even when she would catch me red-handed wearing her clearly marked off-limits clothing.

"Ellen! What the hell was that?"

I look her in the eye for the first time. "That. That was a long story."

"How long can it be, Ellen?!You've only been here for like three months."

"What are you even doing here?" I ask, trying to get everything straight before I start spilling.

"I tried to tell you. I texted you, Ellen!"

I start laughing, because I'm embarrassed and because she keeps saying my name like she's seriously pissed. I can tell she wants to laugh, too. "How long have you been sitting here?"

"A long fucking time. I was about to call the police when this Wendy person showed up with this!" She throws an envelope at me, and I can feel through the pink paper that it's my keys. Both Ryan and I somehow forgot I was locked out, possibly because being at his place seemed so natural. At least now, Audrey will see why I couldn't sleep at home.

"Who was that? Are you sleeping with him?? Did. He. Hit. You!!!!?" she yells, noticing my head. She throws out questions so quickly I don't know where to start, but for whatever reason, as if it's the most important, I answer, "No, he didn't hit me!" and follow up with, "Trevor's cheating on me!" Shifting the blame.

She gives me a look that says, "Yeah, right, Ellen."

I start at the beginning: how he ignores me, is never home (instead of almost never home like he was in Ontario), is uninterested in having sex with me, and then the hotel key hidden in his pocket.

As I explain it to her, I watch it all register on her face, and when she remains less than convinced, I start to panic. Is there a chance I've been wrong?

"Hidden in his pocket, Ellen? Who does the laundry? Do you even hear yourself?" The flippant way she's downplaying everything infuriates me. I slam my hands down hard on the brick and stand up to walk away from her condescending voice.

"Wait a second, here. Do you seriously think he's cheating on you?"

"Obviously, Audrey!" I stand there crying out of frustration.

"You're a mess!" She gives me a hug, and I keep my arms firm to my side and my head down. "Let's go in," she says, looking worried. "I'll make us tea. You go get changed."

But I don't want to get changed.

I unlock the door and we make our way through the downstairs. Audrey gushes over all the character, opens two sets of French doors and takes an exaggerated deep breath, even managing to hide her disappointment when she opens my nearly empty fridge. She puts the kettle on, and just like that she's already settled in. She sends me to my room, not even asking where hers is. I fake reluctance and then head upstairs feeling vaguely triumphant, like I've somehow been let off the hook. I stop quickly in the guest room to light a candle, place some blue guest towels on the bed and think how shabby my decorating is compared to Alice's. Mind you, she has an ocean view and I have Mary's RV.

Once in my room, I close the door almost all the way and dive onto my bed, our bed, Trevor's bed, and practically roll around in Ryan's clothes. I take deep inhalations of his scent, which I know fades more the longer I wear them. I can't be drunk anymore, but I'm as high as I've been in maybe forever. I know Audrey deserves better, she deserves me skipping down the stairs to her, eager to catch up. I pry myself off the bed and peel Ryan's clothes off me, lifting his shirt over my head and lingering under it for just a minute.

"Ellen?!!!!"

I jump, "Audrey, you scared the crap out of me!"

She holds her hand over her mouth.

"What?" I ask, embarrassed she caught me making out with Ryan's shirt.

"What are you wearing?"

Fuck. Not this again.

"Shut up!" I say and throw his shirt at her.

"Seriously, Ellen." She's laughing now. "WHO are you?"

"You know what, big sister? That's a real good question."

Because she persists, I show her the rest of my lingerie stash and she says she's trying it all on. She steals the pile out of my hands and runs into the washroom. Never the shy one, moments later, she comes out like a runway model. "I. Love. This."

"See!! It makes you feel good, eh?"

"Yes. It. Does," she says, looking herself over in the mirror, "I'm keepin' it."

"No, you're not!"

"I absolutely am. You can't be trusted."

As if this morning hasn't been strange enough, we're now both standing in front of the mirror comparing our bodies, her longer legs, my flatter tummy, looking like strippers, when we hear a voice call up from downstairs—a man's voice! We both freeze and try not to laugh.

"Holy shit, Ellen, who is that???!" I shrug, and then the two of us scramble around as we put our clothes on. "Another one????" she teases and the more we laugh the less progress we make.

"One second," I yell.

Audrey follows with, "Who is it?"

I slug her, and we both freeze again as we wait for a response.

Finally we hear, "It's Ryan. Your solely platonic friend, Ryan."

"Oh, my God!" I whisper to Audrey, my face flushing and nerves igniting.

"He's got a lotta balls," she says as we fumble around for a few more minutes, falling and laughing, me wanting to look good and Audrey trying to figure everything out, asking too many questions and driving me nuts.

Finally, we make our way down the stairs, fighting over who goes first. I'm now wearing tights and an army green t-shirt. Instead of lingerie, I have no bra on. Which I'm sure has a similar effect, which I'm fine with.

"Don't be a bitch, k?" I whisper to Audrey. "Nothing happened between us."

"Hey there," Ryan, who is now leaning in the doorway, says as soon as he sees us. "The door was open."

"Hey, yeah, no problem. What's up? Why are you here?" I ask, trying to sound welcoming.

"I'm Audrey," she interjects all business-like, offering her hand.

"You guys look alike. Ryan." He shakes her hand, exaggerating and reciprocating the firmness.

"Yeah, we do," she says, "but I'm prettier."

"Definitely," he agrees and then winks at me. He then holds up my phone. "You forgot this in my car."

"Shoot, sorry. Thank you for bringing it back."

"Want some tea?" Audrey blurts out. I hold my breath hoping he says no.

"Ummm, sure," he says and then looks at me as if asking, "Cool?"

"Of course, come in." I tell them to go sit outside while I make the tea. I need a couple of minutes alone so I can check my phone.

As soon as he handed it to me, I could see Trevor's name among a list of missed texts. A lot from Audrey, a couple from Wendy, but definitely one from him. I put the kettle back on and then peer out into the backyard from the window over the sink, trying to ignore the peeling UV coating that makes the glass look broken. Strangely, Ryan and Audrey are sitting directly beside each other at the large round table. Poor Ryan. Audrey is tough. But he's so good-natured, I'm sure he can handle her, maybe even challenge her a bit. I turn my back to them, take a deep breath and look at my phone. I scroll past Audrey's, *Where are you?????* and click on Trevor's, *I hope my surprise arrived and you're happy. See you two tonight. Love you.*

The text hits a nerve, well, a few different nerves all at once. It's not guilt. It's more like confusion, and then hope, and then confusion again. Maybe guilt. I bite my nails, take a quick gander at my two favorite people right now, and text back, *yes, she's here…thank you.* Before I press send, I consider adding *love you, too,* but I hesitate. Do I love him? Of course, I do. It's more like, do I want to love him? I settle for *xoxo.* I pour the tea, adding milk to all three even though Ryan drinks his coffee black. I'm about to head out when I stop dead in my tracks. I put the tray down, grab my phone and type *I miss you.*

Once outside, I linger behind them for just long enough to hear the always audacious Audrey asks, "So. You sleep with my sister?"

Oh, man. Ryan doesn't appear to be rattled, he crosses his legs and leans back in his chair. "Nope."

"But you want to?"

"I wouldn't mind," he says, totally solemn, making her laugh. At this point, I must break this up. I can tell from Audrey's face that she likes him. He's hard not to like.

The drilling stops when I sit down, but it's awkward because it's not awkward at all. The three of us sit there teasing each other, completely oblivious to the strangeness of this situation, and Audrey and I are clearly forgetting our loyalty to Trevor. Ryan has that effect. He's charming, he's attractive, and he's smart enough not to take anything too seriously. A few times, especially when she swipes her hand across his knee and throws her body toward him in laughter, I'm reasonably sure Audrey is flirting.

After a short while, Ryan stands and says he has to go. I knew it was coming, and he probably should, but I'm disappointed, as I am every time he leaves. Audrey and I walk him out front. He says he likes her shirt and I swear to God she blushes. Before he leaves, he gives me a solid look, his eyes meeting mine long enough to make every inch of me stand at attention. He kisses my cheek and then turns to Audrey to say it was great meeting her. When she reaches out her hand, he leans and kisses her the exact way he kissed me.

"You're trouble!" she says and then looks down, almost bashful.

"I really am," he laughs. "And Ellen…"

"Yeah?"

"I can see your nipples!"

"How old are you?" Audrey yells, as I jokingly cover them.

22

When he pulls away, we plunk down on the warm steps out front and let our bare feet relax in the sun. I feel so much more lucid than when we sat here earlier. We don't talk for a few minutes. We just look around at all the houses and the flowers that are still blooming in November, listen to the sounds of birds, kids playing, and the neighbor's water feature.

After a calming pause, she puts her hand on mine and says, "What are we going do with you, Elly?"

"I wish I knew, Audrey. I'm so confused."

"He looks like a blond Josh Duhamel."

"I know."

"Well, I wouldn't say no!" she jokes, then adds, "I get it, Ellen. I get how you could lose yourself in this place. It's something. And he's something. But this isn't you."

"How do you know it isn't me?" I crash my head into my hands.

"Because I've known you your whole life."

"What if I want it to be?"

"It's not real, Ellen, the people, the perfect hedges. Even Ryan! He's married, and he loves her."

"What do you mean, he loves her? Did he say that?"

"He didn't have to say it. Talking about her made him really sad, Elly. His face totally changed."

"Oh," is all I say.

"And another thing," she says, sounding stern. "What the hell is that?" She points up to a small rod attached to the house.

I laugh. "It's a flagpole!"

"What?"

"You know. Like all those," I explain, gesturing to all the American flags waving at us from across the street.

"You should put a Canadian flag up."

"I don't know how well that would be received. I could put up a hockey flag!" I say, laughing.

"Do it!! 'Ugh. What's hockey?'" she mocks. "But not the Kings."

"Obviously."

We head in, and Audrey goes upstairs to unpack and take a shower. I plop on the couch and return Wendy's texts to let her know I'm alive and to thank her for the keys. Like a veteran adulterer, she texts in code, asking questions about "Ryanne" and if I slept at her house. I answer: *let's have coffee soon!* She immediately responds that Audrey is cute but definitely couldn't be a part of our group. When I ask why, she types, *because she's too happy—I was there twenty minutes and she only looked at her phone once, and when she did, she smiled.*

Well, thanks a lot, Wendy. Audrey is happy, but am I really that noticeably miserable?

Feeling as down as I'm apparently perceived to be, I bury my head into the couch. The bruise on my head feels like it might start bleeding, but I ignore it and close my eyes. For the first time, I acknowledge what I've done. I kissed someone else, I slept at his house, I introduced him to my sister, and I liked it, all of it. All of him. I flip around to my other side, like turning a page, and think about Trevor. What would life be like without his steady guidance, striking beauty, his brawn, his brains? I almost want to scream, to peel my skin off and walk out a new person.

My phone vibrates. Perfect timing, a break from my first-world-problems tortured mind. It's Audrey. She tells me to come out front. What the hell?

I symbolically dust myself off, quickly pee and then open the front door expecting her to be on the steps again, but she's not. She is parked out front, exactly where Ryan dropped me off, in the golf cart that was covered in the garage.

"Get in, loser, we're going shopping," she yells, echoing Rachel McAdams in *Mean Girls*. "What the… Audrey! How did you get this out?"

I've been curious about it but never considered starting it.

"I snuck it," she says. "Put your shoes on and get your wallet!"

"K!" As I walk away, she calls out in a thoughtful tone: "Ellen, so why couldn't Gretchen get fetch to work but fleek was like a real thing?"

I shake my head, laughing, and shrug my shoulders. "That's another fucking good question."

She asks me what the driving rules are and I tell her I have no clue. "Good enough for me," she says, and then heads to the green space at the end of the street. Like her car, she drives the unexpectedly fast cart like she's sixteen, taking the dips and turns without slowing. I haven't laughed this hard for years. She starts singing the Indiana Jones theme song, d da daa daaa, d da daaa, and we both pump our arms goofily to the beat. When we pass people, moms and babies, and nannies and babies, we go silent, holding in laughter as they look suspiciously at us. We circle around when we hit a playground with no noticeable exit. A few toddlers play in the sand and a couple of older ones push each other on the swings while their Soul Cycle, blond mothers sit under a covered picnic table. "Are they drinking champagne?" Audrey asks, shocked.

"I think they are!"

"Holy shit, Ellen! I wanna move here!"

She cuts up onto a main road and heads to the grocery store complex at the end of a busy street. We cross an intersection, playing it totally cool, feeling completely absurd. But this is acceptable behavior here. She pulls into the Exit Only with confidence, waving off a scowling senior with patronizing disregard.

"We're starving, right?" she asks. I agree, and so she pulls the tiny cart into the last gigantic spot, pissing off the driver in the Escalade behind us. We're at some café with a ton of outdoor seating. She asks me if it's any good, but I answer that, as with everything else, I have no idea.

We order our food, two California omelets and more caffeine, then make our way over to a table for two that the sun seems to be warming just for us. We sip on our coffees, and I make sure to ask her ample questions about the kids, Mark, and Mom and Dad. When she speaks of them, she does so with such honest joy and love it seems to radiate from her like the California sun she's now soaking up, stripped down to her tank top even though it's not even seventy degrees. She says I've gone soft, and she's right because I made a point to grab a sweater before we left.

My questions remind her to check in at home. Seconds later she's FaceTiming, and the simplicity of reaching out makes me feel guilty for not doing it more myself. Bad Auntie Ellen. As soon as Kate's little face lights up the screen, I feel a rush of love. How have I kept her so far from my thoughts? I sing the song my father always sings to her, "K-K-K-Katy, beautiful Katy; You're the only g-g-g-girl that I adore; when the m-m-m-moon shines over the c-c-c-cowshed; I'll be waiting at the k-k-k-kitchen door."

"Auntie Ellen!" she cheers. "I miss you so much—is Uncle Trevor there?"

"No sweetie, he's at work."

"Booooooo!" she whines. We talk for a few minutes, mostly about her favorite uncle, and then I pass her over to her mommy who has been listening in with pride and now beams when they're face to face.

I lean back in my chair and watch their interaction, loving them both so much and feeling desperately homesick for the first time in weeks. Blocking them out has been a survival tool for me. And maybe Audrey's right: in the process, I might have gotten lost. I've left myself vulnerable, too open to other people's influences. I wish for a moment that I could undo what's been done and start over from the instant Trevor told me we were moving. But as soon as I think about that painful moment, I quickly revoke my wish. I don't take it back. Maybe his promotion, his career dictating my life, was a wake-up call. If I give him my best years, my fertile years, my present to squander, where will I be when he's able to give me his? An older, even more resentful version of my same neglected self? At what point will he want someone younger? Is that what's going on now?

As much as it hurts, I'm also a bit relieved that when I truly consider my feelings, separate from Ryan,

I know my marriage is probably over. Audrey says good-bye, kissing her phone with her naturally full lips, and then quickly pulls up an email she had Mark forward to her from Trevor. She slides her phone across the table to me and says, "Read this, Ellen."

I start at the bottom and scan through a few boring correspondences with the subject *catching up* and then *re:catching up*, finishing with the most recent:

> *Hey buddy,*
>
> *I hope everyone is doing well. Thanks for booking Audrey's flight. I know Ellen will be surprised. I hope it will cheer her up. She's really not settled here. I feel so guilty leaving her alone all the time. Although I'm not sure she even wants me around. I thought this would be an exciting move for us. I see now I was wrong. Here's to hoping things improve. - T*

I'm not sure what reaction Audrey thought this would trigger. To me, it sounds like Trevor is disappointed in me once again. Disappointed that I am unable to live up to his expectation of adventure. Reading this feels like elementary school when your best friend plays messenger, passing notes back and forth between you and your crush: *Do you think Tommy is funny? Circle Yes or No*

With a sigh, I slide the phone back, not offering any signs of a grand realization.

"You really think he's cheating, Ellen? He seems to care an awful lot for someone who's busy shacking up in hotels."

"Does it matter?" I ask, feeling angry with Audrey.

"Yeah. I think it does."

"Well, I think it's embarrassing that he thinks needs to bring in a babysitter for me."

"I think he thought you would be happy to see me."

"I am, Audrey. But he shouldn't be able to just pass me off."

"You need a counselor."

"Probably."

"And not a hot one."

Our food comes, and we eat in silence. I'm frustrated with Trevor. Audrey's frustrated with me. We still exchange our fruit, my watermelon for her pineapple.

Audrey has one of her brilliant ideas: to cook an amazing dinner tonight. We'll fire up the barbecue, light the outdoor fireplace and drink a lot of wine. The idea of drinking again is accompanied by a wave of nausea, but wanting to be a good host I push my plate aside and say, "Sure, why not?"

We make our way through the grocery store, and I wonder how we grew up with the same parents. Not only is she wholly confident, talking to the butcher like he's on trial ("So you're saying this salmon has never been frozen, correct?"), but she also loses me as she goes on about marinades and wine pairings. She's barely older than I am and on top of her education, career and full-blown family, she also knows how to plan a meal in a few minutes, take charge at the meat counter, and cook like an amateur chef.

What have I done in almost the same amount of time? I haven't even learned how to be grown up. I've spent most of my adult life eating with my parents while my husband was away at school or on night shifts that often bleed into day shifts. Here, entirely on my own, I lazily eat yogurt and a lot of apples. I try to pay close attention, to learn something, but when she debates buying the nearly wilted dill here or driving to Whole Foods, I'm like...fuck this.

Somewhere between dill and yams, my pocket vibrates. Like a teenager, I walk beside Audrey as she shops, looking at my phone. It's Ryan, totally ignoring the three-day rule, hell the three-hour rule, to say he needs to see me tomorrow. Outrageously, he wants to come to our house and pick me up at eleven a.m. I can't just drive off with some man when my husband could be home and Mary most certainly will be gardening. I know all this, but still text back: *you're insane...maybe.*

Not long after, we're working away in the kitchen. Audrey marinates a huge flat iron steak (a cut you can apparently only find in the US), in what looks like a million ingredients: soy, balsamic, lime juice, garlic (ketchup, mustard, mayo). And I'm sitting on the bar stool trying to find a new playlist, finally settling on *Young & Free*; I need all the help I can get in those departments, as I feel extremely Old & (unhappily) Married.

She insists we fix ourselves up before dinner, but more likely she just wants to try on all my clothes and steal what she likes. Not quite an hour later, after she's taken half of my clothes down and I've hung them back up, we settle on a dress that I have in both yellow and grey, and navy and grey. I wear the latter, because who am I kidding, yellow? I braid Audrey's hair, noticing her red shoulders and a tan line that emphasizes her nearly transparent skin, and then I do my own. (At least she can't braid.)

When we are (she is) satisfied, we make our way downstairs, open a bottle of red, and then toast. "To being sisters," she says. "Friends!" I add, clinking glasses again. "Best friends!" And this goes on and on until we're at, "Losers!" and finally, "perfect!"

Audrey takes a long inhale and then swirls her wine around in her glass before she brings it to her mouth. I think this is more for my benefit than about enhancing the taste, so I refuse to imitate, taking a long sip and swallowing instantly.

"So uncivilized," she says, leaving me no choice but to take a swig from the bottle and then carry it and my glass outside.

It's close to six p.m. Trevor should be home shortly. I have a strange feeling in my stomach again, sort of like butterflies, but more likely I'm just anxious about seeing him. Will we be able to see cheating in each other's faces, like you fear your parents will be able to tell you've lost your virginity?

Audrey struggles to start the barbecue, the back-yard flooding with the smell of rotten eggs as gas gets caught in the breeze. She's pressed the igniter button a hundred times despite my warnings, and when I come to the rescue with a lighter, the grill explodes with a huge gust of flames and we both jump back, grabbing our braids.

When she's sure it's settled, Audrey bends down close to the grill as if she is looking for something. "Check this out, Ellen," she whispers.

"What is it?" I ask, bending down beside her.

"See that?" She looks at me quickly and then back at the flames, both of our heads down, still and silent like listening to a secret.

"What?"

"That," she points, "that is what hell is like, Ellen."

I smack her arm. "You're such a loser!" We both start laughing and then jump again when Trevor startles us.

"What's so funny?"

We turn to face him, flushed from the flames and our mischief. Audrey squeals and runs in for a loving hug and I just stare at him, awkward, as if we're already divorced and are seeing each other for the first time at a friend's wedding. Audrey squeezes him tight, and he lifts her off her feet. Trevor is barely a year older than her and yet he treats her like the little sister he never had. Together, they are my family. She is my sister, my blood, and she loves my husband like a brother. And family must come first, even before me.

When my eyes briefly meet Trevor's, I can sense we feel the same way, that our magnetic poles are both negatives, pushing us apart as we make our way to each other. We're trying to be normal but feeling like strangers. He doesn't know me, and even if he hasn't cheated on me, which I don't believe, I don't know him anymore either. How can you know someone when you're never together? How do we fit together after all this?

Troubles aside, he is still the most handsome man I've ever seen. We hesitate as we take the last two steps toward each other, but then he somehow recharges and comes at me with a quick embrace. He uncharacteristically holds me close for more than his usual second, bending down to my level instead of pulling me up like he did Audrey. In his arms, I forget the present for a minute and remember all the moments we've shared like this, too many that I never even really noticed. And so, when he kisses me on closed lips, I kiss him back at the last second, feeling hope that we might still find our way through this somehow.

"You guys look like you're having fun," he says as he backs away, looking down as if to hide his beautiful blue eyes from me.

"We are having fun. I'm a lot of fun," Audrey says as she hands him a glass of wine.

"How was the conference?" I ask him, hearing my voice shake.

"Boring. Really boring, actually. But one of us had to go, and I'm the new guy."

"Brutal. Did you have drinks with anyone?" Audrey asks awkwardly out of nowhere. I give her a sharp look.

"Ummm…," he says, laughing. "Why? Can you smell it? Yeah, I had a couple last night with some guys I knew from NYC." He playfully sniffs himself.

"Must have been more than a couple," I say under my breath, and then regret it, thinking of my night. Too late to wish I hadn't encouraged the inevitable rebuttal question he immediately asks.

"How was your night, Ellen? I didn't hear from you."

"I didn't hear from you, either," I reply, altogether avoiding the question.

"But I never hear from you," he says with a winning smile.

"All right, all right. Sounds like you're both losers here," Audrey interrupts. "Just give each other a kiss and say sorry."

"Audrey! Knock it off," I say, furious, and turn to head into the house.

"Why, Ellen? Is kissing me the worst idea?" He stands there, his expression a bit sad, someone I feel I don't know and I'm not sure how to act around, never mind kiss.

"No. I didn't say that."

"Then c'mere," he says, opening his arms to me.

"We just did."

"That was not a kiss!!" Audrey says, pretending to eat her invisible popcorn.

"Forget it," Trevor says, with a wave of his hand.

I don't want to have this all turned on me, so I say fine and then take long, brisk steps toward him. Once I start I can't stop, so when I get there I don't hesitate. I stretch up to him, my hands planted on his shoulders to anchor me without his help, and then kiss him like I'm trying to win some sort of competition. I start small, but then force his mouth open with insistent lips. At some point, our heads naturally tilt as we give into each other, reintroducing our tongues, history and muscle memory taking over. Strangely, it feels like kissing him when we were first in love; I wonder if kissing at the end is supposed to feel so good.

When we separate, I give him a smile that feels sincere, and he smiles back, finally showing me his eyes, like saying, "There you are." We allow ourselves to stay in the moment, and although it's the smallest moment, I realize it's more time we've spent on us since that awful night at home when he told me about the move.

Audrey brings reality back to the backyard with, "Yay!" followed by "Best idea!"

"Ellen! What happened to your head?" he asks as if seeing me for the first time. He inspects it, touching it gently. I tell him it was nothing, clumsy jogging. He doesn't press for a detailed explanation, which makes me both happy and sad.

Trevor goes to shower and I help Audrey, who gave me creative freedom to layer slices of fresh mozzarella and tomatoes. I'm just about to go overboard with balsamic drizzle when a thought hits me—why shower now? He must have showered at the hotel. This is followed by panic as I picture a certain red t-shirt thrown carelessly somewhere in our room. I drop the drizzle and sprint, thinking on the way up that this is not good, not the shirt, the doubt, the sneaking around. All lies, even if they're not spoken because he hasn't asked.

When it doesn't turn up, I start freaking out, thinking it's in the washroom with Trevor.

But thankfully, like the wonderful and typical big sister she is, Audrey both hid the evidence in her room and then let me freak out for ten minutes before telling me about it.

"Thanks a lot!" I say sarcastically, but I'm so, so grateful.

We set the table outside, light candles, plug in the lights wrapped around the trees, pour more wine and wait for Trevor. Finally, he joins us, and Audrey insists he and I sit together while she brings out the perfectly rested steak, sliced on a wooden cutting board, my spruced up Caprese salad, and yams fragrant with maple syrup and butter. I can't help but feel ashamed that I haven't grilled one meal since we've been in

California, and have never made a meal like this in my entire life. My regret is made worse by Trevor's zealous appreciation. "Wow! Audrey, this is amazing. Unreal! So appreciated!" (Subtext: I married the wrong sister—not brilliant, not successful and not domestically talented.)

While we eat, Trevor tells us witty accounts of first-year residents being abused by their attendings at the conference, belittled with luggage duty, coffee runs and segregated seating. He and Audrey laugh at their humiliation, their nerve. Tilting their perfect heads back, they chuckle like two high-society snobs looking down on the underlings. I can't help but think how alike these two are: Mr. & Mrs. Perfect.

"Wasn't so funny when you were in their shoes," I say like a party pooper, aligning myself with the underdogs.

"Part of the process, Ell. I earned the right to enjoy it. You remember the shit I went through." He takes a sip of wine and puts his other hand on my leg. It startles me, and my knee flinches like he's inflicted pain. "You are so tense, Ellen."

"I know, right?" Audrey adds. "Calm down!" she says sternly, bugging her eyes out.

"I'm fine. I'm just tired. I didn't sleep much last night."

We haven't even taken our last bites when Trevor's phone vibrates, sending it scurrying across the table like a quick insect. I want to snatch it before he does, to cover my hand over it and then lift it up, see her name

NEWPORT JANE

and yell, "Ah-ha!" But I don't. I watch him flip it over, glance at the number without picking it up and then excuse himself from the table.

I give Audrey a questioning look, and she shoots it down with, "What? He's a doctor, Ellen!" And isn't that the perfect cover up. Red flags and warning bells would consume any other wife had her husband exhibited the same behavior. Predictably, he returns a minute later and sheepishly says he has to go.

"But we haven't even had dessert," Audrey says, even though we don't have any dessert planned. (But I like her style.) I sit and spin a piece of steak around on my fork, thinking, *shocker.*

Once he's gone, Audrey admits for the first time that she thinks his schedule sucks and that she can understand how it would be frustrating here without my own career and the company of my open-door family down the street. Her half-committed realization starts a heated debate. I argue loneliness; she counters with boredom. I state my expectations for a husband, and she argues not depending on someone else to make you happy. Finally, I win the verdict when she says, "Have a baby," and I say, "He doesn't want one." She asks how I know that is still true, and I say, "Because we haven't had sex in five weeks."

"Five weeks?" she yells, appalled, as if she finally gets it. Audrey has higher than average expectations; she and Mark do it all the time, like six times a week, all the time. Since we started living together, Trevor and I have always had the lower end of the normal amount of sex, in the two-to-three times a week range, mostly because his schedule and general level of tiredness has never allowed for more.

"Keep your voice down," I say, not entirely sure if Trevor's left yet.

"That's bad, Ellen!"

"Thanks, Audrey. I know."

"Well, no wonder you want to cheat. You just need a vibrator," she says, totally serious.

"Yeah, that will solve everything."

"Well, there is no reason our night needs to be spoiled." She pushes her chair back aggressively and offers her hand to me. I reluctantly accept, and she pulls me to my feet, gives me a buck-up hug and a pat on my ass. "Grab the wine!" She walks over to the hot tub and steps in like she's crushing grapes. She holds her dress up at first but then lifts it over her head and tosses it onto the faux grass. I can't help but laugh. Sisters. Two peas. I follow, and in no time, I've forgotten all about the men in my life and am focused on Audrey's ability to make pre-school drama exciting… and exhausting.

"Ahhh," she sighs and takes the last sip of wine. "I predict you're going to be just fine, kiddo."

"Ha. Who knows?"

"Hot tub time machine?" she asks with a smirk.

"You first!"

"1998. Prom night do-over. Justin was such a giver. I should've at least given him a hand job."

"Justin!" I laugh, remembering her prom date, who was madly in love with her. "You were such a selfish lover."

"Hey, he was lucky! Soooo, where are you going?"

"Second year. 2004, the year I met Trevor. I'd like to see him with these eyes. See if he would sparkle as much."

"You're fucked."

We tidy up and pull the plug on our evening, cut short like most evenings in this house, in this marriage. She must mutter "five weeks" under her breath a million times before she heads upstairs to call Mark, likely to fill him in on her outrageous discovery.

I intend to just blow out the candles and then head up too, but as I lean over the table and extinguish the last flame, I collapse onto the chair and start sobbing. My emotions are a depressing cocktail of sadness, embarrassment, shame and utter frustration. It occurs to me that my forced kiss with Trevor, as good as it was, didn't feel anywhere near as good as kissing Ryan. But then, it was obligatory, in front of Audrey, and at an incredibly bad time in our relationship.

And then again, watching Trevor with Audrey felt like home.

24

Last night, like most nights here, I slept terribly. My mind was consumed with half-conscious thoughts of Ryan and I running away together, to New York maybe; of Trevor and I pushing a stroller around the Port Streets, smiling the proud smile of new parents. For the first time in my life, I can't seem to connect the dots. There's no simple line to follow. Or perhaps there is, but it's faint, and there's a bolder line now, a detour, or maybe it's a U-turn. Either way, I'm at an intersection, a crossroads. I know Jane would go straight. But Jane's not here anymore.

I agreed to let Ryan come pick me up this morning. I thought about lying to Audrey, sneaking out while she was busy on a conference call, but I don't want to deceive her, too. When I told her today, she seemed even less patient with the theatrics.

"Your life isn't a movie, Ellen. In real life, you work things out. You stay loyal, at least until you've exhausted every other option."

She's right. She is. But I'm hurt, and I'm tired, and I feel like loneliness is something you can die of. Am I supposed to stay loyal to a reality in which women settle for unhappiness because it's too late, they're married—maybe because they have children? Women struggling through their days, one disappointment after the other, socks thrown on the floor, missed recitals, porn-riddled search histories. Until the day they wise up and realize that to make it work, they have to forget about being happy. That married life is settling for work and vicarious movie romance, their only sexual pleasure by themselves, when no one else is watching.

At this point of my life, as I teeter between youngish and dried up, I'm more interested in staying loyal to my own happiness before I must think about little doe eyes, eyes that force me to stay unhappily married to their philanderer of a father.

Minutes before he pulls up, Ryan sends me a text asking for a sandwich. At first, I think it's a joke; but when he follows up with *pllllease*, I realize he's pathetically serious. Though it seems quite a bit too soon for food requests, I like the idea of being needed for something. Trevor insists on being independent and never asks for a snack or a homemade lunch. So, I make Ryan a sandwich, and I make it good.

Just as I finish wrapping wax paper around a basic peanut butter and jam, I remember the leftover steak in the fridge and the ciabattas in the cupboard. Thanks to Audrey's experienced shopping, I have all the makings of an impressive picnic. I move quickly so she doesn't catch me—she'll be disappointed when she comes down for lunch and her olive mix and buns are missing. One last touch: despite the smell of them, I throw in a bag of Doritos.

He pulls up in a Range Rover, and because I didn't see it at his house it hits me that Alice must be home. I don't let it get to me, because after all I'm married myself and as far as Ryan knows my marriage isn't falling apart. He doesn't get out, just rolls the window down and tilts his sunglasses down on his nose far enough to give me goosebumps with his persuasive gaze and smile. I smile from the porch, hesitating for a noticeable moment as I wonder if Audrey is peering out the window at me, urging me to make good choices.

"Quick, get in," he yells, looking over his shoulders.

I can't help but laugh and wonder if his humor is a tactic to distract me from the seriousness of our being together. Either way, it works, and I find myself practically skipping to his car, proudly holding up my basket of goodies.

He knows better than to try anything stupid like kissing me here, but he does reach over and place his hand on my leg, a single tap and then a squeeze, as if to say, *relax*. He's wearing a fitted dress shirt rolled up at the sleeves and slightly unbuttoned. He looks over at me, from my loose-fitting tank top to our inaugural meeting jeans shorts, not shy about checking me out. Then he smiles and I feel beautiful.

He doesn't have long, so we pull into a community center parking lot just outside the Port Streets, overlooking a canyon. A few joggers pass on the trail in front of us, and another couple sits in a car twenty feet or so away, likely doing the same thing we are. She has glasses on; he's in a hat. Could be a disguise, hiding from their spouses and friends; could also just be the sun. We, on the other hand, are dangerously casual about our relationship, possibly because we've only dabbled in the cheating area, only a few kisses. At this point, we're still marginally platonic.

He is seriously impressed with the picnic and makes no apologies for begging for food. We eat, both taking big bites and shoving handfuls of Doritos in our mouths, smiling at each other, completely comfortable. I forgot napkins, and as our hands are sticky and orange, he tells me to check in the glove compartment. When I do, I spy a crumpled picture of him and Alice hidden under a manual. I consider ignoring it, but the act of crumpling the picture seems more aggressive, more hurt than I feel about Trevor. I've had my bouts of rage, but I don't feel the urge to destroy pictures of us together quite yet.

Against my better judgment and my respect for Ryan's privacy and suspected pain, I retrieve the photo and smooth the wrinkles out. I run my hand across his distorted face and see how happily perfect they both looked, equally gorgeous and successful.

"You want to talk about it?" I ask, glancing over to him as he watches me hold his heart in my hand. He sighs heavily, and says, "Ummm…not really?" and then looks at me as if asking if that's okay.

"I think you should, Ryan." I say, passing the photo to him. He takes it, studies it with his eyes, eyes I've never seen before: sad, angry eyes. He turns the photo over, resting it on his thigh. "I left her alone a lot. Well, she wasn't really alone—she spent all her time with her boss, some young, good-looking, pompous dickhead." I stay quiet and let him keep talking. He tries to keep it light, but he sounds angrier as he continues. "You know, at first she hated him, always complaining. Then one day she stopped complaining, and I guess I never noticed." He shrugs it off and then jokingly shoves a handful of chips in his mouth, eating his pain.

"Were you married a long time?" I ask, careful not to sound begrudging.

"Ummm, married? No, but we grew up together. She was my sister's best friend."

"That's a lot of history…"

"It is, and it's probably the only reason she tried moving out here. I think she's where she wants to be now."

"You love her?"

He pauses, and then slowly nods his head, "Yeah, I do...but I don't like her."

"Hmmm," is all I say as I fight immature jealousy, but also understand completely.

As if he's worried he's said something wrong, insulted me somehow, he adds, "But I really like you, Ellen. I bet I could even love you." He gives me a sweet smile, absent all the seductiveness of just moments before.

I laugh and say I know exactly what he means. When he asks, I betray Trevor more and fill him in on almost everything: how lonely I've become, how I'd let my family and friends fill the void in my marriage, how exposed that void is now, and how unimportant and useless I feel the instant my eyes open every morning. Embarrassed, I also admit to him, the second person in twenty-four hours, that I haven't had sex in five weeks.

After he unsuccessfully hides his shock, he tells me he knew I was sad the first time he saw me in the wine aisle. That he recognized something in me that he sees in himself, how my eyes looked lost in thought or maybe just lost, how he watched them come alive as we talked, like the energy we created together was more than just happenstance. I wasn't going to tell him about Trevor cheating, maybe because I am scared he'll pity me. But he looks at me as if he knows there's more to my story, so I tell him as if I'm just acknowledging what he already knows. "And then there is the fact that Trevor is cheating on me."

"What?" he says, as doubtfully as Audrey. "I highly doubt it, Ellen."

"No, seriously, he is."

"The guy is as boring as they come. I don't think he's broken a rule in his life."

"Oh yeah, well how do you explain the complete lack of interest in sex with me? And the hotel key?"

"What hotel key?"

"I found it in his pants." He pauses, scratches his chin, processing everything as I stare him down and wait for him to validate my suspicions.

"Yep. He's probably cheating on you."

"I know."

"I don't know how he could sleep next to you for five weeks and not fondle you at least once." He gives me the raised eyebrows and I laugh, but say, "Be serious, Ryan. Fondle?!" I shake my head in pretend disgust.

"I am being serious! I don't know why he'd have a hotel key. And if Alice taught me anything, it's that anything is possible."

As suspected, his validation just upsets me more. "You know, for cardiologists, you two are pretty shitty at love. It's like your own hearts are in your asses."

"Hey, I never cheated on Alice once. Not in ten years."

"Well, did you leave her any choice but to cheat?"

"Ummm, yeah, I think I did." He stares straight ahead, probably frustrated with me and angry with Alice.

"I'm sorry," I say, slipping my hand under his, touching his thigh. "You're not Trevor. But maybe I'm just like Alice."

"I guess that makes me the pompous dickhead."

After a pause that lasts a few seconds, he continues. "You know what? Shit just happens. Relationships don't always work out. We're probably all to blame equally, in different ways." He looks right at me, and I know he's right. It's like he can read my mind, and I know exactly how he's feeling.

I lean over to him, push myself up with one arm and kiss him gently on the mouth until he kisses me back. His hands grip my hair in handfuls, both of us kissing like we're trying to forget everyone else. It doesn't even feel like cheating; it's more like reconnecting. We get caught up: he pulls me onto his lap and I throw one leg over him. He runs his hands down my back, holding onto my hips as our kissing takes on a familiar rhythm, like we're teenagers in a dark parking lot. But we're not—we're adults in broad daylight.

Not until my back presses against the steering wheel and the horn blows do we stop. I can feel him hard beneath me, and the idea that I did that to him turns me on. I climb back into the passenger seat and both of us catch our breath, trying to calm down. At one point our eyes meet and we start laughing as we dry our cheeky mouths.

The holidays are coming up and he asks me to spend Thanksgiving with him. Trevor will have to work the weekend, but Ryan scheduled it off months ago, planning to spend it with Alice's family, who now live in South Carolina. Even before he's given me the details, I'm already trying to figure out how I can sneak away with him. I hardly think it's fair to put Audrey in the position of covering for me, forcing her to betray Trevor more than she already has, but I could ask Annie.

"Let's just say I could make it work. Where would we go?" I ask.

He takes a sip out of an old bottle of water, because unlike Audrey would have, and Alice probably, I forgot drinks.

His chest still moves with exaggerated breaths as he swallows and says, "Well, I was thinking we could hide out at my place. Maria has the weekend off, but she always leaves me all the fixin's. We can eat, drink some wine, walk the beach…"

It sounds amazing and every cell in my body wants to say yes, and not just to his suggestions but also to rolling around together, in the sand, his bed, to finish what we've just started. But my mind isn't clear; it's weakened by surging hormones and a deep pulsing lower in my body.

"I don't know if I'm ready for that…"

"You can stay in your old room," he laughs. "Just think about it."

I don't know if all the self-control in the world could stop me from tiptoeing down the hall to his room. (Their room.) I agree to think about it, likely won't be able to think about anything else. He starts the engine and tells me he can't wait. I slug him and giggle that I only said maybe.

When we're close to home, Ryan asks if I would rather get out at the end of the street. I know I shouldn't risk being caught, although a big part of me doesn't want to admit I've done anything wrong. Like a rebellious teenager, I answer no, out front is fine. We pull up, and Mary is on her porch, rocking on a rattan chair, drinking something in a mug, all alone as always. When I get out, I don't hide; I don't pretend or offer any excuses. I just yell a polite hello. I cross in front of the car, lean into Ryan's window and enjoy another longing exchange, looking deep into the eyes that see me for who I am—I think.

Audrey goes home a couple of days later, and I hope that the good memories outweigh the awkwardness. The day before we spent the afternoon at Laguna Beach, lying on matching towels we bought from one of those tacky, nonsensically expensive souvenir shops. We watched teenage boys play volleyball and joked that they don't grow that way in Ontario, with their shaggy blond hair and bronzed bodies. The boys we grew up with hid under oversized t-shirts and baggy jeans, their white skin never making a mid-winter appearance. It was nice to just talk as the sound of the tide crushing against defenseless sand made it easier to tune out Audrey as she recalled happy memories of Trevor and me.

When I dropped her off at the airport, I couldn't help feeling like I was saying goodbye to the last part of my good sense, my old self. Farewell, Audrey. Farewell, Jane. She hugged me tighter than she ever has and told me she really hopes I can get through this phase without any permanent damage. I promised to call more and then watched her walk away with a confident stride I didn't inherit, stealing stares from men and women alike, her blond hair falling on her sun-kissed back, looking like a California girl off on a business trip.

The house is silent when I get home. No signs of Audrey, not her shoes at the front door, or her files scattered across an otherwise useless dining table. As if trying to hold onto her, and out of the purest form of boredom, I tidy her abandoned room. As I change the bedding, I can smell her on the sheets like a bouquet of flowers. Likely Chanel, but to me it's Audrey. I take long inhalations and know she's the one constant I'll always have; my one true love. And so I try not to feel sad as I throw the sheets into the washer, not to worry I won't smell her again soon.

Trevor gets home unpredictably early, around five. I peek down over the banister and see he is still in his scrubs, which suggest he hurried home or he's soon going back. Either way, I've stopped factoring him into my days, my plans. Audrey and Ryan have significantly cut into my regularly scheduled loneliness this week, so a night alone wouldn't have been the worst thing.

Regardless, I go downstairs to greet him, slower than usual, feeling hesitant but obligated. From a distance, I watch him in the foyer as he tosses his bag and then strips off his scrubs, first his shirt and then his pants. By the time I take the final step, he's standing there in boxer briefs, possibly in even better shape than he was this summer. It dawns on me that I rarely see him work out other than an occasional run. To maintain his perfectly toned physique, he must have a gym membership somewhere, somewhere out there where he lives his life without me.

As I get closer to him I realize he is shaking, his hands visibly trembling. I can't stop myself from running to him, throwing my hands around his neck and burying my head against his bare chest. His heart is racing, and then I feel it, wet and warm on my cheek. I can't remember a time I've ever seen him so vulnerable. I reach up to touch his face and wipe away a lone tear.

"What's going on, babe?" I ask in a careful, gentle voice.

He peels my hands off him, steps away from me before answering and for a second I think he knows.

Finally, he says, "I lost someone. I lost a patient today."

"I'm so sorry, Trevor. Was it a child?"

"No," he says, and pauses, shaking his head as if he's still trying to figure out what happened. "It was a woman. A thirty-five-year-old mom."

I don't respond right away, because I know he's trying to get it out. I take a seat on the bottom step and look up intently to let him know I'm still listening.

"I stupidly told her husband—I promised him—she would be okay…"

"You couldn't have known."

"Exactly. But I was so sure, so cocky. I still don't understand why, or how. She was in perfect shape." He trails off after giving me a slew of reasons why she should have pulled through, some of which I understand, most of which I don't. There is nothing I can say to make him feel better, but I do assure him that he is the most careful, thorough person I know and that it was out of his hands. Although I'm not religious and it almost sounds trite, I say it was God's plan. He tries to smile at me and says he knows he did everything right, but that it wasn't enough.

"Maybe if I had more experience…. When I told him, her husband, he didn't believe me. I had to say it over and over. He finally just collapsed, dropped to his knees. I couldn't imagine losing you like that, Ellen."

He sits beside me and wraps one arm around my waist. Uncharacteristically, he rests his troubled head on my shoulder.

"I'm so sorry you had to go through that," I say. I know now I have to tell Ryan there will be no Thanksgiving, no more private picnics, at least not until Trevor decides to tell me he's in love with someone else. If there is any hope at all for this marriage, I don't want to be the one that ruins it.

As if he reads my mind, Trevor stands abruptly and says he has to shower. First, he collects his scrubs and angrily tosses them in the kitchen garbage, slamming the door.

A few minutes later, I'm still sitting on the step when Trevor yells down, "You want to grab dinner somewhere?"

I hadn't even considered he might be staying. I certainly hadn't planned on a date, my second of the day. I feel nervous and even more hesitant than when Ryan asked. I can't let too much time pass before I answer, but my mind is scrambling. I call back, "Sure." There is something different about Trevor lately, especially tonight. I see something in him that isn't perfect, and I think he sees it too. For the first time in a long while, I wonder if there might be room for me in his life after all.

Twenty minutes later, as I dig my flip-flops out of a deplorably messy front closet, Trevor names off a bunch of restaurant possibilities. "True Foods, Sushi Ruko, Sharky's..." I stay quiet except for a few whispered curse words as I fight with shoes and needless hats and scarves. Just as I locate my missing flop, Trevor asks, "How about Maestros?" I've only driven past it, but I know my outfit isn't going to work. When he adds how much he likes it there, I throw my shoe back in the mess and head to my room to change. I wonder if he has any idea what he just said. I don't give him the satisfaction of asking when he went or who he went with; I just unbutton my false-hearted jean shorts and let them fall to the ground.

I blew my hair dry this morning, so I just slip into a simple black dress and some unassuming wedges and throw on a little mascara. Strangely, when I stand in front of the mirror to see if I look good enough, I can't recall what Trevor is wearing.

Is it possible that I didn't look at him once after he came down? I remember hearing the water turn off, the sound of his elephant steps on the stairs and finally his voice, but not one time did I look in his direction. We've gotten so comfortable in this funk of being cold to each other, I naturally ignored him the way I had willed myself to do all summer. Sadly, I doubt he even noticed, but had he, what must he think of me? What percentage of our failing marriage is my fault?

Guilt-ridden, I will myself to look at him straight away. As I turn the corner, I hear his voice and my stubborn eyes follow. Standing at the island finalizing what sounds to be a reservation, he's hunched over on his elbows talking into the speakerphone like it has a face. Apparently, one he would rather look at than mine, because he doesn't shift his gaze in my direction when he hears me enter the kitchen. Even from here, his dark hair shows a subtle speckle of grey around his sideburns, which is as becoming on him as it would be horrible on me. He wears belted black dress pants below a simple grey golf shirt, his long legs aligning his hips with the granite counter. He suits this place: he's fancy even when considering Five Guys' burgers and fries. This well-dressed man is almost a complete opposite to this woman, who until minutes ago was Coachella to his country club.

"All set?" he asks, as he looks over to me for the first time, no look of love registering on his vacant face, no compliments offered.

"Yep, this okay?" I ask, seeking attention or pathetic approval of my boring dress.

"Sure," he responds, which is basically, whatever.

The valet is equally perfunctory; he opens my door with a half-committed welcome before he quickly moves on to the car pulling in behind us.

The hostess greets Trevor as if she knows him, smiling and whispering to the seater-greeter who then motions us to follow her without confirming our name. Still, I bite my tongue and refuse to play out the jealous wife scene. He pretentiously stands back and gestures for me to go first with a Prince Charming bow. Nevertheless, I oblige and follow her through the restaurant as if it's our first date and I'm dutifully impressed and keeping my lucky mouth shut.

As we make our way through a room full of striking people, I beg my mind to stop with the self-conscious thoughts that surely reveal themselves through my timid walk. I wish I had spoken up and opted for True Foods, where I'd fit in makeup-free and braless.

Fortunately, we are seated on the patio along the window instead of in the center of the room. After our escort leaves, it's just us. Seated directly across from each other, leaving us no choice but to lock our impressive blues and basic browns.

"Knock-knock," Trevor says, breaking the silence just before it becomes awkward.

"What?" I say, taken aback.

"Knock-knock," he repeats.

"Who's there?"

"Juno," he answers, with a proud grin.

"Juno, who?"

"Juno I love you, right?"

Despite my emotional lockdown, I am unable to contain a girlish giggle as I melt. I want to answer that I do know. I don't want to spoil this moment like so many moments, compliments and romantic gestures in the past. But—does he love me? Women who remain silent and accept infidelity in exchange for sporadic kindness and shiny things have always baffled me. But right now, I get it. All I want is to smile and accept the familiar hand that bears a matching wedding band as he slides it across the table to me.

I'm scared though, scared I will fall apart with his touch. It is easier to be angry and vengeful than it is to be sad, or worse, pitiable. To save face, both publicly and personally, I give him a slight nod, a contrived smile that I hope seems genuine, and take his hand.

The waiter, a young man with a stylish faux hawk, returns to the table with wine and Trevor orders for us, which I'm fine with. He's more comfortable than I am in these types of environments. He can professionally order items I can barely read, plus he knows what I like. I try to sit up taller to fill up my side of the table, to justify my date, who essentially fills the whole room with his charm and effortless grandeur. As he speaks, his pronunciation of carpaccio and charcuterie is flawless, while his crystal-blue eyes, eyes that make him look more angel than adulterer, don't falter.

Before he leaves the table, the waiter gives me a polite acknowledgment and then as if it's my birthday and all stars have aligned, pauses and says, "Oh, hey, Ellen!" I'm momentarily baffled, but without missing a beat, I return the welcome greeting with, "Nice to see you!" My mind races, trying to place this gem who just gave me the best and most needed boost of confidence.

"Who was that?" Trevor asks, as our waiter walks away. I say the only thing I can, knowing how suspicious it sounds, especially had the scenario been reversed. "I have no idea." Even though Trevor is over it immediately, accepting my explanation with a sip of wine and a bite of his bread, I feel high. Suddenly all the beautiful and important people around me seem to be just wearing more make-up and nicer shoes.

The pianist starts a rendition of Zayn's *Pillowtalk,* and although I'm with my husband, trying, I start thinking about Ryan, how he makes me feel beautiful and worthy. Just the thought of him reassures me that I'm good enough, maybe even more than enough.

By my second glass of overpriced wine, I feel like the Ellen Trevor first met, the only Ellen Ryan knows. My shoulders and smiles are loose. The food, which I had expected to be blah, tastes amazing. I had half-expected this evening to be something I had to get through, but I'm enjoying myself. Maybe it's just the wine, but I feel happy.

As usual, Trevor tells me stories about work: dis-gruntled patients, Crystal and office drama. I listen, and with the aid of the music, his stories aren't com-pletely boring despite being very like stories I've heard many times before, about people I'll never meet. But when he says Ryan's name, I spring to full attention and then hope it's not as obvious as it feels. Just seconds be-fore, I sat casually in my chair listening with half-assed enthusiasm as I swished my wine around in sync with the piano keys, my eyes roving the room for something interesting. Now I'm upright, and my eyes are focused only on his mouth as he speaks of someone he doesn't know but thinks he does, someone I know but he thinks I don't. As he talks about Ryan, I listen with disguised aggression, like he's talking about something that's all mine—someone who is none of his business.

"I just don't get the guy," he says, as I force myself to try to appear uninterested. "He barely shows up. He's super selective with his patients, like one or two surger-ies a week at most."

"What's wrong with that?" I bark, then smile to minimize the damage.

"It's just strange. He's at the prime of his career. He's renowned, Ellen! And he acts like he's bored, always distracted. You know he hasn't even spoken to me in like, days?"

"There are more important things than work, Trevor. It's a job after all."

"You wouldn't understand. You're not a surgeon. It's addictive; you start to need it…"

I nod my head to be agreeable, but inside I can't help thinking: this is the real problem. Maybe I should thank Trevor's mistress for helping me see I will never be as important to him as his work. Not even close.

"Maybe he's focused on Alice right now?"

He leans in and whispers, even though a shout would barely be audible. "No chance. Between us, the word in the office is that he's a bit of a dirtbag."

"A dirtbag?" I repeat with indignation and raise my eyebrows. Dr. Pot calls Dr. Kettle…

"Yeah, he definitely gets around."

I fight to be expressionless, to be devoid of any reaction. Not positive, shocked, certainly not jealous. I say, "Well, good for him."

"What?!" Trevor's appalled expression is still beautiful as he leans back abruptly, as if my response repelled him.

"Good for him," I repeat. "It's none of our business."

Without letting him respond, I stand and excuse myself as our waiter returns to check in on us. From this vantage point, I recognize this thoughtful young man immediately— he makes my coffee nearly every morning.

"You keep yourself busy," I say to my loyal barista, fully aware that remembering him now makes me appear to be a liar. I touch his shoulder briefly before I leave them, hoping Trevor cares enough to wonder.

On my way to the washroom, I can't help but question if Trevor has any idea how much that two-minute conversation hurt me. When he pictures himself five years into the future, to where Ryan is today, he has no intention of allowing any distractions to come between him and his so-called addiction. He has no intention of making room for me or our future children. I was raised by a strong, intelligent woman to be more than the little Mrs., and I feel like I'm trapped in a nightmare. Despite my attempts to wake myself—wake up wake up wake up—this is my life. I'm Trevor's wife. Full stop. I'm a fool if I think I am any more to him than simply a person who fills a specific, defined role in his life. If not me, someone else.

I push open the bathroom door with an urgency like that final push to the surface of the pool before coming up for air. Once inside, a breath explodes from me and I gasp quietly. Unfortunately, I'm not alone. The bathroom counter is lined with women checking themselves out, washing their hands, careful not to let their outrageous diamond rings slip from their fingers. I lock myself into one of the stalls and finally feel like I can breathe.

Not even bothering to cover the toilet seat, I plunk down and try not to let a distinct dampness put me overboard as I cradle my face in my hands: my self-soothing at odds with the self-deprecating actions that brought me here. Is it possible I was too focused on achieving my own success as an editor to realize our marriage would be a failure? Not once, not even in the beginning, had I considered what life with Trevor in the absence of my own career would be like, celebrating his successes while mourning my failures. I wouldn't have thought any man would be able to fill the hole that being unemployed has left. And maybe no man can, but I'd like to think Ryan could be that filler, that compound.

After a few minutes, I pull myself together. As I reach for the door of the stall, the whispers of two women stop me in my tracks.

"That's for sure him," one says. "That's the doctor Julie was with last weekend."

"Really?" says the other. "He is so hot—those blue eyes!"

I can't hear whatever comes next, partly because they whisper even more quietly and partly because the sound of blood rushing through my furious veins drowns them out. Against my will, my hands start to shake, a neurological reaction that hits before I'm even consciously aware that they must be talking about Trevor.

A better person would open the door and confidently interrupt their conversation, at least to see the faces of the women who know such secrets.

But I am not like that. Instead I take the slightest peek under the door at their shoes. Two pairs of red soles. How original. I stay in my hiding place until I am sure they've left. I can't imagine facing them while facing myself in the mirror, knowing that if they saw Trevor they know he is with me.

My life has become a soap opera. I can't even say that I am too good or too sophisticated for such a role. I feel silly; ridiculous. I've been many things in my life so far, but this feeling is a first for me. It feels like a combination of middle-school bullied and pitiful; like the people here tonight are as Kurt Cobain said, stupid and contagious. A quick count to ten and I brave my way back to the table, keeping my head high despite the shame and grief that weigh me down.

As usual, I don't confront Trevor. As I approach the table, he gets up from his chair. A cheat in gentleman's clothing. The insincerity of his gesture makes me want to throw a glass of wine in his face or smash the tiny vase that holds two pink peonies on the floor. To storm out yelling, "You bastard!" To be the bold to his beautiful, to allow my life to be as dramatic as it is pathetic.

But, if nothing else, and although my behavior of late would suggest otherwise, I have pride, so I sit, replace the napkin on my lap and force a smile at my husband.

Fortunately, while I was gone Trevor received a page from the office, or more likely from his mistress. I couldn't have been gone more than ten minutes, but he's already paid the bill. He stands seconds after I sit, explaining the situation as he gathers his things. It could well be a medical emergency. Or perhaps he spotted the same woman who spotted him. I can hardly imagine him carrying on this dinner, this charade, with a potential whistle-blower next to us.

Still seated, I watch him move about: smiling, fidgeting with something in the barely functional pockets of his overly fitted pants, playing it patient while silently rushing me.

I deliberately take my time, placing the napkin on the table, folding it neatly, and then slowly put my phone into my bag. I stand and then sit back down again to adjust a pretend annoyance in my shoe. I can feel his frustration with me as I look around the restaurant and comment on the ambience, daring him to say something. I don't know that we've ever played games in our relationship, but if he forces me to play I intend to win.

In the car he's finally relaxed, his shoulders settled back into their regular position, now in control of how fast or slow I move.

"Will you be okay tonight?" he asks, as if this is my first night alone.

"Sure will," I respond, my gaze steady out the window, my thoughts moving onto Ryan.

I feel hurt, humiliated and enraged and yet I don't really know if I'm any less guilty than Trevor. The truth is, what Ryan and I have done isn't entirely unforgivable. I can still say no to the direct "Did you sleep with him?!" question, which is more than Trevor can say. But is hopelessly wanting to be with someone else, fantasizing about him constantly and nearly sleeping with him not a worse betrayal than a one-night stand or a purely sexual affair?

Are we really any better than the thoughts in our heads? I think therefore I am, right? My thoughts make me human and determine what type of human I am.

Right now, I guess I'm the type who is sick of living in my head, living my life in fragments instead of all-in.

And so, I tell Trevor the first real lie I've ever told him.

"I'm thinking about taking a trip this weekend with Annie." I spit out the words without a plan, forcing myself to think on my feet.

"Oh yeah?" he asks, keeping his eyes on the winding road.

"Well, it's a holiday and it would be depressing to spend it alone," I say. "I assume you'll be working?"

"Ellen, we're not even American. You can't tell me you're that upset about not celebrating American Thanksgiving together."

"Well, you worked Canadian Thanksgiving, too, Trevor. It's just another weekend other people are with their families and I'm alone."

"Whatever. I think it's great. Where?"

"Ummm, Vancouver?" I answer, unsure.

"Vancouver! Why? It's raining there. Just have Annie come here. She'll love it. Stay at the beach."

Obviously, this is a good idea, but the fact that he just shoots down my plan like it's stupid infuriates me.

"Because I need to get the fuck out of here, that's why!"

"Woah! Settle down!"

"Sorry." I fake settle. "I just need some space."

He turns the radio down and says, "From me?" His voice sounds curious, a mix of sadness and eagerness, like he is hoping I will say yes and initiate a weighty conversation.

"From California."

He takes the longest pause ever. "Well, let me know if you need my help with anything."

26

Ignoring the three-hour time difference, I dial Annie's number as soon as Trevor's headlights disappear from the cul-de-sac that anchors our street. It's been at least a few weeks since I've heard her evenly pitched voice, but I'm hopeful we've at least exchanged a few texts. Because I've erased my phone's entire history for obvious reasons, I can't be certain. I just pray it hasn't been longer than a month. What is wrong with me? It's as if I'm punishing myself for being lonely by distancing myself from even the people who are there for me, who have always been there for me.

As the phone rings, my anxiety builds. I'm uneasy, wondering if she resents my neglect.

I will immediately hear it in her voice, as Annie has never been the type to mince words. She follows more of a guy-logic when it comes to fighting. Knock him out and get over it, no grudges or drama. This is something I've always respected about her. If she's angry, I will apologize and take my lumps. Once she hears there is trouble in paradise, I doubt she will be able to resist hearing all the gory details.

She picks up on the third ring. The way she says my name, with shock and worry, serves as a cold reminder that I've been a lousy friend and an even worse BFF.

"Annie!" I say cheerfully to end the suspense. "Were you asleep?"

"Ummm, no! It's barely ten-thirty. Are you okay?"

"Yes, totally. I just miss you. What are you doing?" I ask. I play it cool and kick my wedges off against the back of the closet before I move into the living room and settle onto the couch, suddenly excited to catch up.

"I'm great, actually. Chris is here," she says, sounding happy. This is good news. Chris is her on-again, off-again boyfriend, the man she goes back to after she is disappointed by someone more successful and better looking—and entirely more douchey. He also happens to be perfect for her. Without being too general, he's kind, has a good sense of humor without being obnoxious, and he's just slightly less attractive than she is. According to Annie, his one flaw is that he is an elementary school teacher, the least sexy job for a man in her view. But I can think of many worse professions. Cheating surgeon, for one.

Annie does exceptionally well for herself in the advertising world. She works for a successful company, heading a small team under her multi-millionaire boss, who she's managed not to sleep with despite many advances and opportunities, including a highly inappropriate business trip to NYC where they shared a two-bedroom suite.

"How is he? Tell him I say, hi!"

"I will," she obliges, and as I hear her pass on the greeting, I realize he is right there. "He says hi back!" Which I know, because I heard him as if he was speaking directly into the phone. "Can I call you tomorrow?" she asks.

After what Trevor pulled with Audrey, I'm not sure I can take a chance on him not reaching out to Annie. As much as I don't want to blow my "simply checking-in" guise—because I do thoroughly miss her—I have no choice now but to spill.

I say it fast and hope that Chris is enough of a distraction to stop her from asking questions. "Of course. But Annie, if you talk to Trevor at all, could you tell him we're spending this weekend together?"

No such luck. I hear her fumbling, and she whispers to Chris; she's clearly left the room, and I'm in trouble.

Out of the two of us, Annie has always been the more confident and outgoing, by far. She would never force me to enter a room first. She leads and I follow behind like one of her accessories, not some costume jewelry from Claire's, but like her prized possession. She is as careful with me as she is her Cartier Love

Bracelet. I always felt safe going out with Annie, like I was attached to her, sharing her confidence. Though she got most of the attention, I never felt unimportant, because I knew I was important to her. It wasn't until Trevor and I were married that I realized Annie depended on me as much as I depended on her. Of course, she would never admit it to me, but according to Audrey, Annie had even once drunkenly confessed that she didn't enjoy going out anymore, that she felt lonely and a bit lost. She disappeared for a while after our wedding. As much as she was happy for us, Annie was more comfortable doing things first.

After the initial sting, I willed myself not to take it personally and hoped that she would come around, and she eventually did. I guess this was my turn to disappear, but I'm back, and once again, I need Annie.

When she's settled with a glass of red and her Hermès blanket, likely seated with her long, impossibly flexible legs crossed twice like a pretzel, she sighs and orders, "Talk!"

And I do.

The story comes out of my mouth with startling honesty and few pauses for air. Annie is family; I don't fear any judgement from her, but I'm curious what her response will be. She's always been wary of Trevor, not worried about his fidelity but more so of his love affair with himself and his grand plans. When I've said all I can say, confessed and backpedaled, explained and justified, I ask again, "So, will you?"

"Will I what?" she asks, confused, stunned.

"Will you tell Trevor that we're spending the weekend together?"

"Holy shit, Ellen! Is this a joke?"

"Seems that way, doesn't it? Maybe the kind of joke that will be funny in ten years, but right now I'm dead serious."

She's giddy, possibly from the wine. Not surprisingly, she has my back and promises to be there for me when this all comes apart. She doesn't offer much advice, as she's never been married or, unexpectedly, unfaithful either.

I don't know if my confession makes me feel better or worse. On one hand, it's a bit thrilling that predictable, good Ellen has wavered. On the other, I feel a sick pit in my stomach as Annie and I basically laugh behind Trevor's back.

When we hang up, I immediately begin to text Ryan, to tell him I'm in, that I've decided to sneak away with him to hide out in his beach house like we're in some romantic movie.

But before my fingers have completed a solitary word I drop the phone like it bit me. As reassuring as it was to talk to Annie, I suddenly feel dizzy, like I've just woken up from a coma and the last three and a half months are a blur. I do know how I got here: negative thoughts, doubts about things both real and imagined and days spent living in my mind. Right now, I feel like I've gone from A to B without really paying attention. It seems impossible that this could be happening to me. The way I felt in that stall at the restaurant, invisible and insignificant; I could never have predicted that. Despite being outwardly average, when I was growing up I always felt like I was destined to be special. Maybe every little girl feels that way, but it was like I had a secret superpower of sorts, like when squirrels and chipmunks ate only from my hand and the way I could will snow days with my strong connection to Mother Nature. You're welcome!

Most (all) of these things went unnoticed by everyone else; but just after turning eleven I won a student writing contest with my short story about my perceived telepathy. The prize was a trip to Montreal, Quebec: it was the greatest and scariest thing that ever happened to me. On the bus ride there, a boy from a neighboring school with wavy brown hair and thick glasses asked me when my birthday was. He then added all the numbers together and told me that eleven was my life number, and it has meant something to me ever since. I planned to graduate university by twenty-two (check), and at thirty-three, something special was in the cards. Which means I have less than one year to get my life back on track.

If I'm honest, I have a history of selling myself short, chickening out. My inhibitions held me back even as a child, like when I won a coloring contest at Shoppers Drug Mart but was too shy to claim my prize because of the skill-testing question, and compulsively skipped recitals, field trips and birthday parties regardless of how much fun I knew I was missing. I'm not interested in turning thirty-three, or forty-four, with a bunch of adult regrets to go along with my childhood ones.

In my case, regret is complicated and could undeniably go either way. I've spent my entire adult life loving Trevor, thirteen years. And in five months I have convinced myself that our love is a sham. Now, throw in Ryan, the ultimate temptation. Would I regret ending a relationship with my husband, my planned life partner? Or will I regret passing up on passion and a connection that I've never felt with Trevor?

Divorce.

It's an ugly word, and although we don't have children it's still a failure, associated with a generation of irresponsible people.

If I text Ryan to confirm our Thanksgiving, I'm setting the demise of my marriage in motion.

I never predicted this: this bitter woman, this failed marriage, these sordid affairs and lying games.

It's only nine o'clock, but I'm exhausted, tired of thinking, tired of feeling both guilty and betrayed. As if I'm the most depressed woman who ever lived, I roll my body from the couch, crawl over to the chair and snatch the generic blanket thrown over the arm, then slowly crawl back to the couch and climb back up one heavy limb at a time. I hold my body tight and tuck myself in under the blanket, fully prepared to spend the night here. I'm not particularly tired in the sleepy sense, but my mind is so full of intertwined thoughts, I can no longer isolate a single one.

27

Dreams come fast and seem to last all night. In the one I have right before I wake up, I open my eyes and the room looks the same, quiet and empty. But something is wrong. I'm overcome with dread and nausea. Seconds later I'm transported, the way you are in dreams, into a washroom where I am throwing up. My breasts are sore, my belly swollen, and I realize I'm pregnant. I stand and look in the mirror. Nothing in my face has changed, yet everything is different.

Ryan is no longer an option. Tiny cracks appear in my skin, not like wrinkles, but as if my face is breaking. As I look closer, the cracks extend; my face shatters, and then even the mirror falls away into pieces. I wake up shaking and panicked. I whip the blanket away and my hands find their way to my stomach and linger there. I'm relieved, but then I do the math in my head.

Fuck.

I have not had one pregnancy scare in my entire life. Audrey and Annie, hell, even my own mother, have had them. Not me. I am regular, responsible and, at the moment, not sexually active. I pray to God this is just my first scare—that I will be given a pass.

As in the dream, my first instinct is to run to the washroom. I lift my t-shirt over my head and toss it on the ground as if I'm trying to strip myself of the dream and this possibility. "No, no, no," is on repeat; I mutter it over and over. I sit on the toilet wearing only my bra, rocking back and forth like a crazy person, trying to process this nightmare.

According to my frantic calculations, I am at least three weeks late. I cup my breasts in my hands, squeeze them firmly and then pinch my nipples. "Oooooowww," I cry, followed by another stream of no's. Without even wiping, I pull my underwear up and sprint up the stairs. In my room, I walk around in circles for a minute before I jump into the shower. It could be in my head, but even the California-conservative water pressure hurts my breasts. Turning my back to the assault, I place one protective arm over them and one hand over my mouth, fixated on the water running down the glass like it's crying.

After I barely dry off, I throw on some clothes, grab my wallet and head to the car. I'm already mourning Ryan, and I feel like the most irresponsible mother ever, likely having already fucked up my child. As if

I got here on autopilot, I get out of the car with no memory of the drive. I can only hope I didn't just commit a hit and run to go along with poisoning my kid with alcohol, unprocessed cheeses and nitrates, while starving it of nutrition and folic acid and whatever else good mothers know about and I do not.

I move through the aisles without any Canadian charm, not smiling or apologizing to anyone. When I get where I need to be, I find the shelf is full of a variety of pregnancy tests, all claiming to do the same thing described slightly differently. After debating and then refusing to be overwhelmed by their advertising, I go with the most expensive, the most sensitive, and even an ovulation one. If their claims of pregnancy detection even before a missed period are accurate, three different tests should give me a definitive answer at three weeks late. If only they were guaranteed to give me the answer that I want.

I do not want a baby. For the first time in years, I do not want a baby.

Once at home, I tear through the packages like a desperate animal and then line the tests up on the counter.

Ryan called twice this morning. I can't bring myself to answer. In a twisted way, I feel like I've cheated on him, cheated us of possibility.

I stand at the counter staring down at the tests, urging myself to stay calm and hopeful. Finally, I grab them in one handful and make my way over to the toilet in a death march. I squat and hold the wand under a dutiful flow of urine that I worry is either too strong or too diluted, too much or not enough. I replace the lid to the first and then complete the last two with trembling legs and a straining stream that seems to get more on my fingers than on the tests.

I wash my hands while I count to sixty in my head. I feel guilty about the wasted water siphoning down the drain, along with everything else. Another sixty seconds until these pee-soaked sticks reveal my fate. In my head, I've concluded the worst; I swear I can already feel my breasts growing and little flutters in my stomach that can only be tiny baby kicks.

Fuck it. I shake the nerves out of my hand and pick up the first test with confidence that borders on aggression. One line. Could be too early. Moments later, the second and third also reveal only one solid red line, no double lines or visible crosses. Even when I shake them, hold it close to my eyes and wait another few minutes, they're still negative. My uterus is as empty as my life.

Thank God.

In a state that can only be described as jubilant, triumphant and ecstatic, I skip down the stairs and find my phone where I stashed it, buried beneath the throw pillows on the couch. Even though he's surely at work, possibly standing next to my husband, I text Ryan immediately, hoping he was smart enough to store my name under some alias, maybe something like Elle, or Cindy, and tell him I'm in.

I don't let myself dwell on why I was so traumatized by the close call and what that means for my marriage, for my future with Trevor. Rather, I am happy to blame diet change, exercise and stress as the culprit, and move past the whole scenario, burying the tests deep into the garbage bin outside like it never happened.

More than ever, I am convinced I am making the right decision, even if ultimately it is wrong. The idea of having a baby with Trevor, forever sealing the signatures on our marriage certificate, is far more consequential than spending the weekend with a would-be lover who I would otherwise spend my life fantasizing about, wondering what could have been had I taken a chance.

So here I am, only a few hours before I'm supposed to be at Ryan's. I don't fret over packing, not the way you do when you're going away with your girlfriends, matching shoes to outfits and handbag hardware to jewelry, or the way you pack for a trip with your boyfriend, sexy dresses and romantic nighties. I simply pack cozy, loose-fitting pants and basic t-shirts, sets of white and black panties and bras (girl next door this time, not escort), minimal makeup and my ever-present jean shorts.

Trevor doesn't ask me for any specifics about my airline and hotel details, the way a somewhat interested partner would, so I don't offer any information.

As a result, I feel less deceptive.

28

It's difficult to say if it's my excitement to see Ryan or the lingering burn of listening to strange women gossip about my husband while I hide that is overwhelming my guilt. But when I lock the front door behind me and get in the Uber, supposedly on my way to the airport, I feel nothing as I drop my keys into my handbag.

Instinct. Survival. Justified.

As much as I love this Dutch door with its promise of neighbors within reach and children watched over lovingly, safe in the yard, it provided none of those things for us. Now it only promises that there is still a way out.

I handle the drive over with the same don't-turn-back approach. Except for a text to Ryan to let him know I'm on my way, I don't look at my phone with its photo of Trevor and me on my parent's front porch.

Instead, I focus on the road or look out the window at all the other people in cars, on their bikes or jogging by with headphones and flushed faces. I wonder where they're going, who they're going home to or getting fit for. I'm not judging or envying, just simply observing, and I realize I'm seeing the streets Newport Beach with a renewed and sunnier outlook on life. For the first time in a long time, I'm looking forward to something, and everything else feels different.

His street is just ahead, less than a couple blocks away. The car seems to slow, and I start to fidget and hold my breath, thinking about Ryan, pushing thoughts of Trevor away. I can hear an imaginary soundtrack in my head, the type of melody that accompanies romantic movies; violins, cellos and piano notes soar as the intensity builds. But this isn't a Nicholas Sparks-type scenario here. I'm not deciding between two great loves; not making a noble choice. What choice has Trevor given me?

The combination of the curvy road and the butterflies I'm feeling makes the final minutes of the drive feel like a rollercoaster. I'm excited, but I'm also scared to death. When I pull up in the Uber, Ryan is sitting on the curb outside of his house. He's lit up by the sun, now on its way down, his elbows resting on his knees. He's not killing time scrolling through his phone. He's waiting for me, and his face lights up when he sees the car. I hadn't expected this welcome and I'm overcome with relief, as I dreaded the awkwardness of knocking on his door.

He runs over to the car as it slows and opens my door immediately, as if not giving me the chance to change my mind.

"Hello there," he says, helping me out, giving me a half hug and taking a long inhale of my still wet hair. "You smell good."

"I showered. Hi," I whisper, leaning up to kiss him lightly on the cheek.

"Well, this is a good start."

He grabs my bag from the trunk and then shakes the driver's hand, a kind gesture that isn't lost on me. I follow him hesitantly, not sure what to expect or what he expects will happen when we close the large steel front door behind us. A moment of awkwardness builds as I stand there, not sure if I should follow him or wait for an invitation. Happily, it's quickly deflated when he initiates some small talk: "So how about those Ducks?" he asks, referring to the local hockey team in an attempt to appeal to my Canadian interests.

Then he says he made us tea. Tea? Right now, nothing sounds more perfect than tea. His easy charm plus the coziness of my hands wrapped around a hot mug are completely unsuited to this cold, stark house. Just as me being here in the first place is more suited to wine or shots of Patron. Some of my most cherished memories of my marriage were our shared early evening teas, usually accompanied by movies or whatever show we were into, which baffled Audrey as she and Mark rarely waste their alone time on TV.

Ryan wraps a blanket around my shoulders, picks up our mugs and leads me out onto the back patio to talk and enjoy each other, the ocean the only distraction. He makes it feel effortless. To be fair to Trevor (as ridiculous as that sounds), Ryan and I are still in the honeymoon period, still finding everything about each other sexy and mysterious. If I listen carefully, I can hear my sister's warnings blowing by in the breeze: "Once the beginning ends, they all cut their toenails on the toilet with the door open."

For now, he is perfect. He's wearing loose-fitting cargos and a navy-blue, long-sleeve t-shirt, unbuttoned two buttons from the top, and I find myself peeking at his chest hair the way men look down women's blouses. He's barely older than Trevor, but he has a ruggedness that makes me feel like I'm with a man, a man's man, an alpha minus the conceit. He helps me onto the lounge chair like I'm breakable, then drapes the blanket across my legs and drags a small table over for our tea. He's attentive in a way that might infuriate me if it were anyone else, but because he knows the turmoil in my heart I feel like he's protecting me, maybe even from himself.

Not long ago the four of us—Ryan, Alice, Trevor and I—sat in these same chairs. Unlike Gwyneth and Chris, we were unconsciously uncoupling, with two of us touching toes in the sand the way we are now. I'm aware of a fear that, with all this build-up and fore-play, starting months ago in a grocery store, whatever happens here tonight may end up being a huge let-down, like when men cheat and are disgusted and full of regret the moment they cum. But mostly my fear is that I'll want more. Sitting here watching him run his hands through his blond waves, chuckling at his own stories and cursing endearingly, makes me want to dump the tea and throw the blanket. I want to wrap myself around this man who makes me laugh and light up, who makes being abandoned by my husband less heartbreaking and more convenient.

"Where are you?" he asks, breaking my trance. I've been so caught up in analyzing his every move; I'm hypnotized by the way his mouth forms everyday words. Nervous and comparing, always comparing... now I haven't a clue what he's been talking about.

"I'm here. Sorry. Just a lot on my mind."

"Are you nervous?" he asks in a way that makes be-ing nervous completely okay. But I'm not nervous, at least not the way he thinks. I correct my slumped pos-ture and swing my legs over into the space between our lounge chairs and take my first sip of the tea, buy-ing myself some time.

After I've put down the cup, I smile at him and say, "No, I'm not nervous."

He follows my lead, sits up and places one knee in-between my legs and the other on the outside, lock-ing us together, our hands resting on our own legs but brushing against each other's. I know I want him, possibly in a way I've never wanted anyone. The simplest of touches makes me wish I was wearing a seatbelt to prevent me from coming on too strong, from propelling myself at him.

He, on the other hand, seems completely composed. He doesn't seem as intoxicated by my presence as I am by his. Perhaps he's just trying not to pressure me.

"I like having you here," he says, and then lifts slightly off his chair to kiss my cheek.

"I like being here," I reply.

I find myself wishing I had braided my hair as it blows and sticks against my face. Compared to Alice, I am small and plain—a petite girl with a lot of baggage. But for whatever reason, I feel beautiful around Ryan. Possibly because he seems so natural with me, never trying to impress me or feed me lines. It's just the opposite: he teases me and then laughs at me, and eventually, with me.

There is something more than salt in the air, something between the two of us that wasn't there before. It's a romantic feeling that goes along nicely with the scenery, but it's also tension. Sexual, but more innocent than lust. Like the nerves you feel on prom night when you and your guy have booked a hotel room, the anticipation that it will probably go down and everything else before that is just filler.

I try hard to concentrate on what he's saying, but all I can think about is which of us will initiate.

Finally, uncharacteristically, I cut him off mid-sentence, something about New York winters, and kiss him, quite bravely, on his neck. There is nothing cute about this kiss. It's all Annie and no Jane—I even throw my tongue in the mix, almost like I am going to give him a hickey. But it's not 1990, and so I move up to his jaw, with my hand placed close to his lap the whole time, holding me up and leaving no questions about my intentions.

I feel him stiffen underneath me and his mouth meets mine halfway. He slows it down a bit, then kisses me hard and gently bites my lower lip, forcing me to open my eyes. We stare at each other for a moment, his dark, lively eyes intimidating me more than what's about to happen. Then out of nowhere, like an animal, or better, Tarzan, he whisks me up and places me down on my back onto the lounge. He's over me, holding himself up in an effortless plank, kissing me like his survival depends on it, like he's dehydrated and I'm water. Any evidence of the composed man of just minutes ago has now completely disappeared.

We're kissing so passionately that for the first time in forever I'm out of my head. It's all body. Sure, we've kissed before, probably even this intensely, but with the addition of his body on mine, his knee now pressed up tight between my legs, I'm completely infatuated. My body responds in all the right ways, moves that are now instinctual, my hips rising, my hand gripping him over his cargos to feel him harden with my touch. His hand is up my t-shirt; completely ignoring my bra, he moves his fingers underneath and is all over my breasts, stretching my bra so much I can feel it lose shape, but I don't care. He kisses my neck and then shifts his body to put his mouth on my nipple over my shirt. I can feel the fabric wet from his saliva, and it's incredibly hot. He moves back to my mouth—his lips are full and moist, and he parts mine with a pressure that's neither too soft or too hard. I have never been kissed like this before.

Although the beach is empty and the dusty pink sky and cool breeze heighten sensations that are already potent, I'm aware of how exposed we are. It's inevitable that we have to stop, temporarily at least, but neither one of us want to move and extinguish what's happening between us or wake up sleeping thoughts.

"Do you want to go inside?" he finally asks, out of breath, smoothing my hair while he waits for my response.

I really don't. I don't want to walk into Alice's house like this, but I don't want to stop and we can't stay here.

"Okay," I say, looking up at him.

Brilliantly, he doesn't stop abruptly; he doesn't remove his knee right away, still putting sweet pressure on my body, keeping me engaged. He slowly retracts his hand from my shirt and then wraps my legs around his strong torso, runs his hands down my back, over my hips and then takes my backside in two firm handfuls. He lifts us both from the lounge chair and then carries me inside and through the house swiftly, effortlessly holding me close. He lowers me onto the bed in the spare room, my bed, and then takes off his shirt, revealing a fit, lean body, not terribly cut but incredibly sexy. He undoes the first couple of buttons on his pants and then positions himself on top of me, kissing me hard and placing his hand where his knee was. "I've wanted to do this since the first time I saw you," he whispers into my ear.

I swallow hard and admit, "Me too," and then shimmy out of his embrace to remove my shirt and my bra. He looks me over, but I'm not self-conscious. I've always loved my breasts despite their size.

"You're so fucking sexy," he says, burying his face into my now naked chest. He leaves a trail of kisses on my stomach before he pulls off my jeans and throws them on the floor.

He leaves my underwear on, but his hand returns to its resting place between my legs as he makes his way back up to me.

"How far do you want to go?" he asks, pulsing his finger and kissing my cheek. The directness of his question catches me off guard. It's not as bad as if he'd asked something like, "What do you like?" but I don't know how to answer...I'd just assumed we'd go all the way. His fingers toy with me, and I know he can feel how wet I am.

We're certainly old enough, so I ask, "Do you have a condom?"

"I do," he says, and then reverses off me in slow motion to remove his jeans. I'm lying there naked except for my thin white panties, watching him as he looks down at me. I really want this, him, and not just his body. If things were different, I know I would love him already, but things aren't different. I feel my heart start to race in a way that is different than before, more fear than excitement. I wish he would just do it quickly and get it over with before I freak out, but at the same time I can't stop worrying about his penis, what it will feel like in my hand, in my body.

It's been a long time since I've touched a penis that wasn't Trevor's.

Ryan is on top of me again, still in his bright blue boxer briefs, and I feel better now. The weight of his body seems to compress my organs, and my heart and lungs are forced to relax. But for the first time, we seem off-kilter: he seems more urgent; I'm more tentative. I'm kissing him back, imitating his movements, breathing heavily, trying to get back to where I was, when he stops.

He somehow knows, senses something is up, which makes me think a woman could never fake it with him and get away with it. He kisses me softly and then playfully swings his body around to pull me on top of him. He runs his hands up my legs, which are now on either side of him, and it's clear we're going to have a talk. He's shaking a bit, which I find adorable. I can still feel him underneath me and know how aroused he is, yet he's so considerate I almost try to lie.

"What's going on in there?" he asks, pressing his thumb gently on my forehead before dropping his hands straight to his sides, not touching me, attempting to calm himself.

"I think I freaked myself out," I say honestly, comfortable enough to not cover my breasts.

"Look, Ellen…we don't have to do this."

"I know, Ry. But I want to. I know I do. I just started thinking…"

"About?"

"Ummm… your penis," I admit and then nod my head, like, "you asked."

He laughs. "Oh yeah? That freaked you out?"

"I think it did," I say, embarrassed, not wanting to explain.

"You're lovely. Okay, what about my penis worries you?"

I start laughing and climb off his lap, flopping down on the bed beside him.

"I can't explain it."

"You're not a virgin, are you?" he teases. "It's been a while since I've been with one of those."

"Ha. Ha. No, I'm not a virgin, it's just…"

"I know you said you haven't done it lately. But…?"

I throw a pillow at him and let out an exaggerated sigh. "It's hard to explain."

"Well, would you like an introduction?" He peeks into his underwear. "Strictly business?" He rolls onto his side. "But you'll have to say something sexy. He's a grower, not a show-er."

"Oh, my God, Ryan!" I laugh. "Okay, let's have a look at the little fella," I joke, pretending to inspect him.

"Wait a second here, calling him little isn't going to help! Besides, I was actually feeling nervous about your vagina."

"You were not!"

"No, seriously. I might need an introduction myself," he says, jumping on top of me as I giggle, "No way," and pretend to push him off.

He hops off the bed and picks up his crumpled cargos. "I know exactly what we need," he says, going through his pockets. He pulls out a clear baggy that appears to hold a couple of small joints and waves it in the air, exactly the way my school friends used to.

"Is that weed?" I say, springing up.

"Yep!"

"But you're a doctor!" He jumps back onto the bed beside me.

"Wow, Ellen, Trevor's a bigger nerd than I thought. It's pot, not cocaine. Plus, this is medicinal!"

"Ahhhh!" I clap my hands excitedly. "I haven't smoked weed since I was twenty years old!"

"Not me," he says with a laugh. "I do it all the time."

"No, you don't!"

"Okay, so I haven't since I was maybe thirty."

"How old are you, anyway? I think I should know, since we've been naked together…"

"Almost naked," he corrects.

"Okay, almost naked," I repeat.

"I'm fifty-two."

"Shut-up, you are not!"

"I'm thirty-eight, almost thirty-nine," he admits and then gives me an eeeek face.

"You're not old. Plus, you're like super immature."

"But super hot, too, right?"

Not long after, we're outside again, ready to ignite a different kind of flame. He insisted I wear his Rochester shirt and this time I didn't object, just pulled the blue t-shirt over my head and relished every second of feeling like his girlfriend. It's cool outside now; the breeze has turned into wind and so we huddle around the lighter as we attempt to light a twig-like joint, a pinner as we would've called it back when. We're both giggly, laughing as the lighter fails over and over. When the tip finally turns red, I watch him take a long breath in and hold it almost like he's swallowing, the defenseless paper shriveling away, shorter and shorter. He passes it to me and I am transported back to my teen years, hoping I don't do it wrong, feeling guilty like I'm about to get busted. I bring it to my lips, inhale for as long as I can and then cough, spitting the smoke out like an amateur. We carry on like this until I can feel the heat of the flame on my fingertips. As is always the case when you smoke pot, it doesn't hit us right away, so we mistakenly light up another, smoke it halfway and then realize we're both inordinately high.

It doesn't matter that we're adult, married, educated people; in this state, we are happy-go-lucky free spirits. After determining that I am unable to sit still, mind-blown by stars that seem to be gaining on us, getting closer and closer, the sand and sky working together to crush us between them, I jump up and tear off his t-shirt like I'm high on ecstasy rather than marijuana. I dance through the sand toward an ocean that roars into shore as if it is running away from itself.

The cold air on my body is shocking, my nipples hard as rocks and my breasts chilled as they bounce heavily with each step, a sensation I've never really felt before, not even when I run down stairs. Every feeling is intensified. When I twirl in a circle with my arms out, my fingers stretched wide, I can feel the wind pass through them like I'm a turbine, somehow creating energy. At the edge of the shore, the freezing water bullies me, pushing me out and then tugging me back in, a movement that nonsensically angers me, especially when I am tackled and thrown lightly onto the sand.

"What the hell?" I yell. Ryan is behind me, holding me in a bear hug. "Let me go!" I shout, fighting him off.

"You could have drowned," he yells over the roar of the waves, loosening his grip as I wiggle away before realizing I was in further than I thought, my white panties now transparent.

"Shit," I say, straight-faced, and then start howling with laughter. "Why are you dressed?"

"Why are you naked?"

"Good question!" I answer, looking myself over, full of intoxicated pride, before rolling into the cold sand and applying it all over my body like sunscreen. "I thought sand was always hot. It's freezing. It's like a freezing exfoliator. Feel me," I say, rubbing up against him. "I'm like human sandpaper."

"Ouch. You're ripping my skin off!"

"But you like it, right?"

"Ummm, not particularly. I'd like it a lot more if we took this inside and you weren't all scratchy."

"How come you're not as high as I am?" I slump back and cross my arms.

"Oh, I am. Your boobs look like eyes; they keep staring at me."

"Well, stop looking at them!"

"Can't! They're following me around. See?" He sways his body side to side, his freaked-out eyes locked on my chest.

When he stops, he admits he was kidding, that he isn't that high. He says we should go in, that I'm going to get sick. But I don't want to hear reason.

"Now might be a good time for that introduction," I say with a wink. "Especially because you can see what I'm packing," I say, pointing at my soaked panties.

"Ha. Didn't know this was a wet underwear contest. This is not the right time for that. I'm cold, and you're so high it would scare you."

"Chicken."

I stand and walk toward the house. I can feel sprays of sand on my calves, so I know he's following me. I'm starting to come down, and my thoughts become clearer and start to race. Walking in sand is never easy, but right now each footstep is laborious, my feet sliding away from me with every push off. I stop and hold my hands up like a child. "I can't walk anymore!"

"We're only a few steps away," he complains as he scoops me up, his strong arms under my arms and legs like he's about to carry me over a threshold.

"Ryan," I say, looking up at him through squinted eyes, "what if Trevor isn't cheating on me? What if I'm the bad guy?"

"Is that what's really freaking you out?"

"Maybe."

"If he wasn't, would you be here right now?"

"I don't know. I know I'd want to be."

"And if he was, would you let me put my penis in you?" He laughs and raises his brows.

"Yes, if I knew he was for sure, I'd let you."

"Okay, I know something, but you can't get mad."

My stomach drops. "Okay. I won't. Tell me."

"Now, this is selfishly motivated, but I know for a fact Trevor has a room at Fashion Island again. I heard him ask Crystal to confirm it."

I'm almost naked, wrapped in the arms of a man I could love, and yet I still feel like I might throw up. "So, he's there now?"

"I don't know. Could be."

29

After less convincing than would have been required had he been totally sober, Ryan agrees to take me to the hotel. We smoke another full joint, abandoning the half we had left as if it were somehow beneath us, and then plan our disguises, which end up more like costumes. Ryan puts on a 1990s mint-green SurfStyle windbreaker and an FBI baseball cap he picked up in a souvenir shop in Times Square. I pull my hair back tight in a French braid, put on a complete Lululemon yoga outfit and borrow some of Alice's oversized sunglasses.

The second dose of THC irrefutably helps minimize the seriousness of this mission. We're not thinking about any discoveries we might make or any subsequent consequences. We're just standing in the driveway doing our best impressions of detectives, talking into our phones like walkie-talkies, as we wait on our driver.

We arrive to a busy, crowded foyer. Of course, we didn't plan on the lobby being in full swing, fifty-year-olds with breast implants dressed in body-con toasting with martinis behind a velvet rope that separates the party-goers from the regular hotel guests. Our appearance clearly marks us as the latter, perhaps a couple from middle America here to explore how the other half lives.

When I approach the front desk to inquire about my husband's room number, Ryan tries to blend in, visibly hiding behind an annoyed bouncer who mans the rope checking ID, flattering the clearly of age.

I manage to get my prepared line out without laughing or losing my nerve: "I've forgotten our room number and lost my key." Alice's old Tommy Hilfiger sunglasses conceal my clearly stoned eyes, but when the desk clerk asks for identification, it's too much. I am who I say I am, and Trevor is my husband, but handing over proof of being here is a commitment. I don't know how long I stand looking at him, because he repeats his request, a concerned expression on his sharply angled face.

"Of course," I say, and miraculously produce my Ontario driver's license for inspection. He looks it over carefully, comparing the last names. Satisfied, he moves his fingers over the keyboard like a child who is pretending to type, pressing all the buttons at once, and says, "Room 505."

As he tilts his head down, his sharp nose looks like a long beak, and I can't help but picture him pecking at the keys like a bird. The image is so effed up that I back away and tentatively reach for the key card as he tentatively hands it over.

"What the hell happened over there?" Ryan asks, popping out of his hiding spot to meet me on my way over to the elevators.

"What do you mean?"

"You dumped your whole wallet on the counter!"

"No way?"

"Seriously! Did you get it?"

"Sure did!" I say, triumphantly holding the key up.

Being stoned is sort of like being stuck in a lucid dream, except opposite: everything that is happening can't be real, but it is. The elevator moves exactly the way you would expect it to in a dream, extremely pro-longed but with chunks of time missing. We went from the lobby to the fifth floor in a blink that happened both quickly and in slow motion. When the doors slide open, the subtle chime somehow wakes me from my dream state—the state that fooled me into thinking this was a good idea.

The expression on Ryan's face as he hesitantly leads me out of the elevator confirms what I'm thinking and in-dicates that he too is sobering up. We both stop to take in hallways that extend so far they seem almost like a mirage, more of a maze than a hotel, concealing Trevor and yet leaving no room for Ryan and me to hide. The two of us are as exposed here as I expect to find my husband.

The room numbers and their corresponding arrows on the wall outside the elevator do little to point me in the right direction. The more I stare at them, the more complicated this basic math becomes.

"I got this," Ryan says, unaware that those are the three sexiest words any man could ever say to any woman. He takes my hand and initiates our movement to the right. On one side, we pass 500, 502, 504, and then stand there frozen. Shivers go up my spine knowing that 505 lurks behind me like the monsters who chased me up the basement stairs as a child.

"I thought we'd have more time," I whisper, not looking up. "The elevator is literally right there."

"Okay," he says. "Follow me."

He ducks into the area with an ice machine just left of the elevators. It's an elementary solution, but to me, it's genius. I take a deep breath, and it releases an intense tightness around my lungs that was making it nearly impossible to breathe. Ryan takes his hat off and runs his hand through his hair, which is becoming one of my favorite habits of his, of anyone's really. He leans his back against the wall and unzips his windbreaker. Extreme public displays of affection are so not like me, but I feel an intense urge to walk over to him and run my hands up his shirt, feel his abs under my fingers and kiss his pouty lips.

"You look sixteen with that braid," he says, interrupting my fantasy.

"Thanks, Ryan."

"Like a very promiscuous sixteen-year-old," he adds, walking toward me exactly as I'd just pictured walking toward him. I pull the elastic off and tousle my hair. "Better?"

"Not really," he says, pulling my chin up and kissing me. I kiss him back but am distracted by the persistent thought that I've lost my mind. Bigger picture here, Ellen.

I could never tire of kissing this man. He uses the exact amount of tongue and lip to put me in some sort of trance; every time, my knees go weak almost as soon as our lips touch. As much as I like being pinned in his embrace, and the idea that I could just wrap my legs around his irresistible hips and let him take me against a vending machine, it's time to behave somewhat sensibly. I place two hands on his chest and push him back. "We need a plan."

"We need a hotel room."

"Ryan, I can't. Not yet."

"Well, just go in there and then we can go back to my place," he says kissing my neck as I wiggle away.

After a fair share of laughing, punctuated by me panicking, we come up with a reasonably straightforward plan. While I remain in our alcove, Ryan takes not more than ten reluctant steps toward room 505. Just before he knocks, he looks back at me for reassurance, and I nod. His knock is hard and unmistakable but before the echo is completely gone from my ears, I realize we didn't discuss what we would do when Trevor answers. Twenty long seconds later, Ryan repeats his initial knock followed by two lighter, quicker taps and yells, "Turn down service," in his best imitation of a female housekeeper. (Because it couldn't possibly be a male housekeeper.) I cover my mouth and dip back behind the wall.

He seems convinced Trevor's room is empty and waves me over to join him. I try to move, but it's as though my feet have been cemented in place. I'm a statue, thinking for the first time how it will feel to know for sure. Only when I realize Ryan has the key card in his hand and is about to enter alone do I force myself to tiptoe down the hall.

"Just open it!" I whisper-yell, feeling the pressure of being so close to an elevator that could open at any moment.

He insists I be the one to insert the key, and as I did I fully expected a little red light to reject us. But instead, I immediately get the green light and hear the unmissable click of the lock opening. For the first time in my life, I manage to open the door in one attempt. After a pause as I consider running, I push open the door.

"Hello," I call into the room before fully committing.

All possible scenes flash through my mind: tangled sheets, scattered underthings, empty bottles of

expensive hotel wine. But what I see is even more up-
setting. At first, all I see is the king bed, still professionally tucked on one side and slightly folded down
on the other, in perfect Trevor fashion. On the night
table are his reading glasses, a copy of Eric Blehm's
Fearless bookmarked more than three-quarters of the
way through, and an empty water bottle.

Even before I've processed everything, my stomach
contracts intensely. I open the closet and feel sick when
I see three of his suits hung carefully next to matching
dress shirts. The drawers are nearly full of folded socks
and underwear. I slam them shut with such fury that
the giant flat-screen teeters and I half hope it smashes.

I fly into the bathroom, close to suffocation as I
haven't taken a breath in nearly a minute, and discover
his toiletries meticulously lined up along the counter-
top. Even though I don't need to at this point, I check
the garbage for disposed condoms but only come up
with an empty contact lens container and a Vega bar
wrapper.

On my way out of the bathroom, I catch a glimpse
of myself in the mirror and everything becomes clear:
Trevor isn't cheating on me.

Trevor is leaving me.

"Ellen, wait!" Ryan yells as I burst out the door and
head straight for the elevator. I know he's come to the
same conclusion. I keep my head up, no longer afraid
of getting caught, almost willing Trevor to be standing
there when the doors open.

Even the idea that he was cheating on me, prefer-
ring the company of some other woman, was not as
hard to face as the fact that he would rather be alone.
I'm sure his intentions weren't cruel, but this discovery
hurts in a way I wasn't prepared for.

"Would you wait?" Ryan calls after me as I step into
an elevator and join a young Asian couple, holding
hands and wearing matching Chanel, who were probably hoping to ride alone. Ryan steps in and the door
closes behind him. We all stand silently, our eyes fixed
on the descending numbers, the two of them probably
mistaking us for a squabbling married couple instead
of the mess that we are.

We make our way through the lobby without speaking, me on a mission. I walk with the indignation of a
scorned woman, all eyes on Ryan as the windbreaker-
wearing culprit while my eyes dart fiercely around the
disco-lit hotel for any sign of Trevor.

For whatever reason, my mind is swimming with
thoughts of Wendy and Scarlet. How I allowed myself
to see my marriage like theirs and put Trevor in the
same category as their womanizing husbands; how I
broke my promise to him and fell for someone else.

More intrusive is the single thought that keeps
surfacing: I'm so humiliated. Humiliated that unlike
Alice, Trevor isn't running away to someone else; embarrassed that unlike my new friends' husbands who
always come home, Trevor creates imaginary surgeries
and extended work weeks. Unlike Mark, who is all over

Audrey, Trevor prefers a good book and unfamiliar sheets. It might have hurt my pride more to discover Trevor tangled up with a Victoria Secret Model, but I could have called him a million names and pointed out how horrible he really was—a cheat. In this scenario, however, which happens to be reality, Trevor remains perfect, and I'm the only villain.

I'm the cheat. I'm the ordinary, unemployed, undeserving, childless, plain-Jane cheat.

Beside me in the car, Ryan tries to be supportive in every way a person needs support in a time like this. His fingertips graze my leg, but he keeps his distance. He does all the talking to the driver, but apart from that, he stays quiet, not offering any grand advice or excuses. I'm grateful, and yet his presence beside me, the rise and fall of his chest in my peripheral vision, makes me feel dirty and ashamed; physically ill with guilt.

It dawns on me that less than six months ago, I had very little to be ashamed about. Sure, I struggled with feeling proud of myself, my accomplishments meager when compared to Trevor's. But I've never, ever felt like this. Suddenly Audrey's advice, Trevor's pleas to try harder and my subconscious doubts are all so crystal-clear; they were there all along begging me to listen. It all seems so obvious now, like when you find out the answer to a riddle. What was so wrong with being a Jane? At least Jane can sleep at night, recognize her own reflection in the mirror.

The drive is short, but at some point, trying desperately to piece together how I was so unthinkably wrong, the combination of mixed emotions and wild thoughts leave me so flooded my mind crashes. I'm left staring out the window with only a depressing humming sound in my head, as if there has just been an explosion or I'm a mental patient numbed by narcotics.

It strikes me that Trevor is not entirely innocent here. He is guilty of wanting it all: his career, the heroics of saving lives, his not-up-for-discussion ten-year plan, and least important but still necessary to complete the package, me. The wife, waiting at home alone, not complaining or sticking my head in the oven.

If he knew me at all, if he thought of me at all, he would have known this move, this entire upheaval of my life, our life, couldn't have ended well. How could it? Had the roles been reversed, had my career taken off and not his, would I have expected him to follow me? More importantly, would he have obliged? We are both career-driven and goal-oriented, so maybe this is another case of a pot calling the kettle black, but I'm stuck waiting for the water to boil as he whistles away. Another disappointing personal revelation: in addition to being humiliated and unfaithful, I'm also jealous and resentful. Ugh. Who knew you could grow up without actually growing up?

When we pull up to his house, I ask the driver to wait while I grab my things. I'm consciously polite to

Ryan because none of this is his fault. He holds the front door open for me, not standing in my way; I thank him but avoid his eyes, not out of embarrassment but another strong reaction, one I try to ignore: disappointment. As much as I'm attracted to him, this isn't just about sex. In fact, not having sex with Ryan means one less thing to feel guilty about. But losing him hurts. He is important to me, and I hope he knows that even though I can't say it. Regardless, we both know this is what I must do.

Minutes later, he closes the door to the town car, with me seated straight-backed and blank-faced behind it. His hands linger on the sleek black roof as if he's holding onto the moment, me, for as long as possible.

I tell the driver I'm ready and mouth, "I'm sorry," to Ryan just as the tires start to turn, the gravel and sand making a grinding noise that cuts our unshakable silence. He gives me an understanding nod and then removes his hands from the car and runs them both through his hair. The idea that I've hurt him makes me feel so irresponsible, gambling with his heart as well as Trevor's and my own.

As we near the end of his street, about to disappear around the corner and into the darkest part of the night, I can't resist turning around, to get another look at the man who sparked life back into me. He's still there, watching me drive away. The image of him like this, getting smaller and smaller, the wind propelling his jacket like a sail, his defeated expression—this is how I will remember him. Tears flow down my cheeks as I think back to the two of us as we were on the beach, foolish and unguarded in the setting sun.

From the instant I put it all together—what Trevor has done and what he hasn't, what I was willing to believe he'd done, and what I have done—I knew my marriage was over. There is no way to put this all back together again, even if I could go back to waiting alone in our beautiful Port Streets home for Trevor to come home. The question now is whether I will ever be able to find my way back to myself. To myself, and to self-forgiveness.

30

The last empty hanger is still rocking on my side of the closet when I turn the light off. Perhaps the extra closet space and less disorder will give Trevor more room to stretch out and find his Zen. On the scale of trouble I have caused, leaving him alone in this giant family home decorated with things we have collected throughout our marriage seems marginal.

Carrying my own luggage will have to be something I get used to, and it seems a small trade-off compared to being in this house alone for the next two years. Despite my intense exercise regimen of the last few months, there are limitations to my strength, and raising fifty-pound bags high enough not to scratch the floors might be it. I ignore the strain on my back and once I get to the bottom of the stairs, I return to the top to get the next one. Other than my clothes, I don't want anything.

The sun is about to rise. My goal of packing and leaving the marital suicide note that sheepishly says *be happy* before Trevor is the wiser is a success. My luggage is stowed in the trunk of an oblivious driver's car, bound for the airport to fly home to a disapproving town that will require a lot of explanation.

It isn't a matter of losing Trevor to find myself; I'm still lost. I just can't carry on in a direction that would ultimately hit a dead end. The hotel room was the saddest scene in the world to me, but if I'm honest, I don't blame him. Had I known it was an option, maybe I would have booked a room of my own somewhere.

There are no justifications to be made, so eight hours and three time zones later, I walk into my parents' house to find them cuddling in front of a movie they've seen a million times, and say only, "I'm home and I'm going to bed."

I'm thankful for the darkness of the room and my mother's intuitiveness as she stops my dad from standing up with a gentle tug on his hand.

"Okay, Ellen," she calls to me as I make my way upstairs, leaving the heavy lifting for the morning.

My room is no longer my room, but despite the addition of a sewing table and Tread Climber and the absence of my framed Cypress Hill poster, hung mostly for shock value, it's the same four walls that held me together through puberty. I allow myself some kindness and drift off to sleep thinking only of the flourishing palms and abundant green of California, knowing I will wake to barren trees and the dirty remains of gravel-tinged snow.

I have a restless sleep, repeatedly waking to confusion and then panic when reality sets in. My mother has covered me with my old blanket; she must have dug it out for me in the middle of the night, knowing something is up. But in my jeans, my legs still itchy from salt and sand, real rest is impossible. I get the most sleep in the early morning after the sun bleeds into the room, warming my face despite the draftiness of my parents' home.

When I finally commit to opening my eyes, Audrey is sitting at the foot of the bed sipping on a coffee. She looks worried but angelic, especially with the sprays of light and tiny bits of dust floating all around her.

"Hi," I say, sitting up, hugging my knees to my chest. She hands me her mug, a sign of true love, as coffee comes second only to her children, and stands to open the curtains.

"You okay?"

"Nope."

"Sure, you are. Or you will be."

"I don't know, Audrey. Everything is messed up."

"I heard."

"You what?" I ask, placing the coffee on one of the now matching end tables.

"He called me."

"Already?" I ask, springing up, looking for my phone. "Shocking he noticed."

"No, not Trevor. Ryan."

"What?" I repeat and scramble back to the bed. "What did he say?"

"He just wanted me to know...to be there for you."

"Oh," I mutter, unable to look her in the eye.

She hugs me tight, no obvious signs of resentment or disappointment. "I'm so sorry, Elly."

We spend the next hour going over the last twelve. I fill in the blanks and add my perspective to Ryan's explanation. She doesn't offer any opinions except for a few gentle attempts to defend Trevor and a lot of understanding nods aimed at me. Mainly she just agrees that things are, in fact, not good.

As I'm sure the suspense is killing her, we eventually invite my mother in and Audrey uses her lawyer skills to put six months of turmoil into a brief, perfectly summarized opening statement.

After a few nods of her head, my mother lies and says she's proud of me for following my heart, even though I haven't followed my heart at all. If I had, I would be with Ryan, but Audrey omitted that piece of incriminating information. I'm not sure my mother could handle the truth right now, that I traded one tragically great man for another. Regardless of her use of the word heart, I know she would have much rather I used my head.

The days that follow are as hard as I expect them to be. It takes Trevor three days to call me, which I suspect had more to do with the length of time it took him to figure out I was gone than with the anger that was clear in his voice when he realized this trip would be permanent. Even so, he doesn't show up on my doorstep; he does not ask me to come back.

I don't tell him about my hotel room discovery. The least I can do is absorb all the blame. I may come across as weak and self-centered, but it feels like the most generous thing I have done for him in a very long time.

Almost three weeks later, as I start to come to terms with the end of my marriage and plan my future, knowing I can't hide in my old room forever, Audrey invites me over for dinner. It's a welcome break from Mom's home-cooked meals.

If it weren't for the fear of hitting someone I would drive to Audrey's with my eyes closed, partly because I'm so familiar with the roads of my childhood and partly because, like a child, I half-believe that if I close my eyes I won't be seen.

Audrey convinced Mark to buy a house in our hometown, on the water mind you, even though they could well afford a home in one of the fancier surrounding areas. She spins it as better value, more bang for their buck. But I suspect my sister is more sentimental than she lets herself believe, which is one of the reasons I never bought her contrived jealousy of my moving away.

I drive with my windows up and my hat pulled down low, the opposite of the way we drove growing up, blaring Courtney Love CDs from our factory stereos as we repeatedly cruised the one strip that makes up our downtown. Now I prefer to go unnoticed.

The driveway into their property is long, with a slight bend that makes it a challenge to see the front door, which is why I assume it is Mark I see sitting on their steps. But the closer I get, the less it looks like the five-foot-ten-inch, slightly chubby, always-jolly dad—and the more it appears to be a striking, unusually anxious, visibly freezing doctor I hadn't expected to see ever again.

Surprise is an understatement here, and something I'm never in favor of, especially if it catches me unprepared, which it certainly has.

Two words: Campus Crew. Instead of my figure-flattering jeans and cool band shirts, my uniform of late, today I chose to deck myself head-to-toe in a forest green Muskoka track suit, with a chunky, cable-knit cardigan over an already bulky sweatshirt in lieu of a winter coat. My father's knitted hat hides my three-day unwashed hair.

There's nothing I can do to improve my appearance, I'm in too far to reverse my parents' car (I'd likely hit a tree anyway), and wishing Audrey hadn't pulled one past me certainly won't change this.

Not that I would change this situation if I could.

He spots me, somehow connecting his dark eyes with mine despite the intensity of the sun reflected on the snow-covered grass, strangely brighter than anything in California, and through the layer of grime on my windshield.

It's funny how people look different when you transport them into a new environment. I'm dressed warmer, but I've been equally disheveled in his presence before. He, however, looks unexplainably different. Maybe it's the unfamiliar winter coat or the way his nose glows red...or because he seems unsure and vulnerable.

Without bothering to look in the mirror, which would be a pointless and probably frightening move, I park and give myself a "here goes nothing," before stepping out of the car with a mix of hesitancy and delight. He walks to meet me, cutting my uneasy steps in half, and leans in for a hug before we've said hello.

"Are you mad?" he whispers into my ear before letting me go.

I rest my head on his chest. "No, not at all."

"Are you happy?"

"Happier now."

He kisses the top of my wool-covered head. "Can we go inside then? I'm freezing."

I'm hoping I will be like the wine we drank that night and get better with age. Maybe Ryan's plans to transfer back to NYC—a paltry forty-five-minute flight away—will fall through. Maybe seeing each other will become too difficult.

For now, I will put the results of my selfish actions to good use, get my career back on track and work on mending some of the holes the last six months have left in my life. I'm going to spend a lot less time living in my head, worrying about being happy enough or living up to perceived expectations about how happy I should be (or should have been).

Enough with happy.

In my quiet moments now, with my family around me, I realize it's been there all along, underneath the layers of doubt, of knowing better and doing worse.

If I let it, when I can convince myself I deserve it again, it will come.

Manufactured by Amazon.ca
Bolton, ON

27150002R00188